WAR OF THE BLACK TOWER
PART THREE

WAR OF THE BLACK TOWER
PART THREE

Lord of Flame

JACK CONNER

The Crescent

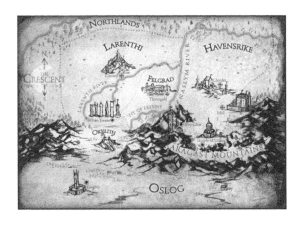

To see a larger, color version of this map, go to:
http://jackconnerbooks.com/map-of-the-world-of-the-black-
tower-trilogy/

Chapter One

Ravening nightmares chased Baleron from sleep.

He shot up gasping, drenched in sweat, to find himself in a small, dark room, propped on a narrow bed. A hideous face hovered over him, tusked and horrible, and he shouted in surprise.

The face drew back, its owner visibly startled.

It was a Borchstog, but a Borchstog unlike any Baleron had ever seen. It was bigger, for one. For another, it was not bristling with hostility, and something in its face even hinted at gentleness.

The Borchstog recovered itself. It held a damp cloth; it had been wiping the sweat from his brow while he slept. A nurse?

It smiled down at him—not prettily, no, but it seemed to be heartfelt, and in this place such a thing was beautiful.

"From the deep pool one comes," it said, and its voice was different from any other Borchstoggish voice Baleron had ever heard. It was ... soft.

He tried to ask it a question, but the effort proved too much for him. He grunted something and fell back on the bed. The world grew hazy for awhile, and terrible beings chased him, drooling, and he heard Rauglir's laughter from the darkness. Upon waking he found himself in the small room once more.

The same Borchstog nurse checked the bandages on his left wrist.

Groaning, he sat up a little and tried to see what she was doing. What he saw surprised him, and he moaned something interrogatively. The Borchstog looked up and smiled again.

"*Roschk ul Kunraggoq,*" it said, a common greeting here. Looking down at the end of his left arm, it asked, "What think you?"

He stared. For, terminating his left arm, was in fact his left hand. *It had been reattached.* A ring of ugly and uneven stitches marked the juncture, and the whole mass was swollen and bruise-colored, and it hurt terribly, but it was there.

He tried to wiggle his fingers. They wiggled.

"Bleh?" he asked.

The Borchstog listened patiently. "I am Olfrig. I am the head nurse here and have been personally assigned to oversee your recovery."

He mumbled another question. He felt very woozy. They must have given him something.

"We nurses see to the healing of our injured slaves—at least, the ones valuable enough to keep," the nurse explained. "I had a dwarf in yesterday, for example: an excellent metalworker. And there's an elf just down the hall who is very good at laying charms on works-in-progress. But you're even more special, you know. Of course you do. It's an honor to serve you, *Ravast-rul.* You're going to help us win the War. You may have already."

He mumbled something.

"That's right, the War. We have both Glorifel and Clevaris under siege as we speak, and the other countries are overrun. It's only a matter of time." The Borchstog seemed very proud.

Despair filled Baleron, and guilt; he'd abandoned his people in their darkest hour. Of course, he reminded himself, the reason he'd left was because he could do them no more good; his time would be better spent avenging them. And so he still would, he vowed.

He had to get out of here—had to get back home. Maybe there was some way he could still help—

A coldness gripped him, like an icy claw about his heart. His Doom had triggered that thought. He knew it. *Father was right,* he thought with a shudder. *How do I know where it ends and I begin?*

Working carefully, he said, "M'ot."

The nurse frowned, then brightened. "Mrot?" *Water?*

Glad to assist, she ladled some water into his mouth from a nearby bowl, and he drank it down greedily. Rank and bitter, it was the best thing he had ever tasted. Feeling much better, he wiped his mouth and said, slowly and carefully, "You're a female?"

She laughed, and he tried not to cringe. "Yes," she said. "Olfrig is very female. Olfrig has over a hundred sons."

"A hundred?"

She patted his thigh. "We Borchstogs have few daughters, but we are large and can fend for ourselves. The males do what we say or we eat them."

He cleared his throat. "Did you say Glorifel is still under siege?"

"For five, six months now."

That sobered him. He'd been tortured for more than a quarter of a year. "What of Larenthi?"

"Clevaris is the only city left, and it's ready to collapse, its rivers poisoned, its gardens aflame. The Queen's powers are exhausted, and most of her House are slain."

Olfrig seemed very cheery about all this, as if she didn't understand that Baleron was on the opposite side. Though the attitude vexed him, it was good that his nurse felt on the same side as her patient, and he didn't disabuse her of the notion.

"Prince Jered?" he said. "Does he still live?"

She scratched her scarred face. "He's been in some battles ... Olfrig has heard name ... but can't remember."

"And the other countries ... Esril, Felgrad, Crysmid ... all of them ... they're overrun?"

"Oh, yes. They sent their armies to Clevaris to break siege. Grudremorq destroyed them. Their homes were defenseless. The Flame and the Shepherd both sent out hosts to raid and burn, and the Master sent more. Some of our foes still live, but they run and hide, they do not fight. The Crescent is fallen. All that is left are two cities, and Master builds another army, the greatest yet, to bring them down utterly Himself."

Dismay filled Baleron. If it were possible to escape, he wondered if there were some way he could aid the Crescent. But if he tried, what guarantee was there that he wasn't simply carrying out his Doom? He was alive for a reason, after all, and nothing in his life since Gulrothrog had been an accident, it seemed.

To keep her talking, he brought up something she'd said that puzzled him: "You said the nurses treated your ... slaves. What of the injured Borchstogs? Don't they need healing?"

"Not in Krogbur. Here the strength of our Lord is at its greatest. It's here where the strands of His web cross each other, and one of His children who is wounded need merely bask in His power, and he is healed."

"Your kind must like this place then. Is it to replace Ghrastigor as his fortress?"

She shrugged. "Not privy to Master's designs is Olfrig. I do know, yes, that He has planned long for this, for the raising of His Tower. The Shadowneedle. The Rooted Lightning. The Doorway. And you helped bring it about. You must be very proud."

Catching him by surprise, she pinched the small finger on his left hand. He yelped.

"Is well," she noted. "Feeling has returned."

Later, when exhaustion tugged him back down into slumber,

he dreamt that his left hand bristled with wolf fur and attacked him. Claws extended from its fingers, and a snapping wolf mouth had opened in the palm. Rauglir's laughter chased him.

Olfrig nursed him back to health over the next few days, putting salves on his abrasions, giving him medicines and potions to drink, applying poultices, removing and replacing bandages. Slowly, he began to recover, though he did not know to what end.

In the beginning he would ask her why he was being seen to, why he was being made well, but she never had an answer—it was not her place to know, and she didn't—so gradually he quit asking. He thought he knew without being told: the Dark One was ready to use him again.

For the thousandth time, Baleron thought about killing himself. But he remembered Elethris telling him that Gilgaroth had made him a sword that could be used against its maker, and he remembered Vilana telling him he could yet sway the war in the Light's favor, and he hesitated. Yet if he did end himself, he might be reunited with Rolenya. To see her, he might risk eternal damnation. He dreamt about her, and his dreams were not brotherly. He longed to feel her embrace, smell her hair, press her body to him.

Just as often he dreamt of Rauglir. Creatures mocked him in his slumber and hounded him so that he got no rest. Soon he dreaded sleep.

Something was wrong, he felt, wrong with *him*—with his body, with his mind, he did not know.

He was suspicious of the hand. Sometimes he would hold it up to the light and stare at it. He would flex it and twist it; it obeyed him. The fingernails were growing back, the scars fading and the cuts healing, faster than normal thanks to Olfrig's potions. Just why had Gilgaroth forced him to cut it off, then ordered it reattached? The Dark One did nothing without reason.

What bothered Baleron nearly as much was Olfrig's and the other Borchstogs' conviction that he was *ul Ravast*. Surely they were wrong. Gilgaroth might use him as a tool, but he hadn't been *born to be that tool*. It was merely an accident of circumstance that he was the sort of person the Wolf needed to further his designs, someone who could have access to the nobility and sorcery of both Havensrike and Glorifel. Otherwise, why Baleron? Why not a human that already served the dark powers?

One Olfrig entered the room and said brightly, "You're awake. Is good. Master invites you to the Feast tonight."

"Your Master ... wants me to come to dinner?"

She nodded happily.

Stranger and stranger.

And strange it was.

Chapter Two

The Feast was held in a huge high chamber, the Feasting Hall, the most bizarre dining hall Baleron had ever seen, and he'd seen dining halls in numerous palaces from four out of the six Crescent States. The domed ceiling stretched high overhead, so wreathed in smoke from torches and braziers and pipes that it was nearly impossible to see. The long wooden dinner tables were tiered on a sloped floor, somewhat like that of a theater, but where the stage would be was in fact a sunken pit— a sand-floored arena, in fact.

Thousands of Borchstogs roared and laughed and talked at their seats or standing up. Their din shocked the prince, used to the silence of his hole. Most of the Borchstogs seemed to be chiefs of their broods or cities. They engaged each other in braggadocio and fights and contests of various sorts. Two stuck pins in a thrashing elvish captive, chained to a wall. They gambled on who could make her scream the loudest. A group of Borchstogs sat around a table littered with gore; they competed to see who could assemble the best musical instrument out of the provided body parts: a flute with a thigh bone; drums with skin stretched tight over a pelvis; a stringed instrument with spine, ribs and cartilage.

The creatures' smell repulsed Baleron, which surprised him; he thought he'd become accustomed to their stench by now. But there were so *many* here, and the smell so concentrated.

Growling wolves, pets or companions of the Borchstogs, lounged under the long wooden tables or fought each other for scraps and bones. Many wore spiked collars with chains attached; others were loose.

Huge greasy platters of silver and gold heaped with raw-looking meat (which Baleron did not want to inspect too closely) lay in large quantities upon the tables, and the Borchstogs picked at them with their fingers and ripped at them with their teeth. A few experimented with crude forks, though more than one of these wound up in another Borchstog's eye.

They drank wine or mead from slopping, jewel-encrusted goblets, and Baleron wondered if they'd share. He could use a drink.

Many shouted *"Roschk ul Ravast!"* as he passed. Several dropped to their knees before him, and one even shouted something that sounded like, "Take my soul!" This Borchstog offered him a dagger and bared his throat.

Baleron took the dagger. His guards did not stop him. "If only you were all this accommodating," he said, and slit the demon's throat.

Borchstogs cheered the sacrifice, and wolves began gnawing at the dead one's still-twitching body.

Grimacing, Baleron continued on, and his guards led him down toward the arena. Would he be shoved into it?

Gilgaroth sat on his great black throne on the other side of the sunken arena. Dressed darkly, his living shadow had been drawn about himself so that his fiery eyes blazed from the darkness, as if charcoal clouds passed twin red suns. One of his armored hands stroked the neck of a massive wolf to his left. To either side of him lay one, an impressive form of beast Baleron had heard call *cuerdrig*.

Gilgaroth's crowned, veiled head swiveled in Baleron's direction, and Baleron's guards stiffened, then shook themselves and hastened to lead their prisoner down the stairs to the bottom row, immediately overlooking the arena. There were already some Borchstogs seated there, and by their wide girths Baleron judged them to be leaders of a large Borchstog city. His guards chased them off and shoved him into the place where they had been. The guards remained standing, protecting Baleron lest one of their feral brethren attempt to put a blade through his back, whether in bloodlust or amusement. *Ul Ravast* or not, they *were* Borchstogs.

Baleron glared up at the Dark One, who inclined his head to him in a silent acknowledgment. Baleron did not nod back.

Gilgaroth raised a hand, and the wild throng stilled. All save Baleron's guards quit their pursuits and sat down respectfully.

"All hail Lord Gilgaroth," they chanted, and not dully either. He was their father, their god, their reason for being. What would it be like, Baleron wondered, to have such clear purpose and favor?

"*Welcome, my children,*" Gilgaroth said. "*We have an honored guest tonight. Raise your cups and toast Prince Baleron, my Champion, for he has delivered the heads of many of my enemies—and he will deliver more still.*"

The Borchstogs raised their goblets. "Prince Baleron! *Ul Ravast!*"

"*Thanks to him,*" continued the Dark One, "*we shall end this stalemate that has trapped me here for thousands of years. We shall go forth into the world, and make it our own!*"

They cheered lustily, hooting and banging on the tables. Baleron clenched his teeth.

"So, to amuse Our benefactor, let the games begin!"

Baleron had not noticed before, but there were large, barred doors set into the sides of the arena. Two of these slid away with a groan, and a pair of corrupted, monstrous Giants stormed out into the pit on opposite sides. Both their faces and forms were nightmarish, and without preamble they flew at each other. The Borchstogs howled in delight as the towering creatures struck with an earthshaking crash.

It was a short and bloody fight. The one with the pincers sliced and killed the other one, but in its dying moments the fallen Giant bit the victor, injecting it with a deadly poison, and the two twitched out their lives side by side on the ground, until they lay utterly still.

Several rithlag attended the Feast. Gilgaroth indicated one, who descended into the arena, where it reanimated the dead Giants and, like a puppeteer, made them dance and make merry. Musicians played eerie stringed instruments as the dead things cavorted. The Borchstogs hooted and laughed.

Eventually the rithlag sat down and the Borchstogs shouted out, eager for the next act, which was not long in coming.

Baleron did not bother to hide his disgust, but as the fights went on, he couldn't help but become engrossed in the sheer spectacle of it all. The thundering giants and monsters ... the blood, the noise ...

He saw sights undreamt of, terrors that defied his imagination. One fight showcased a monster the like of which he had never seen. It resembled a giant squid, but it floated, hovering above the ground. It could spray a red cloud to confuse its enemies—in this case, a host of wraiths, the demonic spirits chained to Gilgaroth's will. Like living shadows, they assailed the great squid-thing, tearing at it with ghostly claws. It pulsed with eerie lights. The wraiths shrieked and howled, and the watching Borchstogs clamped their hands over their ears. The squid's tentacles lashed like whips. At times it snared one of the phantoms and shoved the ghost into its maw. Ultimately the squid was destroyed, ripped apart by its enemies' talons, and the wraiths ascended to hide above the layer of smoke that obscured the ceiling.

The next fight featured a Grudremorqen fighting a gaurock, one of the giant Serpents. The Grudremorqen and the Serpent battled furiously, one with fiery sword, one with venomous fangs. Finally the Serpent knocked the sword away and drove at the demon. The Grudremorqen grappled with it, and they wrestled about on the blood-soaked sand until finally the burning claws of the demon gave blackened death to the gaurock, and the latter's death throes shook the Hall.

And so it went. Many times Baleron blanched, but he couldn't deny the allure of the barbaric, the primal. Still, he tried not to watch, but one of his guards jabbed him with a crude fork every time he mashed his eyes shut. And then, at last, Baleron discovered why Gilgaroth had brought him here tonight.

A door in the arena slid open, gaping darkness.

The Borchstogs had been clamoring and crying in the intermission between bouts, but now, overcome by curiosity at what new marvel waited their pleasure, they leaned forward, red eyes a-goggle, breath catching in their throats.

Baleron watched, too, but his gaze was wary.

Shortly the darkness in the doorway stirred, and, to Baleron's surprise, a beautiful woman was ushered out of it and into the arena—an elf, he saw by her slightly pointed ears. Dark hair cascaded down her shoulders and over the creamiest, whitest skin he'd ever seen. Clear blue eyes, moist now, gazed out defiantly from her angelic, delicately-boned face. Full red lips refused to tremble.

Baleron gasped. It could not be ...

It was impossible.

Some sort of trick, he told himself. It had to be.

He sat up in his seat when she was ushered out into the arena, prodded by a scarred troll carrying a spiked pole. She looked lost and scared, but her back stayed stiff and her eyes forward. She didn't spare a glance for the bloodthirsty crowd.

Baleron shouted her name, but his voice was suddenly coarse.

Impossible, he told himself. And yet, he wanted so desperately to believe. *But she's dead! I saw her body. I ... did more than just see it. Gods help me, I did.*

The last time he had seen her, or at least seen her form, had been in Worthrick Mountain. But that had been a trick of some sort, it made no sense otherwise. So then the last time he had *truly* seen her body was in Havensrike. Surely Rauglir, possessing her form, had not escaped Glorifel and made it all the way here without being caught or killed ... but what other explanation could there be?

A trapdoor slid away, slewing sand, and a ten-foot pillar thrust up through it into the arena. Though she struggled, the troll tied Rolenya (or whatever she really was) to the pillar none too gently. Evidently fascinated by her, the troll kept poking and prodding her with its fingers. She bore it all stoically. Her eyes were very blue, and very hopeless. Gone was the fire that had led her to stand up to Ungier. Gone was that spark of rebellion and mischief. And yet, there was something in her eyes, some light, some ember, that Baleron remembered, that had been missing in Rauglir. It was a depth, a serenity, a telltale of her soul ...

Despite everything, he began to believe.

Tears stained her high, pale cheeks and glistened on her red lips. Her long black hair hung in sweaty tangles down past her swan-like neck. She wore a beautiful if less-than-new dress. Dirt smudged her ivory skin in a dozen places. Yet, Baleron thought, she was as lovely as ever. He longed to hold her—as a brother, as a lover, in whatever way he could.

But it could not be her, it just could not be, no matter how much he might wish otherwise. How big a fool did they think he was? He'd already met one false Rolenya. He had seen another when Felestrata's body changed. What was more, he had been regularly conversing with a ghostly Rolenya in his pit until they moved him to the hospital wing. This, then, must be another forgery. The real one was dead, her body encasing Rauglir still, unless the demon had been driven out by the body's demise. And even Rauglir had admitted that her soul now dwelt in the ephemeral flames of the Second Hell. So why did Gilgaroth expect him to believe that this could be she?

The Dark One watched him all the while, calculating, and Baleron returned the look with what he hoped was open hostility.

Rolenya, if it were she, shone like a moonlit diamond in this smoky, foul-smelling chamber, a chamber full of grease and blood and baseness and primal urges. She shone like an angel.

The Borchstogs drew back in their seats, awed by it, by her Grace, and a hush fell over them.

At last her eyes found Baleron. Surprise filled her face. She shouted out to him, and his heart swelled, but he couldn't have returned the greeting if he'd wanted to, and at the moment words failed him completely.

She seemed sad to see him here, like her a prisoner of the Shadow, yet he thought he detected a secret joy in her to see him again, under any circumstances.

"*Behold, prince,*" said Gilgaroth. "*Your sister.*"

Baleron shook his head, unable to speak.

"*You deny her?*"

"Rolenya's dead," Baleron called across to him, having to force the words from the obstruction in his throat.

"*Yet she lives.*"

"It's true," said the figure that looked so much like Rolenya, issuing the words in a small voice that still managed to carry to his ears. To everyone's ears, he imagined. "Bal, it's me. Really ... it's me."

"How?" he challenged. "How could this be possible?"

"I forged for her a new body," the Dark One said. *"Into it I poured her soul. Her essence. I released her from Illistriv."*

Baleron paused. That *might* be plausible. Gilgaroth had spawned races, had raised mountains. He could forge one small body.

"I don't believe you. *Why* would you do such a thing?"

"I need your loyalty, Baleron. I need for you to do my bidding. For HER sake you shall."

So angry at this that tears began to roll down his cheeks, Baleron shouted, "You bastard! You can't *do* this to me! You can't!"

Seeing his tears, Rolenya sobbed too. "Oh, Baleron! Bal! It's true! It's me." Her voice grew small, lost, confused: "Unless this is a dream ... some strange dream. Is it? Could it possibly be?"

He could not answer that. His dreams lately had been too painful, and this might be the most painful yet. He shot a challenging glare at Gilgaroth.

"Prove it," he said.

Gilgaroth regarded him levelly. Smoke drifted between them. *"How?"*

Looking down to the image of his sister, he said, "Sing."

For a long moment, there was silence. Not a Borchstog in the assembly stirred. Torches crackled, but that was all. Not even a wolf could be heard yowling, or a shoe scraping. All was as a tomb.

Then, finally, Gilgaroth inclined his crowned head. His fiery eyes flickered downwards to the slim pale figure bound to the stake below.

"Sing, Rolenya," he bade her. *"Sing."*

Baleron's heart caught in his throat. Could she do it? Would she do it?

To his astonishment, she nodded. Then she lifted her head, stared Baleron directly in the eye, took a deep breath—her chest straining against the ropes—and let out one long, crystal-clear note.

Baleron reeled backward, gasping. Could it be?

Her eyes closed, and tears leaked out, rolling over her high round cheeks and gathering under her jaw. Her voice rolled on.

Suddenly Baleron could not catch his breath.

She sang on, the notes changing, high, then low, then even higher than before. He knew that the words were in the language of the Elves in a far northern land that she favored in song. They were foreign to him but all the more beautiful for that; he could not understand them, but he could feel their grandeur, their greatness. He remembered tales he'd heard as a child, fairytales of elvish princesses who could weave spells with their voice, and recalled that Rolenya's mother was said to have raised entire forest-gardens with her song.

He couldn't believe his ears. Rolenya's voice was filled with Grace—true Grace. No demon sent by Gilgaroth could sing like this. It was Rolenya. *It was Rolenya.* His chest burned. After all this time ...

Her clear, smooth voice cut like a hot, righteous knife through the gloom of the Feasting Hall, lancing the darkness like a beam. Baleron half-expected the ceiling to crack and the walls to shake under the barrage of her purity, her goodness. It was with such a voice that Queen Vilana her mother had raised entire forest-gardens to her liking. She had walked along bare hills, singing, and grass and trees had grown at her feet.

The Borchstogs sat back, thunderstruck.

Even the Dark One seemed to sit back and listen in admiration, spellbound by her voice.

Baleron, himself enchanted, wished the song to go on forever, but at last it ended, and again Rolenya opened her eyes—her clear, beautiful eyes. They gazed openly up at him, happily, sadly, full of feeling and despair.

"Rolenya," he said softly, acknowledging her.

"Baleron," she whispered.

The Dark One's eyes blazed. *"Quite touching,"* he said. *"Quite ... moving."* Then he barked out, *"Thorg!"*

Instantly, the great wolf to his left rose and leapt down into the arena. It pawed the ground with an outthrust claw and snorted. Steam issued forth.

Rolenya screamed.

Chapter Three

*O*f *course*, thought Baleron as he watched it happen. A sickening feeling grew in his gut. *I should've known.*

Throgmar had said it himself: Gilgaroth's true talent lay with inflicting pain. He had given Baleron back Rolenya only now to take her away again—raising the prince's hopes only so that he'd have something to dash.

Her wide, panicked blue eyes shot from her brother to the black beast that shared the arena with her. Its lips lifted back from long, dripping fangs. Its awful, intelligent eyes narrowed to cruel slits.

The Borchstogs, for once, did not cheer for it; they were still too moved by Rolenya's song to root for her bloody demise.

Baleron watched on helplessly.

The cuerdrig, Thorg, stalked arrogantly over to the princess, weaving through the mounds of wrecked bodies and body parts strewn by previous fights. He stuck his black face up close to her small pale one and sprayed her with his steaming breath. She shook in fear and wrenched her head away.

Outraged, Baleron screamed, "Nooo!" and attempted to rise.

A Borchstog cuffed him and he sank back down, still bound to the chair.

Below, the great black wolf began circling Rolenya. Tearful, she shook her head, denying the reality of it all.

Gilgaroth issued a sound that may have been a laugh.

"No!" Baleron shouted again.

"Ah, but yes," said Gilgaroth. *"I want you to see her rent to pieces. My pet can go as slow as I wish."*

"Don't kill her! Put me in her place."

The Dark One said simply, *"No."*

"Fine," Baleron growled. "Then give me a sword! You want sport? I'll give you sport!"

"I do not want sport."

"What do you want?"

The Dark One leaned forward. *"I want you to do my bidding, and you are now too aware of your Doom for it to act without your consent."*

Baleron began to sweat. His left hand throbbed painfully. Sound began to drift in and out of his hearing, and the world began to tilt.

"I will *not* serve you," he shouted. "I am not your Savior. I will *never be* your Savior."

"Serve me and have purpose. Serve me and save ... Rolenya."

"No," Baleron said, half to himself, shaking his head wretchedly. "No. I can't."

Lord Gilgaroth raised an armored hand as if clutching something invisible, as if summoning something, and once more, Rolenya screamed. At her feet, the ground cracked and a huge serpent unwound from the earth, thick and spined and hissing. It coiled about her bound body, squeezing, caressing, winding slowly, almost lovingly, about her—then began to constrict.

She tried to cry out but could not draw breath. It would mash her into boneless jelly.

"NOW what do you say?" asked Gilgaroth.

Baleron glared at him. Said nothing.

The Shadow raised his other hand high, as if grasping something far above, and then yanked it down dramatically. A horde of shadow-wraiths dropped from the smoke-wreathed ceiling. Some had the forms of demons and beasts. Some were hooded and cloaked. Still more had no real form at all. But one and all fell like a wrathful cloud from the heights and swarmed about Rolenya, their mouths opening, if they had mouths, and a terrible, unholy din pouring out. Covering their ears, Borchstogs screamed in fear.

"*I COMMAND THE HOSTS OF HELL,*" Gilgaroth roared, and it was no boast. *"I can summon horrors upon your beloved that you would weep to see—and I will, lest you submit."*

Haunted by the wraiths' screams, Baleron could only see Rolenya here and there through breaks in the swarm of shadows. He could not tolerate them touching her. They were unholy things, unclean things, and their mad screams drove him past his limits of endurance.

"Release her!" Baleron shouted.

"ARE YOU MY CREATURE?"

Baleron hung his head.

With a wave of the Dark One's hand, the wraiths ended their assault and ascended past the layer of smoke once more and were lost to sight. The snake, its shining coils about Rolenya, its colorful scales rasping her smooth skin, uncoiled itself and retreated below ground once more. At its departure, the hole closed up behind it.

Rolenya could breathe again.

Baleron lowered his gaze, too ashamed to think straight. How could he do this?

Below, Rolenya called out to him: "Don't give in, Baleron. So I die ... I've died before."

She was right, of course. He thought of Larenthi, and Havensrike, and all the people he'd led to their deaths for his Doom. Even for Rolenya's sake, how could he betray anymore? He would not be the Dark One's spider. He *would not.*

Thorg continued to circle the arena, his circles drawing closer and closer to Rolenya, until finally he was almost touching her.

Gilgaroth must have seen Baleron's indecision, for he said, *"Decide, Baleron. You don't have long. Thorg looks ... hungry."*

Thorg stuck his steaming snout in Rolenya's face, and his drool dripped on her breasts. His sharp teeth pressed against her cheek. She trembled and closed her eyes, turning her head aside. She was preparing herself for the end, Baleron could tell. How could he let this happen? There had to be something he could do.

The black wolf's teeth left red impressions in her skin. She quivered in fear.

Thorg grazed her arm with one of his fangs, slashing open her tender flesh, and she flinched and let out an involuntary gasp.

"Stop it!" Baleron shouted. "Stop!"

"You will serve me?" asked Gilgaroth.

Baleron said nothing. Rolenya opened her eyes. When he glanced at her, she shook her head mutely, too scared of Thorg to say anything. The terrible beast pawed the ground before her.

"You smell delicious," Thorg told her in his black, unnatural voice. The cuerdrig's red tongue probed her wound, licking at the blood. "You *are*," he added.

The Dark One said, *"Cut her again."*

Thorg bit her, and again. With each surgical slash of his fangs, she cried out, and Baleron strained against the Borchstogs that held him down.

"Decide," said Gilgaroth.

"I'll never do your bidding again!" Baleron said. "Torture me how you like, that will not change."

Silently, Gilgaroth inclined his head to Thorg, who bowed and drew back from Rolenya a few paces, then turned to face her, his mouth open and steaming. He was one great, lethal furnace of pride and fury, and he was aimed straight at Baleron's once-sister, once-lover, forever beloved. All Baleron had to do to save her was betray his kind and kin and all they stood for, and doom the world entire.

He said nothing.

Fire licked from Thorg's maw.

"Baleron!" Rolenya shouted in terror.

"Rolenya!" he called back.

It was the last thing she could have heard.

The great black wolf opened his mouth, and a column of fire issued from his awful jaws, burning Rolenya alive.

This time, when Baleron closed his eyes, no one stabbed him with a fork.

That night, they did not return him to the relative comforts of Olfrig and the hospital wing but cast him down into a pit again—a different one than before. They did not want him getting cozy. He sobbed in the darkness as scorpions and other vermin stung and bit him. He felt that he might as well be in a hell—the First, Second or otherwise did not much matter to him, save that Rolenya would be in the Second. He ached for her. She had suffered so much because of him.

Why did Gilgaroth torment them like this? Was it because the Dark One enjoyed it, or because he wanted to squeeze just a little bit more out of his favorite pawn? What more could Baleron *do* for him, anyway?

Baleron didn't think he could take anymore.

Several hours after the events in the arena, Borchstogs under Ghrozm's command hauled him up from the bottom of the pit in a rusty cage and led him off to a torture chamber, where they tied him up again and brought out the whips and blades and pliers and needles and white-hot pokers. Savagely, Ghrozm and his apprentices whittled away at him.

"You should have given Master what he desired," Ghrozm said, jaw clenched tightly.

Baleron endured it all stoically. His mind was far, far away. In a way, the torture was almost a relief.

Eventually they dragged him back to the pit and lowered him down it. He crawled out of the cage, bleeding and empty, and curled up on the dank stone floor. Worn out, he fell asleep instantly as things crawled over his inert form and stung him mercilessly, and the cage ascended, creaking, above. He dreamt of Rauglir again, and the laughter of the werewolf mocked him as he ran through an endless aviary, dizzied by the bright colors of the frantic birds. Somewhere his mother called to him, and he ran on, blinded by the birds.

The voice changed to another's. Someone *else* called him now, rocking him, and summoning him from slumber.

He opened his eyes, and started.

For Rolenya—dear, sweet Rolenya!—was cradling his bloody head in her lap, stroking his sweaty hair.

"How—?" he gasped. "What—?"

She gazed down at him with such sadness and love that it broke his heart to see. She had to be a ghost born of his weakening sanity, he thought. But then he realized it: *none of his ghosts had touched him before.*

"Rolly!" he choked and sat up. The effort made him grimace.

Somewhere high above a torch burned in the upper chamber, but its illumination was scant indeed. He could see only the orange glow reflecting off the side of her face, the swell of her cheekbone, the sweep of her black hair, the shine in her blue eye. He could see but one eye, as the other side lay in shadow.

"Baleron," she said, and hugged him tightly.

He drowned in her warmth, in her loving embrace. He gripped her and squeezed her to him, and she felt small and frail in his arms, in need of protection. Her breasts pressed against his chest, and he tried not to notice.

They rocked in each other's arms, crying in relief and despair.

At last he pulled himself away. "But I saw you die! How's this possible?"

She lowered her eyes. "He forged me another body, Bal, and slipped me—my soul—into it." She looked glum about it.

"To what purpose?"

"I ... don't want to know."

They looked at each other for a long moment.

He stroked her soft cheek. "When I saw you die—" He shook his head, unable to finish the thought. Instead, foolishly, he asked, "Did it hurt?"

Tears ran openly down her cheeks and dropped off her jaw as she nodded, and scorpions scattered as the tears splashed the floor, not wanting the liquid to touch them.

"That's twice now I've died," she said. "I can tell you, death doesn't get easier with practice."

"But why are you here? I don't understand."

"Neither do I. I was just funneled into this body, and they brought me here."

Suddenly, unexpectedly, he smiled. It was the first time he'd been alone with his sister in a long, long time. A thought occurred to him, and he hesitated. Finally, he forced himself to say, "Rolly, I ... do you know that we're ... well, I mean that you're an ..." He stopped.

The sweet ghost of a smile graced her face. She reached out and brushed a strand of hair from his cheek. "I know. In Illistriv ... someone told me. You and I ... we're not what we thought we were."

"No."

"No." She looked at him steadily. "But maybe that's not a bad thing."

That gave him hope, but he said nothing about it.

For some time, they didn't talk much, just held each other, and to him it felt somehow *right*. He felt they were meant to be together.

But, then, didn't every lovelorn fool think the same thing? He didn't want to talk about it. Why ruin things? Yet, the longer she was near, the more he longed for her and the harder it was not to look at her and touch her as he'd grown accustomed to in Havensrike.

Eventually, he asked softly, "The Second Hell ... is it terrible?"

She made a face. "That depends on where he places you. At first he put me in a safe place, a place of gardens and streams—it was nice, though I was scared, and there was an awful forest near—but after you refused him he was wroth and threw me into a sea of fire where his Warders ... savaged me." The memory, so near the surface, broke free, and she sobbed and flung herself against him. He stroked her hair and cooed in her ear.

"It'll be all right," he said. "It'll be all right."

He held her all night, and it seemed strange to him that Gilgaroth would allow him this, this one moment of happiness. Her heart beat against his chest, and he spoke of happier times. That seemed to comfort her somewhat.

After awhile, she whispered, "You always could make me feel better, Bal. I've missed you."

"And I you." He paused, cursing himself, then plowed forward. "Rol, I've ... got something to tell you. At Gulrothrog, after we escaped—well, that *was* you, right, the night Salthrick came? Or the thing pretending to be him."

"Yes. That was me."

"Well, when I returned, when we attacked it, we found ... another Rolenya. Someone pretending to be you. And she ... he ... it ... well, we ..." He coughed. This was worse than he'd thought it would be.

"I know," she said.

"What?" He nearly jumped away from her.

"In the Second Hell, in Illistriv, just a few months ago, he ... that is, Rauglir ... he came to me, boasting. He wanted to shame me, shame you—to hurt me. He's the one who let it slip that we weren't truly brother and sister, and he told me how you ... how you felt about me ..."

Heart in throat, Baleron waited. "Well?" he said at last, his voice rasping.

"To tell you the truth," she said softly, not moving away from him, "I wasn't as surprised as you might think."

He tilted her chin up so that he could look into what he could see of her eyes. "No?" he asked, his voice even more a rasp now than before.

"No."

They didn't say anything more about it, though they looked at each other for a long, long time. He wanted to kiss her then, but was afraid. After all he'd been through, somehow this still managed to terrify him. It amused him, and shamed him. So he just held her, and she held him, and eventually they passed into sleep.

Upon waking, two fiery eyes loomed over them.

He sat bolt upright, waking Rolenya, and she gasped and shrank away.

No, Baleron thought. *No, it CAN'T be. Not again.*

But it was. The Dark One had taken the guise of the Great Wolf, but he was even larger now. His slavering jaws dripped hissing saliva that smoldered against the stone floor. His eyes burned, pools of fire in the blackness. He growled deep, and Baleron shook with fear. The Wolf's musk-stench filled the pit.

"Gilgaroth," Baleron said, awed.

"I have come," declared the Wolf.

"Thank You ... for Rolenya."

"I have come for her, not you. Unless you have ... reconsidered."

"What? You cannot ... you cannot *do* this! You can't give her to me and then take her away, *again*. It's not *right*!" He understood how foolish the words even as he spoke them, but he couldn't help it.

Rolenya huddled against the far wall, her eyes, angry but

scared, transfixed by the Shadow's. She did not seem able to bring herself to speak.

"*WILL YOU SERVE ME?*" asked Gilgaroth.

Baleron understood now why Gilgaroth had given Rolenya to him. He'd given Baleron something precious so that it would hurt more when he took it away. It was the same in the arena, but this was worse, as the gift he'd given was greater: time.

In a small, trembling voice, Rolenya said, "Don't give in, Bal."

Baleron tried to meet the Wolf's gaze, but couldn't.

"I am not your creature," he said.

Enraged, the Great Wolf bounded forwards, knocking the prince aside and leaping on Rolenya. She struggled, but she could not fight such a being. The Wolf's jaws crushed the life from her, and her blood spattered the stone walls and scattered the lurking scorpions to their holes.

Gilgaroth, ignoring the prince's shouts and fists, devoured Rolenya, right before Baleron's horrified eyes. Baleron beat at the Great Wolf's sides so fiercely that he exhausted himself and sank against the wall as far away as he could get, and, weeping bitterly, turned his face away. He closed his hand over his ears to muffle the wet, meaty sounds and awful growls of the Wolf.

Finally, a secret door slid away in the pit wall with the sound of stone grating on stone, and the Dark One backed into it, his red stare never leaving Baleron. Rolenya's blood dripped from his muzzle.

"*I can make her and destroy her a thousand times, Baleron. How many times can you stand to watch?*"

The door slammed shut, leaving Baleron alone in the pit.

Gilgaroth was true to his threat, for the next night it happened all over again—and the next.

Every night Gilgaroth created a new body for Rolenya and every night he destroyed it after Baleron's refusal to aid him.

Sometimes he would give them time together first, sometimes not. The prince watched his beloved die time and again, sometimes horribly and slowly. He began to go mad, talking to himself when no one was there, pulling at his hair, which (he knew from the fistfuls) had begun to show even more streaks of silver. Killing himself would be pointless; Gilgaroth would only make him a new body. His only defense was to lose himself in his own mind.

He could not obey the Shadow, could not help destroy the world. If he and Rolenya had to suffer for it, then suffer they would. Eventually the war would reach a point where his contributions would matter little and the Dark One would kill him or forget him. Either way, this had to end sometime. He only had to hold on till then, no matter the cost to Rolenya. She agreed, as she said many times when they were put together. "If all I have to do to save the world is be tortured and die, I'll do it," she said. Over and over she urged him to be strong for both of them, to resist the Enemy's demands.

As Olfrig had alluded to, a huge army of Borchstogs and corrupted Giants and Men and others had gathered at the base of the tower, beyond the reach of the Inferno. Baleron overheard his guards and torturers discussing it. Ghrozm was openly boastful. The forces had been massing for months and their ranks were still not swelled fully yet. When the army was all gathered, Gilgaroth would send them and the dragons north to break the sieges at Clevaris and Glorifel, then to sweep across the whole Crescent, destroying what bastions of the Light remained, and they were few. Baleron knew he had only to wait until then, to that unimaginable day, the day when all hope died, when his usefulness to the Lord of the Tower would surely be at an end.

One day, Borchstogs led him out from the pit and down corridors he'd never been down before, and suddenly he smelled fresh air.

Outside!

Excitement coursed through him at first—he'd lived to see the world beyond Krogbur one more time—but then he grew uneasy. *What now?* He steeled himself to face whatever new horrors awaited him, and Rolenya.

His captors led him to an outside terrace, where a red Worm waited. Much smaller and leaner than Throgmar, it was more serpentine, and it hissed at the prince, lashing its tri-pronged tail. Nonetheless, it allowed the Borchstogs to strap him into a saddle, while two of their number strapped in behind him.

On a nearby terrace he saw Rolenya likewise being lashed onto the back of a similar dragon. Former brother and sister looked at each other sadly. Neither knew what was about to happen, but it could not be pleasant.

The wind roared and, despite everything, Baleron enjoyed it as it swept through his hair and over his skin. He hadn't seen the outside world in months, and he blinked at its brightness, even if the sky was covered with storm clouds and all was dim and stark. A tongue of lightning lanced the ground to the left, and he recoiled at its brightness, having to mash his eyes shut. The thunder nearly knocked him off his feet.

When he could see again, he marveled at the vision before him, at the mountains in the distance, the smoking volcanoes, the river of fire off to his right ... It was so big that it took his breath away. He'd become accustomed to tight environs.

As always, hundreds of dragons circled the tower in neverending loops, screening Krogbur from unwanted guests. Baleron thought of that day when he'd tracked Throgmar here. Then he had supposed the moat-Worms had sensed Rondthril and allowed him to breach their ring, but now he knew the truth, as he'd half-suspected at the time: the Wolf had let him in. Gilgaroth had, as was his way, been playing with Baleron.

Baleron's mount tilted and he received an unwelcome glimpse over the side of the terrace. His stomach lurched. It was a *long* way down. Krogbur reached to the very clouds and higher still, and the terrace they perched on was well above the Black Tower's equator. Small wisps of clouds drifted below. Below *that* raged the terrible Inferno of Illistriv. Souls, millions of them, flashing like silverfish, darted through the leaping flames pursued by nightmarish terrors, the Warders.

On the ground beyond the fire spread a restless darkness: the army. The soldiers were too far away to look like even ants; all Baleron could see was the formations and a myriad of tiny pinpricks that must be their bonfires. Still, he was struck by the size of the gathering: it was *immense*, stretching off towards the horizon. No might that the Crescent Union could summon could stand against it.

The realization shook Baleron. *This army, coupled with these hell-Worms, is the doom of the Alliance.* And when the Alliance fell, so would all of Roshliel.

He glanced to Rolenya. She, too, had caught a glimpse of the hordes, and was staring at them with a tight, pale face. Nervously, she looked up from them and shared a grim glance with Baleron.

The dragons bearing prince and princess took off. Flying in tandem, they spiraled down around the thick trunk of Krogbur, taking their time. Overhead, the black stem of the tower rose to the charcoal roof above, ringed by lightning. Thunder shook the heavens.

They passed terraces where powerful Worms lazed on mounds, some of treasure, some of bones and rotting bodies with flies buzzing around them. More blood-spattered Worms hung like bats from jutting beams and ramparts.

On other terraces stood groups of Borchstogs and other demons, come to get a glimpse of Baleron. When they saw him they pumped their fists in the air and chanted, *"Roschk ul Ravast! Roschk ul Ravast!"* Some dropped to their knees and slit their arms with knives, flinging their blood in his direction.

The Worms angled out, away from the tower, and just in time, too—any lower and they would have flown through the very flames of Illistriv. Sparks leapt up from the Inferno and the

29

dragons flew through the fiery sprites that swayed and swarmed with the searing currents. Baleron hunkered low, feeling scalding pains on his thigh and back.

Peering over his shoulder into the fires, he saw at close range a white-hot soul pursued by a long, serpentine dragon-shape, something like the creature in the Labyrinth of Melregor below Gulrothrog—part wolf, part spider, part Worm. He wondered if perhaps the fleeing soul was that of Salthrick. He would be in there somewhere, having died in unholy lands.

The dragons leveled out, gliding just twenty feet or so over the heads of the teeming Borchstogs whose camps sprawled across the plain. The creatures hooted and cheered. Baleron saw a group that had been torturing an Elvish captive stop their games and gaze upward, blood dripping from their mouths.

Some pointed back toward the tower, and a great clamor rose up. Baleron felt a thrill of dread. Reluctantly, he turned.

Saw.

Cold fingers touched his spine.

For—emerging from the very flames of the Second Hell—was none other than the Breaker of the World.

In a form Baleron had never seen him take before, Gilgaroth —it could be no other, such was his awful might and splendor— exploded from the fires that wreathed the Black Tower and shot directly toward Baleron and Rolenya. Rolenya gave a startled cry.

Gilgaroth came as a great black dragon, long and sinewy, with a wolvish head, horned and whiskered, trailing smoke from his terrible maw. His tail cracked like a whip, making Baleron's eardrums vibrate. Having no wings, Gilgaroth seemed to swim rather than fly through the skies, moving through the air like an eel. His eyes blazed Hell-fire, and he radiated an awesome power, darkness embracing him.

Wonder overcame the Borchstogs, who knelt or cheered.

For his part, Baleron was startled. He had heard that Lorg-jilaad was called the Great Dragon but had not known Gilgaroth could assume the same form—and such an awful one. He wondered if it could have been this form that he'd seen that day in the Black Temple—as he had come to think of the dark place where he had lost his hand. He remembered the flaming eyes and fire-lit maw of Gilgaroth seemingly suspended, bodiless, in the center of that great empty space. Yet perhaps the darkness had concealed the sinewy shape of the dragon and Gilgaroth had not been discorporated after all. Or perhaps he had been in some sort of cocoon stage, *growing* this new form.

In any event, Gilgaroth drew abreast them, flame licking his lips and smoke trailing behind him like a second tail. Baleron could feel his heat and smell his smoking breath.

Gilgaroth wasted no time on greetings. "*Baleron,*" he said, "*I tire of games. Today We end this.*"

Baleron tried to say something, but his mouth was too dry. He felt his hands tremble as they gripped the red Worm's reins.

Gilgaroth's eyes crackled. "*Submit to me, Baleron, or I will throw Rolenya down ... to them.*"

The teeming Borchstogs below, tens, no, *hundreds* of thousands of them, cheered the passing of their great lord. Lust and cruelty and malice burned in their eyes. Baleron looked down at them, then to Rolenya. She was deathly pale, and shaking.

"*They will not kill her,*" added Gilgaroth unnecessarily.

Below, the hordes swarmed to the passing shadow of their Master, fighting each other to be in it. Baleron felt sick, thinking of what they would do with Rolenya.

"*Decide now,*" Gilgaroth commanded. "*My children will use her for days, weeks. They may never kill her.*" He added, giving the final nudge, "*You are your sister's last hope.*"

It was too much for Baleron. He had tried to be good, tried to be strong for the sake of his kingdom, for the sake of the world. But this was beyond his limits to endure. He would not let her be thrown down to them, like a bone to feral dogs.

He hung his head, and Rolenya gasped, sobbing, too scared of her fate to fight him this time.

"I will serve you," he told Gilgaroth. "May the Light have mercy on my soul."

Baleron and Rolenya were taken high into the tower and shown to a lavish suite, which they were told would be their home for however long they stayed at Krogbur. The Borchstogs left them, though a servant could be summoned by ringing a bell, and former brother and sister were alone and in comfort for the first time since those few stolen moments at Gulrothrog.

Baleron wasn't ready to enjoy such comfort, though, and he suspected that neither was Rolenya. When the Borchstogs left, prince and princess just stood there at the threshold of the suite, staring dully.

"What now?" she whispered.

He wrapped an arm about her and said honestly, "I don't know."

Despair clung to him. How could he have given in?

She seemed to see his pain. She pressed herself against him and, surprising him, kissed him on the lips.

Startled, he stared at her, and she drew back.

"Thank you, Baleron. I ... " She looked at the floor, ashamed but at the same time clearly not sorry to have avoided her fate. She seemed to want to thank him more but did not think it appropriate. He understood. How can you thank someone for damning the world?

"I know," he said.

She glanced up. "Don't let it eat you up, Bal. He breaks everyone. It's what he does. He's the Breaker. He makes things just to destroy them. Believe me, I know. I don't blame you. I ... I think you were strong. *So* strong. You held out, and held out. I ... *I* couldn't have done it, if he'd been doing those things to *you* and *I* was the one he wanted to bend."

He swallowed. "Do you hate me, Rol, for letting you die all those times?"

She searched his face. "Hate you? How can you think that?"

"Then do you hate me for failing at last?"

She shook her head. Trembling, she said, "No, Bal. I ... I love you." Suddenly she looked away.

Many torches, urns and fireplaces lit the rooms. It was a lavish suite, huge and magical. She moved off into it, and he followed.

The beautifully wrought terrace did not look outward, or inward for that matter. Instead, the view was of some majestic snow-capped mountains that did not exist in Oslog, if at all. Their slopes were green and the skies blue, and from somewhere birds could be heard chirping.

"What is this place?" he asked. "Is it all an illusion?"

"It's all part of Illistriv, I think. That's what this place is, the whole tower."

"But how?"

"Might as well ask me how the stars are born. All I know is that in this one place, he's brought his own realty to ours. And when he's stronger he'll spread the fires of the Inferno. Everything that falls within that ring will become part of Illistriv. That's what he wants, for the whole world to be ..." Her voice trailed off.

"Then if I help him, I truly will be *ul Ravast*."

She took his hand and led him from the balcony.

Inside the suite ran several babbling brooks that came through the walls, and they channeled here and there into little pools that, though steaming, were not too hot to bathe in. Baleron and Rolenya explored the suite with interest, and its marvels took his mind off his shame and confusion for a time. The rooms were surprisingly warm, covered in rugs of animal fur that masked the cold black floors and walls. The couches and chairs were upholstered in hides and furs, as was the bed.

There was only one bed.

Brother and sister stopped when they came to it. Butterflies tickled his belly.

"You take it," he said at last, speaking around the lump in his throat.

She looked at him levelly. "No."

"No, truly," he said, trying to sound casual. "The floors are more than warm enough for me. Let's catch us a rest, shall we? I'm tired. I don't know if I can sleep, but I'm tired. Then it's baths and breakfast."

"Baleron," she whispered.

He raised his eyebrows.

"Don't make me say it," she said.

He opened his mouth, then closed it.

"Bal—"

He stopped her with a kiss. He wrapped her in his arms, and she melted against him. It seemed as if the world dissolved, simply folding away, and there was only the two of them. Her lips were hot and moist.

Suddenly, she made a frustrated sound and pushed away. Shaking her head, she stumbled back. "No, no—"

"What?"

She covered her face with her hands. "No, it's not—"

"Not right?"

She nodded miserably.

Slowly, he moved towards her. "I've loved you my whole life, Rolly. I never knew I wanted you like I do, but, Omkar help me, I do. I really, truly do. I love you in every way I can. After all I've been through, all I've seen, and done, and survived, I won't feel bad about this. If this is all the happiness life can afford me, then I will *revel* in it. I won't have you feeling ill about it. About *us*. We're *right* together, Rolenya. We're very, very right."

He took her hands away from her face. Teary-eyed, she stared up at him. Her lips trembled.

"Say you love me," he said.

"I love you." Her voice quavered.

"Say you want me."

"I want you. Omkar help me, Bal, I never thought about you like this before now, but I do."

Suddenly, she stood on her tiptoes and kissed him. She tasted sweet and pure, and he wanted more. He kissed her back, heatedly, and she responded in kind.

They kissed and touched each other, whispering fervent things in each other's ear, and gradually they helped each other to disrobe, blushing shyly at each other's nakedness. He had never felt more awkward with a girl before, and never more alive. Her body, new-formed, was much like her old one, and it was beautiful and erotic and lush.

They moved to the bed and slipped under its warm furs, caressing each other more boldly, and drowned in each other's touch.

Afterwards, they bathed. He luxuriated in the feel of the hot water against his skin.

Soap had been laid beside the pools, and she said, "Allow me" and began soaping off his grimy, whip-scarred back, sitting behind him in the water, her long legs about him. Gingerly, she cleaned him, avoiding the sensitive areas.

"Look what they've done to you," she whispered. "May the Light protect you."

Later, she said, "Stand."

"What?"

"I said, stand."

Self-consciously, he obeyed.

"Turn around," she instructed, and, having to resist the urge to cover himself, he turned. His eyes found her. Her breasts, soapy and wet, were only half-concealed by the water.

He felt hot, and saw her own cheeks redden. She was all too aware of his arousal, yet she didn't skirt it when she helped him wash.

They took their time soaping each other up and rinsing each other off, and as he touched her, and she touched him, his feelings solidified. Deepened. It began to feel real, their being together, and the taint of Rauglir faded.

Soon she took his hand and led him toward the bed again. He stopped, but she continued to it without him, turning when she reached it. Her towel slipped from one delicate white shoulder, revealing the top of one smooth, round breast.

She stretched out her hand to him, beckoning.

For a moment, he hesitated. *The world might end*, he thought. *Because of our love, the world might end.*

But then all he could think of was her, her red lips, her round breasts, and he stepped forward.

A human servant knocked at the door and asked if they were hungry. Baleron was famished and ate with enthusiasm when breakfast came. It was comprised of eggs and toast and sausage and bacon, with sides of fruit and juice, just like he might have eaten back home; likely Gilgaroth's spies had gathered the information necessary to make it. Just the same, it was the best meal he'd had in a long, long while.

Afterward, they lounged on the terrace and watched the snow-capped mountains against the clear blue sky. They didn't speak much, just held each other close. She smelled clean and fresh and new.

After lunch, they made love again, then they lay in each other's arms and spoke of sweet things. They made no plans for the future, for what could the future hold for the likes of them?

About mid-afternoon, a Borchstog necromancer, dressed in

exotic robes, burst through the doors of the suite and thumped his sorcerous staff on the floor.

"I am High Priest Ustagrot!" the Borchstog said. "You are invited for an audience with Master. Come!"

They dressed and followed him from the suite, and when he led them to a lift operated by sorcery, they boarded it, Baleron's stomach lurching as it rose. When it stopped, the necromancer stepped off, and Baleron and Rolenya followed, casting wary gazes about them. Ustagrot led them onwards, up huge flights of stairs, and Baleron, tired already by his and Rolenya's exertions, breathed heavily, and so did she. Before long, they were leaning on each other for support.

"What could he want with us?" she panted.

"I don't know," he responded. "And I don't want to."

The necromancer led them to the grand staircase that led from the highest terrace—where Gilgaroth had met Throgmar— up, presumably, to the Dark One's Throne Room. Then, to Baleron's consternation, Ustagrot began ascending these stairs. Reluctantly, they followed, mounting the high black steps one by one. The stairs seemed endless, but finally Ustagrot marched up the last one, and so did they

"We go to the Throne Room," the necromancer said, as if they could not have figured this out.

Baleron saw the massive doors that framed the portal and felt dread creep over his soul. *Beyond those doors lies Hell*. He knew it. He could feel it in the air, feel it in his bones. Beside him, Rolenya began to shudder. A steady red light, emanating from within the Throne Room, poured out between the great doors and washed the black stairs with a fiery glow.

"Be strong," Baleron told Rolenya, seeing her fright. "The worst is past."

She nodded, and he hoped his words were true. He could not help but think that soon he would learn the price for her salvation. What would Gilgaroth have him do?

They passed through the massive, obscenely engraved doors, and Baleron gaped at what lay beyond. Through them lay another world.

Through them lay Hell.

Lit by towering bonfires stretched a massive stone cavern so tall its upper reaches were hidden in shadow and its walls were so far apart they loomed in the distance like mountains. The bonfires threw a red light upon the cave walls and floor and colored everything the color of human blood. The higher reaches were dark blood, and the highest reaches black. Shadows leapt and danced in sinister seduction. The cavern was so large it could have contained a city, and it did. Twisting spires and profane domes dotted the floor between the towering stalagmites, some of which had been carved into terrifying forms that loomed overhead, while others had been carved into palaces and temples and other more recognizable buildings. Demons great and small lurched and crept and stomped all about, and wraiths like living shadows sped here and there through the infernal city on mysterious errands of their own.

Two Colossi stood in the wings, mountainous creatures a thousand feet high, their features somewhere between Man and Borchstog and Spider. They had four muscular arms each, and a long, triple-pronged tail. Baleron had never believed in them before: they'd been mythical monsters to him, said to help shape Gilgaroth's mountains, and when they were angry, they were said to pound the earth, breaking it apart and reshaping it.

On the far side, rearing over the city of the damned, thrust a jagged peak, and from the top of this hill sprouted a palace of twisting, interlocked towers and erotic mounds. The fires colored it red, though Baleron thought it might truly be made of red stone.

"That is our destination," Ustagrot said, gesturing toward the distant palace.

"Dear gods," breathed Rolenya, squeezing Baleron's arm nervously.

"Which ones?" he asked.

Ustagrot led them into the infernal city and to either side of them rose bizarre buildings, while strange smells, some pleasant, some not, drifted through the air. Screams of anguish and screams of ecstasy chased each other through the air. In the heat, sweat beaded Baleron's skin. Strange demons, some sinister, some alluring, strode through the boulevards or flew through the air, or simply drifted. A beautiful woman with hooves for feet and with dark-feathered wings jutting from her back shot him a lascivious smile. At an intersection blazed a bonfire of living corpses and about it swarmed a host of wraiths, screaming and wailing. A corpulent demon with nine heads of various sorts stood watching the spectacle, laughing.

"Just where are we, exactly?" Baleron said. "Are we ... *in him?* In Gilgaroth?"

"Yes," said Rolenya. "This place, it's all part of him. Illistriv is within him, and if we're in Illistriv ..."

"But how can we be *in* him if we're going to *meet* him? Then he would be inside himself!"

Ustagrot wheeled on them. "Infidels!" he hissed. "You know nothing!"

"How can your Savior be an infidel?"

"Do not find your own ignorance so amusing, Fallen One. You know nothing of the nature of the world, of how the Omkar created it, and of how my Master could create another world that could merge with this one. So hide your shameful ignorance and still your tongue!"

He resumed the march. They entered a wide, open courtyard dominated by a huge black fountain of a thirteen-headed dragon; out of each mouth poured what Baleron hoped was red water that trickled down their long throats and bubbled in the gruesome pool. The heads of the dragon were wound about each other most lewdly.

A wraith stopped before their path, and Ustagrot bowed to it.

"We have come to see Master," he said.

The wraith bowed back and seemed to hiss, "We have been expecting you. Let us aid your journey."

It gestured, and thunder shook the chamber. Startled, Baleron looked to the right as a Colossus stepped forwards. Bending down over the towers of the city, the giant creature stretched out a massive grayish hand, holding it just above the courtyard floor. Baleron reeled; the hand was large enough to hold Throgmar!

The necromancer climbed onto it and bade them do likewise.

Grimacing, the prince followed and held down a hand for Rolenya. When they were all situated on one of the titan's fingers, the Colossus carried them the length of the Throne Room, toward the palace on its mountain. A moat of high black flames surrounded the sharp peak, and white-hot souls writhed in the moat of fire. The Colossus raised them to the tallest, serpentine tower of the building and with surprising delicacy set them on its highest terrace. Then it withdrew, shaking the ground as it went.

The terrace wrapped around this level of the spire, which was open, the roof supported only by a few obscenely-ornate columns, and in the center of the floor stood the Black Throne of Gilgaroth.

It was occupied.

Ustagrot bowed.

A veil of shadow surrounded the Dark One, and his eyes of fire shone like lamps from the smoky blackness.

Baleron noticed that Gilgaroth's two great wolves, Slorch and Thorg, stretched out to either side of the Throne. Rolenya began shaking when she saw them, but Baleron held her tightly.

"Welcome," said the Lord of the Second Hell.

Rolenya squeezed Baleron's hand, and he squeezed back.

"Bow!" Ustagrot snapped at them.

Awkwardly, Baleron knelt, and Rolenya followed suit. This soured the prince's stomach, but he had to pretend at obedience for now. Hopefully there would be a time when he could stop pretending, when he could seize some advantage, some oversight on Gilgaroth's part, and deal the Shadow a crushing blow, or at the very least rescue Rolenya, escape, and avoid fulfilling his Doom.

"Rise," said Gilgaroth, and they did. *"Come."* The Lord of the Tower stood, a column of darkness that seethed with unimaginable power, and led them to the terrace facing away from the infernal city.

Baleron sucked in his breath at the view. The palace stood at the end of the cavern and the terrace overlooked the valleys and mountains that lay beyond. There were high peaks, roads, buildings, countryside—a whole world. But everything was twisted, distorted by the evil of its maker. The trees leant at mad angles and their branches stretched like tentacles. The lakes burned with fire. In the village squares demons tortured the souls of men Gilgaroth had devoured. Baleron shuddered, and out of the corner of his eye he saw Rolenya turn away.

"Behold Illistriv," said Gilgaroth. *"My Creation. My truest home."*

"It is beautiful, Master," said Ustagrot, half bowing, voice quavering.

"When my Champion completes his labor, the whole world will be as this. Now—to the business at hand." He returned to his throne, and they followed. *"It is time, for you, my Spider, to complete your web. You will obey me in all things or burn in the fires of Illistriv forevermore. You will never see Rolenya again. The world will be just as damned; its damning will only take a few days longer to accomplish. Do you understand?"*

Baleron nodded.

"Good," he continued. *"If you both obey me, and if you both live to see the other side of my war, you will have a place here, or elsewhere in my realm. You may rule, if you wish, some outer province. You will be king*

JACK CONNER

and queen of some distant land, in thrall only to me, and I will not bother you ... much. I can make you both young and beautiful forever, or I can let you grow old and die. Most any wish or desire you have I can make reality, and in time you can become valued allies of mine and my Sire's." He paused, and his tone grew grave. *"Now, for the price."*

Baleron could not meet Rolenya's sidelong look.

"Baleron, you will return to Glorifel. You will gain the confidence of your father and of the others in his Court. Then you will slay him."

Baleron's breath caught in his throat. Rolenya's pressure on his hand became a death grip.

"You will also kill Logran Belefard, the Archmage, and destroy the elvish artifact he wields. Next slay any heirs your father has appointed; all his other sons save Jered are dead, and Jered is at Clevaris with the Elf Queen, where I have placed him—for he is another spider spinning my web—so the only direct heirs can be your sisters. Kill as many of them as you can, starting from the oldest. But especially the Archmage and his artifact. That done, the city will fall." Gilgaroth's voice deepened, and his eyes seemed to reach out and ensnare Baleron. All the prince could see was whirling fire, and his whole world was that one voice: *"You will know all this, yet you will be unable to convey it to anyone. My powers stretch that far, at least."*

"Yes," Baleron heard himself say, though it seemed he had not willed the words himself.

"That is well. Now, when you have finished your labor, allow yourself to be captured and my agents shall return you here to Krogbur, where you will be reunited with your ... Rolenya." He patted the wolf to his right. *"Slorch,"* he snapped.

The wolf rose and sauntered over to them, carrying a satchel in his fang-ridden mouth, and Rolenya flinched as it drew near. It dropped the satchel at Baleron's feet, which hit the floor with a heavy clank. The monster growled and returned to his Master's side.

"Look inside," Gilgaroth instructed.

Baleron obeyed. Within he saw the unholy length of Rondthril, glimmering darkly, nestled amongst belt and scabbard like a snake coiled to strike.

The sword that could kill a god ...

There was no way it could work. No way at all. To use it now would be folly.

"Don it when you reach Glorifel," came Gilgaroth's voice.

Baleron shook his head. "They won't let me past the walls. My father hates me and won't admit me, not even to save my life."

"He will. If you wear that blade, he will. My foresight has shown this."

Rondthril's handle gleamed seductively, drawing Baleron's attention. *No*, he cautioned himself. *That way lays madness.*

Yet he was mad.

Acting with a suddenness that surprised him, he tore the Fanged Blade from the satchel, unsheathed it, and in a flurry of motion hurled it end over end at the Dark One's breast.

For a moment, hope rose in him. It would strike true!

But the Fanged Blade was loyal not just to Ungier, but Gilgaroth as well. It seemed to hit an invisible wall five feet from Gilgaroth and bounced off, clattering to the floor.

Baleron stared from it to Gilgaroth, waiting, and a long, tense moment passed. Somewhere a demon screamed. Rolenya let out ragged breaths, clearly afraid for Baleron.

Amused, Gilgaroth called the weapon to him, and it flew to his hand. He appraised it with interest, turning it over and over.

"Rondthril. A mighty blade, yes—Ungier's finest. A gift from father to son. My grandson's first blade. And, thanks to you, his last." He tossed it at Baleron's feet. *"Did you think I would not foresee that? You are a fool, Baleron Grothgar. Do not act so rashly when you are about my business, or you—and your ... sister—will regret it most severely. Ustagrot, take them from my sight!"*

The necromancer rose to his feet and snarled at the royal pair, "Follow me!"

They followed him down the steep flight of red steps that led from the dais of the Throne of Shadows and through the palace interior to the moat of black fire, which parted for them, then sealed behind.

"Because of your insolence," snapped the necromancer to the prince, "we will have to *walk*!"

It was a long stretch through the infernal city to the doors of the room, and neither of the Colossi volunteered to help. Baleron knew he had been a fool.

Rolenya squeezed his hand. "It was a good throw," she whispered.

At that, he almost smiled.

Wraiths and demons circled them, mocking, and the necromancer cursed him all the way. Eventually they passed the threshold of the room, and Baleron was never so glad to be rid of a place. Ustagrot led them down toward their suite.

Feeling the weight of Rondthril dangling from his hip, Baleron eyed the high priest's back. He harbored dangerous thoughts and almost went through with one, but in the end he stayed his hand. It was too dangerous, the risks too high. Ustagrot was, after all, a sorcerer, and it was a long way to freedom even if the Borchstog should meet his end.

Ustagrot led the prince and princess to their suite and left them. Baleron and Rolenya locked themselves in their apartment, and he half thought of blocking the door with furniture and barricading themselves inside. He had a hard time meeting her eyes.

The Dark One wanted him to kill his father. *Their* father.

All his life he had wanted only his father's love and respect, and now to save his sister from a fate worse than death he would have to kill the man, and doom everything he stood for.

He and Rolenya held each other under the furs of the bed, and she sobbed against his chest, lost in despair.

"It will be all right," he told her, stroking her hair.

"How?" she asked him. "How can it possibly be all right?"

He thought of the perfect lie. "This is all part of my plan," he told her.

She looked at him curiously. "What plan?"

He smiled confidently. "I didn't agree to aid him just to save you," he said.

"You didn't? Then what did you do it for?"

"Because I knew he would send me back, and that's just what I wanted. He walked right into my trap. Don't you see, Rolly? *Someone* needs to warn the Crescent of the army he's massing here. Someone needs to prepare them. They need to brace for its coming in whatever way they can." As he said it, he knew that it was true, and he embraced this new cause with enthusiasm, though he had only thought of it moments before.

She looked at him with her big blue eyes, and at last she smiled, despite everything, and kissed him. "Oh, Baleron, I love you," she said. "You're a big liar, but I do love you."

Without knocking, several glarumri entered, and Rolenya yelped in surprise. The Borchstogs were impatient and dressed for riding.

"It is time," snapped their leader.

The glarumri waited restlessly for Baleron in the main room while he readied himself.

"Oh, Baleron," Rolenya said, clinging to him, a sheet thrown about her nakedness. She put her lips to his ear and whispered, "Forget me, Bal. Do what you know is right."

"I could never forget you."

"Then the world is doomed."

"It is doomed regardless."

She shook her head. "He needs us, my love. He needs *you*. That's his weakness. Use it against him. It's the only way."

"No. No, it's not. I ... know another."

She looked at him strangely, but he did not have time to explain, and it would probably be unwise to in any case. It was time to go.

Their guards allowed Rolenya to accompany him to the glarum platform, which was large and teeming with the foul, black-feathered steeds. They cawed and snapped and stirred uneasily, and suddenly Baleron missed Lunir. Scalding wind howled around him, coming off the Inferno.

Borchstogs seated him on one of the great crows, and the riders found their own birds and mounted up. The leader yelled out, and the squad took off from the terrace, cutting a wedge through the dragon-moat.

Baleron looked back once to see Rolenya standing there on the platform, her wind-whipped black hair flying, her blue eyes wet, her long legs bare. Her small shoulders huddled as she held the sheet about her, shivering in the high air.

She receded with distance, and, when the Worms closed up behind the fleet of glarumri, she was lost to sight. Baleron wondered if he would ever see her again.

Rolenya sobbed as she watched Baleron dwindle to a speck in the sky, her shoulders shaking, tears running down her cheeks. She didn't bother to wipe them away. The wind turned cold, and she shuddered.

Abruptly, she felt a Presence behind her. She could smell an all-too familiar musk, and feel an unearthly heat. For a long while, she could not bring herself to turn, could not bring herself to face him, and to her surprise he didn't force the issue. He just loomed there, behind her, watching her. Waiting.

At last, she set her jaw and turned. As she gazed up into his fiery eyes, her strength fled, and it was all she could do to remain standing.

In his dragon form, Gilgaroth was huge and black, his whiskers trailing like tendrils about his wolvish face. He took up the whole of her vision.

She took a step backwards and placed a hand over her mouth to hold in a scream, but she was so scared that she forgot to scream.

"Rolenya," breathed Gilgaroth.

"M-my lord," she managed, hating herself for calling him that but knowing no other form of address for him.

"Why do you cry? Do you miss him so soon?"

She lowered her eyes. "You wouldn't understand."

He did not speak immediately. Finally he said, *"I too know pain."*

Curious, she looked up. His eyes, twin abysses of fire, mesmerized her, terrified her, but she refused to look away.

"You do?" she said.

"I knew it when you sang."

"You did?"

He nodded. *"Long had I heard rumor of your voice, whiteling. But until you sang for Baleron I had never heard it. It ... was lovely."*

"Th-thank you. I think." Why was he telling her this?

"I want you to sing ... for me."

"W-what?"

"Yes. You will sing."

She tried to think. "But, if it was painful, why?"

"It ... was a good pain."

She screamed as one of his claws ensnared her. He flew off the terrace and carried her away from Krogbur, and she saw it diminish between two of his black nails as the wind tore at her. Yet she felt his heat, his immense, burning heat, and was warm, if not happy.

He carried her to the high, jagged peak of a mountain jutting up from the surrounding wasteland and set her on it. Then, like a serpent, he wrapped himself about the rocky spire and gazed up at her.

"Sing," he said.

Fear seized her, and confusion, but slowly she got a grip on herself. *What else can I do?* she thought.

Unable to help the stammer, she said, "W-what would you l-like to hear?"

"Just ... sing."

She emptied her mind of fear and turned to thoughts of Light and Grace. Marshaling her resolve, she lifted her face to the heavens, and sang. The song poured out of her like a spring flows from the ground, coming to her naturally, and as it flowed she drew strength from it, and her voice grew stronger, echoing off the sharp peaks far away, and off the black roof of clouds above.

Gilgaroth listened, seeming to drink up her voice like wine, but she did not look at him, as the sight of him would drive the song from her. And so she closed her eyes and sang, and as she sang she wept, and thought of Baleron.

Chapter Four

The once-green fields and forests of Havensrike were black and smoking as Baleron flew over them, and with every breath he swore bitter oaths of vengeance against those who'd done this. He and his escort flew for days, rarely stopping, and when they did the Borchstogs kept a close guard on him. He watched for his chance at escape, but it never came. He thought of Rolenya often.

At least he'd reclaimed Rondthril. With any luck, if he could command his Five Hundred again, if he could lead another attack against Ungier, perhaps ...

He tried not to think about it. Gilgaroth could read thoughts, after all.

The glarum riders hated daylight, but they braved the bright skies anyway, never waiting for nightfall when it was time to depart their brief campsites. Their elongated, wolf-like helmets protected their eyes from the sun.

As they drew closer to Glorifel, Baleron saw a great mass of dark clouds above that wondrous city blotting out the blazing Eye of Brunril, throwing an artificial nighttime on its attackers, shielding them from the sun. The glarumri neared the high walls and Baleron saw the teeming army of Borchstogs and their allies camped outside the city. Glorifel was on its last legs; Trolls and beasts and corrupted Giants, even a battalion of Men, numbered among those laying siege to the city. Here and there rose large scaly mounds, glittering in the moonlight: dragons, sleeping.

How can this be? he asked himself. *How can it have come to this?*

The Borchstoggish army was impressive, but not nearly as grand and terrible as the host massing at the roots of Krogbur, the hammer that would destroy the remnants of the Crescent Union, which was the dam holding back the dark river of Oslog— a dam that was about to be broken and the foul tide unleashed. How could Baleron aid that cause? How could he be its Champion?

He pictured Rolenya, and then he pictured her fate if he should fail in completing his web, and then he pictured the fate of Roshliel if he *did* complete it. Where was the solution?

He must free Rondthril with Ungier's death and confront Gilgaroth with it. He could think of no other way. But how to slay Ungier?

Again he tried not to think too long upon it.

The glarumri set down amidst the rabble of Borchstogs near the largest bonfire, near where the command tents were pitched. Various beasts and monsters skulked about or were chained to the earth, snarling.

The riders dismounted and Baleron was instructed to wear his cursed sword. This puzzled him, but he did it. Next the glarumri captain said, "We go to *ul Qrodegrad*." *The Shepherd.*

Hope rose in Baleron, but also fear. Ungier was his only route to salvation, but the Vampire King hated him and he did not relish the prospect of being at Ungier's mercy. Nevertheless, he didn't resist as the glarumri shoved him through the filthy ranks of the Borchstogs toward the command center.

The demons grouped around steaming cauldrons of *srodnarl*, or tortured prisoners, or had slaves pleasure them, or prayed to

Gilgaroth, or a hundred other unsavory things, yet wherever Baleron passed the Borchstogs ceased what they were about and turned to him. Some bowed or muttered prayers. Some offered their souls to him and slew themselves on the spot.

He ignored them.

Lord Ungier, as it happened, sat on a throne made of human skulls and was surrounded by six armored Trolls. He was casually sipping wine mixed with human blood from a jewel-encrusted golden chalice. Bristling murmeksa, the monstrous wooly boar-things with sharp tusks, thronged about the Trolls, grunting savagely.

"Well met, Maggot," Ungier said as Baleron was brought before him. "Deliverer of Doom, King of Catastrophe. Yes, you are a welcome sight, my old friend. You herald the end of the siege and the rise of my new domain. For I will plant my seed in the withered womb of Havensrike, and I will call it Ungoroth."

Baleron was in too foul a mood to exchange barbs with Ungier, and at this point barbs might be counter to his purpose.

The glarum riders bowed to the former Lord of Gulrothrog.

"Kneel to Lord Ungier," said one.

Baleron was dismayed to see that the Vampire King was surrounded by such a force. How could he get close enough?

"Kneel!" said the glarumri leader, and shoved Baleron onto one knee.

Ungier smiled. Red stained his sharp teeth. "Good to see a son of the Fallen Race assume his rightful posture." He added, "And thank you for coming, as I meant what I said: now that you're here, your city's days are numbered."

"Only if they let me in." *What am I going to do?* He needed to kill the vampire to release Rondthril from its service to the dark powers; it was his only chance against Gilgaroth.

"May I kiss your ring?" he asked.

Ungier glanced at the gold ring he wore, bearing as it did the image of the Great Wolf. *How he must hate that*, Baleron thought. But Ungier would have to keep up appearances.

The vampire's black eyes studied Baleron, then shrugged. "Please yourself."

Baleron shuffled forward, head low, past the first two Trolls and dropped to his knees before Ungier. As he did, he drew Rondthril, and, in one motion, hacked at the vampire's leathery neck.

He prayed it would work. After all, Ungier had shown fear of the sword before, and, as the blade hissed toward the vampire now, he seemed frightened again. His eyes widened, and his fanged mouth became an O.

The blade bounced off an invisible wall and Baleron was thrown back as if knocked by a strong wind. Instantly, a Troll placed its foot on his head and chest and pinned him down. Stars danced before his eyes. He could not draw breath.

"Wait!" shouted Ungier. "Leave him be!"

The Troll removed his foot, and Baleron took a deep breath.

Sneering, Ungier picked Rondthril up and admired its craftsmanship. "Asguilar's blade ... I would love to have it back." His voice held tones of genuine lament. "It took me long to forge it, you know. Oh, I was so proud. My first true son ... " His eyes narrowed. "He was a great one, you festering pus, you vermin. How could the likes of you slay such as him? He was mighty. He alone of all my sons that followed loved me. He alone would never have lifted a hand against me. Ah, he made me so proud!" Black-blooded tears welled in his eyes, and the hand that held Rondthril actually shook. He pointed the Fanged Blade at Baleron's breast. "*You* did that. *You* took him from me. And you and your curse took away my home, my brides, my Rolenya ..." Rage overcame him, and he lifted his head and howled like a wolf. In response, the true wolves of the host lifted their heads and howled, too, and the Borchstogs followed so that soon the whole night reverberated with Ungier's pain.

To his surprise, Baleron was actually moved.

At last the great, mournful howling died away. Seething, shaking, the vampire cast Rondthril down at the prince's feet, then collapsed back into his gruesome throne. "Would that I could kill you, but you are denied me. Would that I could keep that sword, but apparently your labor requires it. They won't let you inside the city without it—why, I don't know."

Baleron propped himself up. "You must have some idea."

"I suppose you'll find out the why of it soon. Tell me, did you really think Rondthril could kill me?"

"You were scared of it before, at Gulrothrog."

"I didn't know what sorcery the Elves might've worked on it, but now I sense it's the same as it's always been. Good."

A great horn sounded out from atop the city wall, and a familiar voice, amplified by sorcery, called out, "Has Prince Baleron returned?"

Logran! They must've seen us fly in. Baleron almost smiled, but couldn't. *I'll have to come up with some other plan, damn it.*

Ungier nodded to a tall, cloaked Borchstog—a necromancer. The necromancer lifted a horn to his lips and blew twice, loudly, turning to face the Walls.

"Yes, he has returned," boomed the Borchstog, his voice amplified, as Logran's had been. "The time has come to exchange prisoners, if that is still your desire."

Long moments passed with no word from the wall. Baleron shifted uneasily.

"Go on, decide," said Ungier anxiously, half to himself, his black eyes fixed on the South Gate, as if willing it to open. "What's taking so long?"

"They're studying him. Don't worry," said the necromancer. "He has the sword. They'll take him."

Sure enough, the horn sounded out again and Logran called, "We'll lead out your son, Ungier, and you will present us with Baleron. Any deviation on your part will be met with a hail of arrows, and the first one will slay Guilost."

"It is agreed," returned the Borchstog necromancer.

What's this? Baleron thought. *What interest can Logran have in Rondthril?*

"Farewell, Prince," said Ungier. "We will likely not meet again."

Baleron leveled his eyes at the vampire. "Don't be so sure."

He was ushered toward the high gates, and the archers in the towers to either side watched his approach anxiously. The gates themselves were thrown open and a vampire under heavy guard was led out from the city, where the procession stopped.

Baleron and his handlers stopped a hundred feet away.

The Havensril knights unchained their prisoner and prodded him forwards. Gratefully, the young rithlag—Guilost—made his way back to his people, and Ungier seemed genuinely glad to see him, which surprised Baleron, who'd just heard that only Asguilar had truly loved his father.

Baleron's handlers shoved him forward. This all seemed strange to him—wrong, somehow. Obviously this prisoner exchange was a staged affair, a half-hearted effort on the enemy's part to fool the humans into thinking it legitimate, but there was more to it than that. The Men had an agenda of their own, and the enemy knew about it, was playing to it.

The human soldiers drew around him in a tight, gleaming knot, and he wondered if any of them had been with the Five Hundred.

Suddenly their swords pointed at his breast and throat. "Sorry, my lord," said their leader. "But we have to do this."

He recognized that voice. "Halthus?"

"It's I, sir."

"Excellent!" Baleron clapped Halthus on the shoulder, ignoring the other knights' tension. Halthus had been one of his lieutenants when he led the Five Hundred.

Lifting his visor, Halthus did not look so friendly at the moment, however. "Sir, you'd better come with us quietly."

Baleron withdrew his hand. He hadn't noticed it before, but one of the knights carried coils of chain over his shoulder, and he brought it out now and bound the prince's hands. Baleron, not quite mystified, allowed it.

"I'm not a werewolf," he said.

Halthus shrugged. "That's for the mages to decide."

They led him inside the walls as though he were a prisoner, and the gates closed behind him with a crash that echoed in his ears for long moments afterward. He may be in chains, he thought, but he was home.

The knights led him to their horses and put him astride one. Without wasting a moment, they raced off through the streets with him at their center. It was surreal, after so much time among the horrors of Krogbur, to be home again, to see people—*people*—and hear the sounds of playing children and the barking of dogs.

Even so, it was grim.

Baleron was dismayed to see large parts of the city still burnt and in ruins from Throgmar's passage. The Grothgar Castle, or its blackened remains, reared like a lightning-blasted stump from the highpoint of the city, while masses of emaciated homeless people tangled the streets and looked out of grimy hotel windows. They must be refugees from all over the kingdom, their own towns and cities consumed by the devouring armies of Oslog.

Baleron turned to Halthus. "Did General Kavradnum ever mass an army out of the soldiers of Aglindor and the other cities?"

The knight snorted. "Some army! They botched the attack on Ungier. Our sortie was nearly unable to reach them." Darkly he added, "Only a few survived. And their cities were left defenseless. They did not stand for long."

The knights rode to the largest surviving palace in the city, home to one of the noblest Houses, the Husrans, who, Halthus explained, had offered up their abode to the king and had taken up residence with another great House with whom they shared many ties, the Esgralins.

The knights stopped at the palace's gate and were inspected by a coterie of five sorcerers, who took custody of Baleron, bringing him into a room within the outer wall, not far from the hastily-erected barracks. His chains were removed, and the mages made him stand in a circle of chalk while they all pointed their staffs at him and closed their eyes, chanting in a hypnotic baritone. The ends of their staffs glowed, and he felt hot. They made him remove his sword, and began again.

For four days they kept him there, testing him, scrutinizing him, and for four days he counseled himself to be patient. He could not blame them for their caution. After Rauglir's deception, they *should* be paranoid.

At last—to the delight of Baleron—Logran himself attended the proceedings. Baleron was happy to see him again, but the sorcerer did not look glad to see Baleron. The Archmage just frowned sadly at the prince and waited until his subordinates were finished. When that time came, their leader turned to him and said, "We've done all we can do for the moment, Master Belefard."

"Well?" he asked them.

"It's him, as near as we can tell, but ... there is a taint."

Logran nodded. "Yes, I can feel it."

Baleron said, "It's me, Logran. It's me."

Logran's frown deepened. "The sad part is," he said, "that it just might be. If it is—if it's truly you, Baleron—then I apologize."

Baleron felt a knot of ice form in his bowels. "Why?"

"Because we must consider you dangerous, a threat to the king. Look at it from our point of view and you'll see we have no option. If it were up to me, we'd simply cast you out ... or destroy you."

"*What!?*"

"The wolves are at the door," Logran said, "and now in comes one pretending to be a sheep—a black one, perhaps, but a sheep nonetheless. The only logical thing to do would be to put you down."

"Logran, it's me! It's really me! I've been to Krogbur, the Black Tower of Gilgaroth!"

"There is no such place."

"There is, and ..." Baleron wanted to tell it all, about the tower, and the army—all he could remember—but Gilgaroth's spell bound his tongue, and he realized he could say no more. All that came up was a dry cough, and then he started to suffocate. There was suddenly no air in the tight room. Agonized, his lungs on fire, he sank to his knees, holding his hands to his throat and wheezing for breath.

Logran's hairy eyebrows crinkled, and the other mages drew back as though expecting Baleron to slip into monstrous form and run amok.

Gradually the dizziness and shortness of breath receded, though, and Baleron fell back gasping.

"I ... I cannot ... can't tell you anything," he managed. "I'm—sorry."

Logran shot a strange look to his lieutenant, and they frowned together. The others looked wary, their staffs all leveled at the prince as soldiers would level crossbows, and with the same gravity.

Logran said, "In any case, it is not up to me. The king hates Baleron too much to slay him, and no words of mine will convince him that you're not his son. He may not believe your lies, but he can't entirely discount the possibility of your survival, either." He sighed. "He wants to see you."

Accompanied by a gaggle of knights and half a dozen mages, Baleron was shown inside the palace proper, which was a beautiful and graceful affair, much unlike the stark Castle Grothgar; these spaces were light and airy and cheerful, or had been. Now all was bleak and gray and cold, and the high spaces only made Baleron feel forlorn as he passed through them.

He was shown to the new Throne Room, which had been converted from the grand ballroom of the Husrans. Social occasions here had been a thing to remember and to talk about for weeks afterward; Baleron could remember he and Sophia dancing across this very floor, gay music playing. Sometimes, when the Husrans had employed a sorcerer for the evening, the revelers could even waltz through the very air amidst glowing balls of multi-colored light ... but those days were gone now. Aristocrats would have to amuse themselves elsewhere.

A grim-faced King Grothgar sat his throne, wearing all black, still in mourning for his wife and sons. He'd been lost in brooding contemplation before Baleron's entrance, and he only looked up distractedly—but, when his eyes found Baleron's, they hardened. They turned to ice.

The prince was reminded once more of what a forceful presence his father had, and what cold and penetrating eyes. Yet, for all that, there was a glimmer of hope in them—more so than in Logran's, anyway.

Guards shoved Baleron to within twenty feet of his sire, then forced him to his knees for the second time that week before Albrech said, "You may rise."

Baleron rose, finding it difficult to meet his father's gaze. He'd been sent here to kill the man. Yet for some reason he felt warmed by his father's presence. Was it, he wondered, the call of blood and kin, or was it the protected feeling a father brings to his children, or something else?

"Tell me," said Albrech, "are you my son?"

"None other."

"How can I be sure?"

Wondering that himself, Baleron said nothing.

"I was fooled before," mused the king, "and it cost me dearly. Then I failed to notice the telltale sign; Rolenya did not sing. *Would* not sing. That was a distinctive characteristic the demon couldn't mimic. As for you, the only distinctive characteristic I can think of is a penchant for fouling things up, the more profoundly the better."

"Father, I—"

"*Don't you call me that!* How *dare* you!" Albrech leapt down from his chair and stalked over to Baleron, knocking knights and sorcerers aside.

"Lord, don't!" advised Logran, stepping between father and son, and forcibly halting the king with a hand on the latter's royal chest, just as, on a previous occasion, he had prevented the king from embracing Rolenya. "It's a demon. It has to be. There is no other reason Gilgaroth would have arranged this but to loose another of his agents in our midst. The only reason we allowed him to enter, remember, is that he brought the sword with him. *Remember.*"

Trembling, the king nodded and took a step back. "You're right, of course."

"Right about what?" Baleron said. "What use is Rondthril to you?"

But Logran never got the chance to answer.

In that endless moment, it occurred to part of Baleron even as he was asking the question that he was as close to both Logran and the king as he might ever be. They might kill him. They might imprison him. It was unlikely they'd ever let him this close to one, much less both, of his primary targets again. If he wanted to save Rolenya, now was the time. After all, Ungier was seemingly untouchable; there was no way Baleron could kill him and so make Rondthril a threat to even higher powers. This left Baleron with no plan and no recourse save to either let Rolenya be thrown to the Borchstogs or else save her by guiding the fall of Havensrike.

A creeping coldness came over him. Tendrils of ice snaked their way throughout his body, even his mind ...

Urgently, he pushed it away.

My Doom! Damn it all, this is it! Steering me along my path. It makes me do what I'd tend to do anyway, but it makes sure that I do it, and do it to the Shadow's satisfaction. That is why Gilgaroth holds Rolenya against me. Not just to lay a claim on me, but to give my Doom something to work with, some leverage to move me by.

But I will not be moved.

He thought all this in the flash of an instant. Even as he put the question about Rondthril to Logran, he made his decision and forced down that creeping, icy tendril, tried to lock it away within himself.

Rolenya will be cast to the Borchstogs!

I will not be moved!

He shoved that icy tendril down, down, though it squirmed and twisted, and its voice reverberated throughout him. He saw an image of Rolenya being tossed to the ravening hordes, the hordes that viewed torture as the ultimate act of veneration to their dark master ...

He fought it.

His Doom was strong, though.

And it was not alone.

Baleron and his left hand shared the same blood, and, as Baleron reasoned afterwards, the foul spirit of Rauglir tainted that blood, spread the demon's influence throughout his entire body.

Just the same, it was indeed the left hand that darted to the side at that moment, just as Logran was prepared to answer the question (or not) put to him. The hand struck like a snake, moving lightning-quick, wrenching a dagger loose from one of the knights, where it was strapped to the man's side.

Stepping quickly forwards, Baleron, or at least his body, drove the curved blade into Logran's backside—the Archmage had been facing the king—severing the sorcerer's spine and puncturing his left lung.

Blood burst from the sorcerer's lips, as Baleron saw when the man twisted in pain, and the mage's brown eyes flew wide.

Rauglir only seized control of Baleron's body for a moment, while Baleron was still wrestling with his Doom. As soon as Baleron felt the alien intellect surge through him, he was able to fight it, to wrest control away from the demon.

But too late.

Logran sank to his knees, the dagger still in his back, blood trickling down his brilliant robes and from the corner of his mouth.

The king looked from his ghastly face up to Baleron's, and rage took him. He gave a great bellow and jerked out his own sword, steel ringing.

Baleron, his left hand covered in Logran's blood, stumbled back, blinking, not quite sure what had just happened. Had he just *murdered Logran*? And what had been that *other* presence inside him? It had not felt like his Doom—

All the sorcerers had their staffs leveled at him, and the knights had drawn their blades, but the king roared, "Stay your hands, damn you! He's mine!"

Reeling drunkenly backwards, Baleron tripped and fell to the marble floor, then stared, confused, as his father loomed over him. The king raised his blade so that it glittered in the torchlight, and there was a mad look in his eyes.

Baleron raised his hands to ward off the blow, shouting, "No! Father, don't!"

From somewhere, he heard laughter. It coursed through him, echoing in his mind, bouncing almost painfully in his skull, and with a start he recognized it.

Rauglir.

The top hand he had raised had been his left.

King Grothgar frowned at the gruesome stitches, but he didn't stop swinging. He raised his blade as high as he could, then brought it down savagely. The large sword hissed as it cut the air.

Baleron had lived through too much to die like this. He rolled aside.

The mighty sword smote the marble where he'd lain, sending up chips and sparks. The impact was so great it tore the weapon loose from Albrech's hands, and the sword clattered loudly to the floor.

For a moment, Baleron and his father looked into each other's eyes. Lord Grothgar moved.

Baleron was faster.

With fear-spurred reflexes, he seized the sword. His legs lashed out, swept the king's feet out from under him, and the monarch toppled with a cry. Even as he struck the ground, he found himself in the grip of his son. Baleron pressed the sword to his father with his other hand, and rolled them both away. The mages and knights scattered.

When he was clear of the press of people, Baleron jerked his father to his feet and pressed the edge of the blade to his throat while the other arm he locked about Lord Grothgar's left arm and chest. He backed up against a wall.

"Don't move against me," he warned the gathering.

One of the sorcerers dropped beside Logran, putting his hand to the dying man's chest. An orange light suffused the skin of his hand.

Albrech struggled in his son's grip, but when the blade drew blood from his throat he quit.

Baleron's left hand shook. It tried to, *under its own power*, reach around and throttle Albrech. Startled, Baleron exerted every ounce of his will on it. Sweat wept from his pores. A cord on his neck popped out and the clenching of his jaws nearly shattered his teeth. At last, though, he mastered the hand and forced it into submission.

"You dog," Albrech was snarling. "You filthy little worm. I should've known the Wolf would corrupt you. You always were weak."

"No, Father," Baleron wheezed. "I'm cursed, but I'm no traitor. If I was going to kill you, you'd be dead already, and the gods may damn me for sparing you yet, as by doing so I'm condemning Rolenya to a fate worse than death."

"What are you babbling about?"

Before Baleron could answer, all the soldiers in the palace seemed to run into the room. A gaggle of archers aimed their weapons at the renegade prince, yet no man dared fire lest he strike the king.

"Rat!" hissed the father to the son. "Snake! Weasel! Traitor!"

"I am not a traitor!" Baleron said, hearing the desperation in his voice. That icy feeling was returning. A cold tendril tried to force its way into his mind. He blocked it, barely. His left hand shook.

"Murderer!" Albrech said.

"That I am, but not for Logran; there's something inside me, Father. I think—yes—it's the same demon that possessed Rolenya."

The knights and sorcerers erupted in a clamor, demanding the king's release. Baleron ignored them.

"Listen to me, Father," he said. "There is no way you can win out against the Dark One."

"Craven!"

"I've seen his resources, and they're beyond anything you or the Union can summon. He's grown strong in his time sealed off from the world, free to breed his minions at will. There's more. He's brought his own demons over from the Second Hell. He's built a huge tower, Father, a doorway to Illistriv. Flee, Father. Break through this rabble of Ungier's and take your subjects north —far north. Take them to Wethelion and the Tower of the Sun.

Assemble there with your allies and prepare a defense. If I should die, remember that."

"You would have me run away like a coward!"

"I am your *son*!"

The king sneered. "I have no doubt of that. Oh, I know it's you, Baleron. Only *you* could make such an awful mess of things."

Baleron looked about at the assembly of soldiers and mages, and they glared back. None spoke now. All was silent as a tomb.

"How do you propose we get out of this?" Baleron asked in his father's ear.

"I propose *we* don't."

He acted fast. One of his hands reached up over his shoulder and clawed at Baleron's eyes so that the prince reflexively released his hold on his father's throat; at the same time Albrech gripped the naked blade with his bare hand and shoved it away. Rubbing his throat, he stumbled aside, giving the archers an open shot.

They took it.

A score of arrows split the air.

Baleron had time to curse, but that was it.

Yet suddenly all the arrows stopped in mid-air, paused, and fell to the floor. Stunned, Baleron stared at them.

"Leave him be," said a strained voice, and the press parted to reveal Logran, bleeding and dying on the marble floor, his voice frothy. A faint smile tinged his lips. Apropos of everyone's confusion, he said, "You heard the king. That's Baleron—the real Baleron. A werewolf would be chewing Albrech's corpse by now."

With that, he slumped to the floor and was still.

The sorcerer that had knelt over him looked up and said, "Come, brethren. I think there's still time."

The mages gathered in a circle about the Archmage, aimed their staffs at him, focusing their power, and the circle glowed a bright, morning yellow, tinged with orange.

King Albrech, still rubbing his throat, turned to Baleron and said in a growl, "Welcome home, son. Guards, take him away!"

Chapter Five

Rolenya sang, pouring her heart and soul into her song, driving back the darkness that encircled her.

Dressed in white, a white light seemed to glow from within her, suffusing her, and she was the only light in the neverending blackness, which was full of a seething tension. She stood at the edge of the high platform that jutted out into what Baleron had called the Black Temple, that vast space at the core of Krogbur where the Shadow's presence was the strongest.

Somewhere in the enormity of all that blackness, *he* was there, listening, watching. She tried not to think about it, about him, tried solely to focus on her song. It was difficult. She was alone with Gilgaroth, more at his mercy now than at any time since she'd been freed from Illistriv.

She sang on. Every night since Baleron's leaving, Gilgaroth had asked her to sing for him.

Now below her yawned a black abyss that seemed endless and might very well be; this temple, this well, could run all the way through the roots of Krogbur and beyond, into the very bowels of the earth, or into some strange netherworld, for all she knew. She stood in the very place where Baleron had lopped off his own hand; his blood likely still stained the ground, if she could but see it. She hated this place. Its evil almost suffocated her. The very air vibrated with malignant passions, and made her feel unclean.

Yet this is where Gilgaroth had brought her every day for the last week. She would sing, and he would listen, spellbound, for hours. She found it hard to believe that such a terrible being could appreciate what meager elements of Light and Grace she could offer in her voice, and it made her wonder if Gilgaroth might not have some of those same qualities after all. If so, he was an even more pitiable creature than she'd imagined.

On this day, after she'd been singing for over an hour, two flaming slits opened in the dark well of the temple, above her and before her, suspended over an abyss that made her shiver just to contemplate.

The eyes of fire widened.

"Beautiful," breathed Gilgaroth. His voice sounded like flames licking stone, and she didn't know if he were referring to her or her voice.

She refused to look at those burning eyes, refused to be sucked into his mesmerizing stare. She sang on, loudly and with all the force she could muster.

"You are my treasure," spoke the Tempter of Man, watching her with what appeared to be genuine fondness. *"It's been too long since I've listened to the silver song of a daughter of the Light."*

The eyes dimmed and closed. The Shadow, subdued by her voice, relaxed ... and drifted.

She sang on.

Should I? she thought. *Should I do it now?*

She paused, fearful, and her heart trembled.

She almost did it—almost—but her courage failed her, and she continued to sing, until at last, she thought again, *Now! I must do it now!* But still she was afraid.

It was a mad idea. A mad, impossible plan. But what else could she do? She'd thought about it all this last week, but so far she couldn't bring herself to do it. Growing up in Havensrike, she'd often read tales of Elvish princesses that could stop the heart of a thing of darkness with their song, and such stories had been among her favorites. Those princesses could weave spells with their songs. They could entrance a listener and bind the listener to them—they were spells of love, some of them, but some were spells of power.

Now that she knew she was Elvish, she'd began to wonder if she could do this, if she could sing such a song. After all, her mother, her true mother, was said to be able to call entire forest-gardens into being with just her song.

Come! What do I have to lose?

But what if he finds me out? What then?

She steeled herself. Reaching deep within, she searched out the well of Light she knew to be inside her.

There! Slowly, very slowly, she began to weave strands of Light from that well into her voice.

Gilgaroth's eyes remained closed.

She sang on. Could it be done without schooling? Could it be done on instinct alone, fueled by sheer desperation?

Give me courage, beings of the Light, she thought. *Give me strength.*

She sang on, faster and faster, as loudly as she could, but now she injected something new into the song. She tried to weave a spell, a web—tried to lay a foundation for ensnaring the listener. She could feel the tools to do this with, could feel how it might be done, and it was far more complicated than she would have thought. How had those fairytale princesses done it? How had her mother?

Against her will, her thoughts turned to Baleron, but she forced these thoughts aside. She had to concentrate, had to dredge up those latent abilities of binding and unbinding.

The Shadow's eyes sprang open, and Rolenya almost screamed. She'd been found out!

"A visitor comes," he said.

She relaxed, breathless, then caught the sound of air being split by something large. She wheeled about, her song forgotten, as the huge black multi-legged mass of the Mogra rose up from the shaft, ascending under her own power, drew abreast of the platform, then leapt on the stage directly behind Rolenya.

Eyes wide, Rolenya stared up at the horror that was the Goddess of Mists and Sacrifice and stifled a scream.

"Lovely," said Mogra. "A golden voice in a lightless gloom."

"My songbird," said Gilgaroth, his terrible mouth a gash of flickering red in the darkness. Fires from his throat bathed his sharp teeth in a lurid red glow.

"I hope that singing is *all* she's done for you, my Lord. Now go along, little pigeon," said Mogra, "for Lord Gilgaroth and I shall make our own sweet music now."

Caught between these two implacable forces, Rolenya froze. Should she go around Mogra, or under her, threading her way through the forest of huge spider legs? The thought petrified her.

Mogra made the decision for her. The Spider Goddess coiled her many-jointed limbs and leapt straight over Rolenya's head and disappeared into the blackness where Gilgaroth waited. The Dark One and the Shadow-Weaver wrapped each other in an unholy embrace within a darkness so deep even Rolenya's elvish eyes could not penetrate it.

"Go," commanded Gilgaroth. His fires were no longer visible.

There seemed a great movement in the dark—restless and wild, full of need and desire and ancient wrath. Shadow swelled and swayed and pulsed. A great power throbbed in the blackness.

"Go!" bade Mogra.

Rolenya turned her face from the unholy union and descended the endless stairs without another word, glad to be away. As she went, she emitted her own radiance—an ability granted by her heritage and transferred with her soul, not her flesh. This was fortunate, as there was no other light to be had. Her white light revealed one stained black stair at a time, her pale bare feet touching down one after the other.

She wondered why Mogra had come. Perhaps the Shadow-Weaver had heard rumor of her songs and in jealousy had decided to visit the Black Tower? Rolenya doubted it.

She wondered if her spell-song had begun to work on Gilgaroth before Mogra's arrival, and if she should try it again next time. The thought terrified her.

As she descended the spiraled stairs that wound along the temple walls, terrible noises chased her from behind, roars and screams and howls and grunts—an unholy din as though Hell itself had been unleashed, and perhaps it had. She did not look back.

It seemed he spent half his life imprisoned, Baleron mused as he languished in the palace dungeon, which had been converted from the Husran catacombs. In fact, the room he now occupied was not a prison cell—not originally—but a crypt. Oddly appropriate, he thought.

It was a comfortable enough cell, though, dry and warm, very much unlike the pits of Krogbur. He was becoming a connoisseur of prisons. Sadly, it meant that though he traveled between different peoples, he existed outside any one country, any one family. He was utterly an outsider, treated as hostile by all sides.

He would be glad when this was over. Then perhaps he could find a place where he belonged, even if it was only a place for his spirit. He didn't expect to come out of this war alive. He would die, he knew, and his spirit would spend the rest of eternity dwelling on his mistakes; he had to minimize those mistakes now, or he'd be one woeful spirit.

But it seemed that any decision he made was the wrong one. Every choice he faced led to some unendurable consequence, whether it be the fall of the Crescent or the misuse of the woman he loved.

And what did it matter, really? Rauglir had made the choice for him. Ironically, Gilgaroth's backup plan (Baleron now realized that that's precisely what Rauglir was) had landed him here, where Rauglir's targets were safe from him. Baleron only hoped his father and Logran stayed far away. He didn't want to rot in prison, but it was far better than the alternative.

When his first visitor came, he'd been stuck in the crypt for two days without food or water, and he was sorely in need of a drink, his throat parched and his stomach gnawing at itself like a weasel in its den. His dreams continued to haunt him, and he could feel Rauglir like a shadow inside him. An iron collar about Baleron's neck weighed him down, and chains sprouting from it rooted him to the floor. Iron rings to either side of the collar bound his hands.

They must think he was some wild, ravening beast that needed to be forcibly restrained, he thought. The worst part was they might be right.

His visitor was Logran.

"You're alive!" Baleron said. He rose to his feet, the chains clinking around him. He took a step forward, all the chains would allow him, and two members of the prison guard brandished their swords at him.

"Don't try any of your tricks," warned the senior officer.

"Please, captain," Logran said, "don't poke any holes in him for the time being. Agent of the Dark One or not, he *is* the Heir."

The soldiers lowered their blades uncertainly.

"The Heir?" Baleron said. If he was the Heir, that could only mean ...

"We'll get to that," the sorcerer promised.

"But how? How are you here? *I felt your spine sever.*"

"Yes," Logran admitted. "That is not my fondest memory of you. And it nearly did for me, true enough. But somehow my brethren managed to put me back together again. Our art has come far in the last few years, I really must say. Though I must give credit where it belongs, to Elethris and his Flower. They're what really saved me."

Soberly, Baleron said, "It's good to see you again."

"Likewise." Logran looked about at the guards. "Why don't you leave us alone for a moment? I promise to keep both eyes on him at all times."

The captain nodded reluctantly. "We'll be right outside if you need us." The soldiers withdrew, the captain throwing one last scowl at the prince and saying, "You'd better not try anything or it's me you'll have to face."

Despite himself, Baleron laughed. After all the horrors he'd been through, this pudgy, squinty-eyed little man thought he could intimidate him?

Logran had water. As Baleron drank greedily, he noted that the sorcerer seemed hale and hardy, much improved from when he'd resided at Grothgar Castle; Baleron now supposed that then the sorcerer had been wasting away in grief over Elethris and Celievsti, but purpose had rejuvenated him.

Logran smiled, and Baleron frowned. It was good to know he hadn't killed the old man, but it was annoying to find the sorcerer in such good humor.

"What did you mean, I'm the Heir?"

Logran's good humor fled. "Prince Jered was cut down this morning upon the walls of Clevaris. He was battling a powerful Grudremorqen, one of Grudremorq's oldest and most powerful sons."

Baleron let out a breath. After he'd found out that he and Jered suffered a like affliction, their Dooms, he'd often wondered what it might be like to consult with his brother—to compare notes, as it were. Now he'd never get that chance.

"And Kenbrig?"

"Also fallen. Killed shortly after your departure by ... *that thing.*"

"Rauglir."

"Yes. I had the satisfaction of destroying him myself, at least."

Baleron gritted his teeth. Rauglir mocked his every move. Baleron didn't know the nature of his left hand, not exactly, but he had suspicions.

"What ails you?" the Archmage asked, perhaps seeing his expression.

"Rauglir ..." Baleron stared at his scarred left hand and tried to waggle his fingers. Almost to his surprise, they waggled.

"Rauglir is loose," he muttered.

"What was that?"

"You should've trapped him."

"What do you mean?"

"You said you felt a taint in me." Baleron flexed and clenched his left hand. "I think he's inside me, Logran. I think he's the one that stabbed you."

"Are you sure it was not your Doom?"

"I'm sure. Otherwise why would Gilgaroth have had me chop off my hand, then reattach it? See the scars if you don't believe me."

Logran looked noncommittal.

Baleron's mind returned to Kenbrig. Baleron and his brother had never been particularly close, but he would miss him.

A more pressing issue faced him, though: what did it mean that Jered had been slain? Did the Dark One betray him after he'd fulfilled his Doom? Would Gilgaroth do the same to Baleron? But surely Jered's purpose had not been fulfilled, or Logran would have told him that news first.

"The Queen, the City," he said, just to make sure. "How do they fare?"

"Clevaris stands, but barely. Grudremorq has fouled the River and corrupted the Larenthellan; he sends his sons into the moat and their heat boils it away. It kills them, but they weaken it, and he's dammed up the Larenth upstream. The elves would've run out of water by now, but Queen Vilana stopped the flow in time, and since then a dam has been constructed at the northern end of the City, and they have water enough to last ... for a time. But Larenthellan, the moat that protects Clevaris—it no longer serves as a barrier, and the Fire God can now lead his troops across it to assault the walls of the City directly. Meanwhile the Whiteworms and Swans protect the City from the air, but their numbers dwindle, and the Darkworms and glarumri seem endless—although where these Worms come from I can't imagine. There should not be so many ... "

Then Jered had not accomplished his task. The mystery of his death deepened, and Baleron was determined to find out the why of it. After all, the spawn of Oslog knew not to slay Baleron, so why didn't they know to spare Jered? Was it because Baleron was *ul Ravast* and Jered simply a pawn?

"Several of Vilana's highest and most powerful elves have been murdered," Logran continued. "Right in the Palace, too. There's a traitor amok, and no one has any idea who."

A sudden headache bloomed fiercely, yet the prince managed to say, "I don't think he'll kill anyone else," before the pain overwhelmed him and he fell back, gasping.

Logran knelt over him and placed a hand on Baleron's head. The Archmage concentrated, closing his eyes, and quickly Baleron began to feel better, but Logran gasped and hastily removed his hand. He staggered back, as though afraid of Baleron.

"What—?" asked Baleron.

Logran let out a shuddering breath. "The Wolf's touch," he murmured. "I felt it upon you ..."

Baleron maintained eye contact. Slowly, steadily, he said, "I don't serve him, Logran. I don't. It's Rauglir, he's in me. It sounds absurd, but it must be."

"You're tainted ..."

"*He's* the taint. Don't you see? Give me a sword, I'll chop off my own hand right now. *Then* you'll trust me, and I'll be free ... of Rauglir, at least. My Doom will still—"

"I doubt anyone's going to give you a sword again, Baleron, not for a long, long time."

"But you believe me, right? I'm. Not. Evil."

Logran regarded him sadly. "I don't know what you are, Baleron." He gathered himself together and stared at the chained prince with sad brown eyes. "Your father has instructed me to determine your status, whether good, evil, or other. Tell me truly, Baleron. Are you an agent of the Wolf?"

Baleron paused, lowered his eyes. "Almost, Logran. Almost. Even now I'm not sure what the right thing to do is, *if* there is a right thing. But no, I'm not working with the Enemy, though later I might wish I had. Just by cooperating with you, I'm ... well, you would not believe me if I told you, but trust me, it will have terrible consequences on someone I love."

"Why should I believe you?"

"Because it's me, Logran. You've known me all my life. You know what I would or wouldn't do. You must trust me."

"*You stabbed me in the back.*" Logran breathed heavily. After some moments to calm himself down, he said, "I clearly can't let you walk around freely, can I? Your father has given me custody of you. He says that since it was my life you tried to steal, you are mine now."

"Your sorcerers have already tested me."

"Tested and failed, but there are further tests we can do ... though they won't, I fear, be pleasant." Logran sighed. "I need to rest. We'll see each other again soon. Try not to kill anyone in the meantime."

"No, wait! What of Rondthril? Why do you need it? I must know."

Logran paused, seemed to steel his resolve, then disappeared out the door. It shut with a harsh clang, and Baleron was left alone once more.

Sinking back to the floor, he eyed his left hand. Could it really be Rauglir? Once again, he flexed and clenched it, and it obeyed him ... but for how long?

"You don't fool me," he told it.

Suddenly he heard dark, familiar laughter inside him, and his eyes widened.

"So it's true! You're really *here*. Gods!"

More laughter.

Something cold crawled up Baleron's spine, like little spiders made of ice. *My body is not my own.* Without warning, a feeling of utter horror overwhelmed him, and he shook in a sudden convulsion, lifted his head and screamed. His voice echoed off the walls of the crypt, and the guards looked nervously in at him, but they did not enter. Hastily they slammed and bolted the door.

For the rest of the morning Baleron languished in the catacombs, contemplating his hand, before finally he received his second and last visitor.

King Grothgar entered the crypt and stared down at him, still chained to the floor. Baleron, who had been brooding unproductively, trying to mentally grapple with the alien spirit inside him, glanced up with astonishment as the door flew open and his father marched in accompanied by half a dozen guards, two of which held crossbows aimed at his breast.

For a long moment, father and son just stared at each other. Baleron could feel the disappointment radiating off the king like heat off a hot road.

"Your brother Jered is dead," Albrech said abruptly.

"Logran told me."

"Did you also know that Kenbrig had died, murdered by the same fiend that took your mother and possessed your sister—the same fiend that you rescued from the depths of Gulrothrog and led amongst us—not once but twice?"

The prince's head hung a bit. "I know."

"You," said Albrech in disgust, "are now the Heir."

Baleron had heard it before from the sorcerer, but he'd been so focused on the mystery of his hand that he had not had time to think much on it.

"Have you formally announced it?" he asked.

"No," said Albrech. "I haven't wanted to. I thought you dead, or worse. It turns out to be the latter. When I heard you were back, I wanted to see if you demonstrated any characteristics that would lend you to the job, and you can see the result of that. I suppose I'll have to circumvent tradition and appoint one of your sisters in your place; there is one or two that seem competent enough, though the lot are involved in typical womanish schemes and silliness."

"Appoint one of them, then. I'm clearly not fit for the job."

"You're a creature of the Dark One!"

"You said yourself that you know it's me."

"Yes, and you've *given* yourself to him. You're weak, selfish, base." The king began pacing like a caged lion. Suddenly he stopped and stared at his son acutely. "What were you gibbering about your sister the other day?"

"Would you believe me if I told you?"

Again the king stared at him sharply, appraisingly. "No," he grunted at last. "Probably not." He cleared his throat. "You missed her funeral, by the way. It was a small affair—one among many. We didn't have the time to stage anything more elaborate, and it would've seemed crass to do so what with all the others. So many funerals, Baleron. So much death and destruction, and here we are in the End Days when we will see even more. Soon Glorifel will fall. I should not say it, but of that I have no doubt. Tell me, Baleron, how does one have a funeral for a city?"

"It doesn't have to be that way, Father. Take your people north. Regroup with our allies. Build up your strength, then strike and strike hard. It's the only way you're going to win. Trust me. I know what you face."

"And I know that every word that comes out of your mouth is suspect. Either you're a willing agent or, as Logran tells me, you're tainted, whatever that means—but either way I can't afford to trust you. What I can do, however, is acknowledge you're still family, and allow you to Jered's funeral this afternoon—not that you'd know what time it is from this infernal night that hangs over us constantly."

"Jered's ... funeral? But isn't his body at Clevaris?"

"It is, and it will be buried there. The Queen feels most strongly about that; he was truly like a son to her—more so than to me, I'm sure. She builds his tomb even now. But we will hold a ceremony here, as well, for he was after all our kin, not hers." Albrech moved towards the door, then turned back. "We'll have some of your clothes brought down. You don't want to be wearing *that* to see your brother off in."

"Rolenya—does she also have a tomb?"

The king looked pained. "She does," he admitted. "Thanks to you." His voice turned sour. "Never forget that it was you who caused this, Baleron. Her death, our fall, all of it—it's on your head."

Scowling, he swept from the room, taking his men with him, and they slammed the door shut behind them.

An hour later, a full dozen guards escorted the prince—now washed and in clean attire, which was a relief—up into the street that ran before the palace, where there waited a long string of black coaches pulled by black horses. Baleron was led into the back of a prison coach, nearly the last vehicle in the funeral procession, where he was locked inside, and, with a cry and the crack of whips, the procession was off.

They wound through the war-torn city, and Baleron gazed out from his barred window at the desolation of Glorifel. They passed the Street of the Arts, and Flower Lane, and the great temple to

Illiana on Morning Row. Starving and desperate people thronged the streets, huddling against the chill of the false night.

At last the procession reached the royal cemetery, and Baleron (under heavy guard) was led with the others to the newly built tomb—surely less impressive than the one the Queen of Larenthi was having built, but handsome just the same—where an empty coffin would be installed on the dais within. Griffons, Great Swans and Whiteworms were carved into the tomb and wound along its white pillars.

A chill wind blew, black clouds blotted out the sun, and thunder rolled.

The funeral was a slow, solemn affair, as the royal family, or what was left of it, huddled together in the cold and listened to a priest of Brunril and Illiana say kind words about Prince Jered and his brave sacrifice defending the world against evil. Baleron ignored the sermon. He wondered how Jered had handled being in thrall to Gilgaroth, and why he'd died. It must have been a mistake, Baleron decided, a bloodthirsty Grudremorqen caught in the heat of battle.

Saddened by Jered's death, Baleron found himself disappointed that he would never get to discuss Dooms with the legendary Prince of Clevaris who'd been the golden son, and yet not a son, of Felias and Vilana. Baleron had thought of Jered as his golden shadow, the prince who was everything a prince should be, and loved and renowned. But now it was Baleron, corrupt and rash and broken, that had survived. He wondered if perhaps Jered had simply found the only way out he could: to die in battle with a worthy foe. Baleron knew he would be lucky to do the same.

The funeral ended and the royals picked their way back to their coaches. No Glorifelans had been told of Prince Jered's true identity, so there was no one to console the royal family, no crowd of supporters.

The king intercepted Baleron.

"I've been to many funerals of late," Albrech said. "Most of them my own kin. My wife, my sons, Rolenya, even two true daughters lost when the castle fell. Baleron, you and I have never been close, but you're the only son I have left, and I don't want to attend your funeral, too. Neither will I allow a son of mine to rot in prison if I can help it. Report to Logran at once. He's told me that there *is* a procedure he can perform—a Purging, he calls it. I won't lie to you, son. It may kill you. He says it kills many. And it's very painful. But perhaps it can burn this demon out ... and your Doom, as well." He paused. "I'll let it be your decision. Either make the dungeon your home, or submit to this Purging. Decide now."

To Baleron, there was no question. "Do it," he said.

"Guards, take him to Logran's tower."

As before, Logran had made his home in the highest tower of the palace, but this time a servant opened the door and led Baleron and his guards into the sorcerer's inner sanctum.

"Shhh," said the servant. "He's performing a spell." When they reached a comfortable living room infested by low, soft couches, he said, "Why don't you take a seat?"

Too anxious to sit, Baleron moved out onto the balcony and surveyed the once-peaceful city. He knew all of its parks and museums and culture centers, all its grand monuments, its history and customs ... and yet from this high tower he could see beyond the walls. He could see the endless campfires of the Borchstogs, the dark hordes that waited just beyond, and from somewhere out there he heard war drums banging. *Boom doom boom.* Smoke stirred on the breeze. They would attack soon, he thought. *Would that I had my old command.*

Logran cleared his throat, and Baleron whirled around to see the Archmage framed in the doorway.

"You startled me," Baleron said.

"A bit tense, are we?" Logran looked to the guards, then back at the prince. "So you're mine, then."

The captain of the guard said, "You're to do your Purging."

"I see." To Baleron, Logran said, "You *do* understand this will more than likely kill you. There is only a very small chance you'll survive, and even if you do it's not certain the demon, or your Doom, or both, will be destroyed."

Baleron shrugged. "If I die, they cease to matter. Just be sure to destroy my corpse when you're done."

Logran looked at him steadily for a long moment, as if to satisfy himself of something, and at last nodded. "I apologize that I didn't make it to the funeral. I was ... working on something."

"Rondthril?"

The Archmage nodded uncomfortably. "Yes, as a matter of fact."

"Please, can you tell me just why that sword is so important to you? Why would you only admit me into the city if I had it with me?"

The Wielder of Light stepped out onto the balcony and joined the prince at the balustrade. Leaning on it, he peered out at the city. It was so large and so full of sparkling lights, like a reflection of the night sky on a still lake, that it took Baleron's breath away. He could see Logran's appreciation for it, his love for it, shining in his brown eyes.

"Beautiful, isn't it?" said Logran.

Baleron knew him well enough to know he was leading up to something; he hadn't come out here to discuss the view.

"Yes," Baleron agreed, playing along.

"I've lived here for many decades, Bal. I was your grandfather's and your great-grandfather's closest advisor as well as your father's. I've played a large role in shaping and preserving this fair city." He paused. "It was I who guided the rash King Grothgar the First into preserving the custom of the Swap."

That surprised the prince. "You mean you're the one responsible for ... Rolenya and me ... ?"

Logran smiled. "I think your loins had more to do with that than I did, Baleron. Nevertheless ... yes, without me you would never have known her, let alone known her well. And, I suspect, a great deal of this whole despicable affair never would have come to pass, at least in its present incarnation."

"What do you mean?" Baleron said warily; he did not want to push the limits of what he could reveal, did not want to needlessly face the pain again.

"I strongly suspect that Gilgaroth is using your sister against you in some fashion, though how exactly I cannot guess."

Baleron held his breath, saying nothing.

"He's possessed you, or part of you, somehow, Baleron. I believe you now. But he would never use one method alone to control an agent such as you. He would use your own heart against you. It is his way. It is, I suspect, how he was able to manipulate Prince Jered—oh, yes, I know about him. The Queen and I keep in constant communication, and she had doubts about him since the first murder."

This was of great interest to Baleron, but he still said nothing.

Logran looked at him levelly. "And of course you're here in Glorifel to fulfill the same function."

Baleron didn't deny it. "Can you drive it out of me—Rauglir?"

The sorcerer made a pained face. "I ... will try, Baleron. But I make no promises. If indeed this Rauglir is inside you, it may well be that you and the demon are ... entwined."

Baleron grimaced, then laughed bitterly. "With it and my Doom both, my soul should not be lonely. If only I could just lop off my hand and be done with it! But then, I suppose, my Doom would still be there." He groaned. "Do your Purging, Logran. Do it now."

The Archmage shook his head. "It will take time to prepare. We will begin on the morrow."

Baleron noticed that Logran would not meet his gaze. The sorcerer's eyes were wet and troubled. *He knows the Purging will kill me*, Baleron realized. *Or if it does not that it will fail.*

Strangely the prospect didn't bother him. He almost longed for it, for the final answer to his Doom.

That icy feeling throbbed uneasily in his chest, and he smiled grimly. *Yes, be afraid. On the morrow you die, my constant companion. You too, Rauglir.*

He looked out at the lights of the city. "And my sword?"

The Archmage raised his eyebrows. "Your sword, alas, has been a disappointment."

"How?"

"Well, as I was saying, I've taken tremendous pride in helping to steer our great nation over the years, and I had hoped, with your sword, to be able to steer it from this present brink."

"*How?*"

"It knows the Dark One's will," said the mage. "It can sense it, interpret it, and it will not defy it. I had hoped to be able to use Rondthril, to tap into it somehow, to be able to divine his will myself and so predict his future actions, or at least be able to prepare a defense against his current ones."

It was certainly a worthy notion, and Baleron could see why the sorcerer had been so keen to get his hands on the sword.

"But it didn't work?"

Air hissed out of the sorcerer's long, aristocratic nose. "Alas, its primitive sentience—if it can be called that, which I begin to doubt—is too rudimentary. It knows the Wolf's will, can sniff it out like a dog can sniff a smell, but it can't be made to tell me what it knows, just as a dog couldn't describe a smell." His face looked deadly serious in the darkness. In a low voice, he added, "It was my last hope."

Baleron started to answer, when suddenly horns and alarm bells sounded an alert, starting at the walls and spreading inwards.

"Gods protect us all," Logran breathed. "Ungier attacks."

Chapter Six

Baleron felt the blood rush to his face as he watched Ungier's hordes charge the walls. From here he could see them simply as a great, surging shadow against the darkness. Alarm bells rang throughout the city, and all able-bodied men and women, even the homeless refugees, would be rushing to what arms they could. Even children would lend aid.

Baleron could not sit idly by. Heatedly, he looked to the sorcerer. "Give me the sword," he demanded. "Give me Rondthril."

"There is no need. You're safe here."

"Yes, but I'm not *staying* here, am I?"

"Of course you are. You're no longer a leader of men, Baleron. You're a prisoner. Your Five Hundred is no more."

Anger coursed through Baleron. He desperately wanted to join the fight, to lose himself in the violence. Also, he wanted to redeem himself somehow, to smite the wicked armies of Gilgaroth. At that moment, he felt the craving as though it were a physical need. He felt he would die unless he fought.

"I'll bet my father isn't staying here," he said. "I'll bet they're bringing a coach for him even now, and if I'm fast I can be on it. I'm a good fighter, Logran. A good leader. They need me."

"Baleron, I can't condone this. You're possessed, tainted, call it what you will—you can't be trusted with a sword, much less Rondthril. And you certainly can't be trusted to lead troops."

Baleron gripped the older man's arms and looked deeply into his eyes. "Logran," he said urgently, "I must do this."

Wind whistled shrilly. Horns and bells echoed throughout the city streets. Logran must have seen the madness and desperation in Baleron, and slowly he began to put it together; Baleron saw it in his eyes and the tightness of his lips.

"You want to find what Jered found," Logran said at last.

Baleron didn't look away.

"You want ... death," Logran said.

The prince ground his teeth. *"I want freedom,"* he hissed. "I want out the only way I can. It may damn someone I love, but it was she who told me to do it. If I live, I'll only spread death and misery. I'm *ul Ravast*, Logran. I tried to deny it, I tried not to believe it, I even tried to change it. But look at me, look what I've become! Let me do this, Logran. You've always been a friend to me. Sometimes I thought of you more as a father than my own. Let me do this one last thing, and I will ask you for no more ever again."

Logran studied him, seeming full of thought.

"You have custody of me," Baleron pressed. "My life is in your hands. The king cannot gainsay you. It is all up to you, Logran. My friend. Please, don't let me end my days mewling on the floor under your Purging, burnt to a crisp in an effort to do what we both know's impossible. Let me end things my way. Give my life back to me. It will not be in my hands long."

Tears actually clouded the sorcerer's eyes, and he had to look away. When he spoke, his voice was thick. "Very well. You may have it. You may have your freedom."

"And the sword! *I must have the sword.*"

"Have it, then."

The sorcerer left to retrieve the weapon, and Baleron followed him inside and waited with the guards. They shifted uncomfortably, their eyes looking outside. Obviously they wanted to be away, just as he did, to join their brothers on the wall.

"Soon," he told them. "I will lead you out myself." His blood burned hot, eager for battle.

Presently the Archmage reemerged, bearing the resplendent length of the Fanged Blade, which shone brightly, twinkling in the lights of the room. The flames of the fireplace leapt high, crackling, reflecting brilliantly on the unholy steel.

"It certainly is a fine weapon," Logran said, "but I feel corrupted just holding it."

"We have always worked well together, it and I," Baleron told him. "It's saved my life more than once."

Still a bit wary, the sorcerer passed the sword to the prince, who grasped it eagerly. As soon as his hand touched the handle, as soon as his fingers closed about it, he felt its darkness, its raging bloodlust ... its power. It sang a song of death and carnage in his mind.

And, despite himself, his Doom answered.

It happened swiftly. Coldness seeped out from his chest, icy tendrils spreading throughout him.

At the same time, Rondthril began to rouse the spirit of Rauglir, whom Baleron had been managing to suppress, and the demon reared its head and answered the Fanged Blade's song with a song of its own, a grisly wolf howl.

Logran frowned, seeing sword and master together.

"Something's wrong," he said. "What is it?" When Baleron didn't answer, Logran muttered, "But I can see that you're meant for each other, you and this sword. Don't lose it, Baleron. Yes, you can do much with it, and no other wielder can do what you can."

Baleron paid little attention, as he was fighting his own battle. Rauglir grappled with him, and as the seconds wore on, Baleron began to panic. Rauglir struggled mightily, and the power of Rondthril was aiding him, the two dark entities working together, helping each other carry out Gilgaroth's will, and, bolstered by Baleron's Doom, they were winning.

An icy tendril tried to force its way into his mind. He blocked it. It shoved. He strained against it, but it was strong. Baleron shook like a string under tension. Every muscle bulged. His veins stood out with the effort, and sweat beaded his brow.

They were going to overcome him.

Frantically, he tried to drop the sword. His fingers would not obey his call, even though they were on his right hand. Rauglir was seizing control.

"What is it?" he heard Logran ask. The sorcerer, fearful, took a step back.

Baleron felt that icy tendril slam him aside, bursting the door in his mind. He wrestled with it, struggling to force it out, but while he was engaged with his Doom Rauglir slipped through and seized full control of his body.

Baleron tried to scream out a warning. It was too late.

Helplessly, he watched through his own eyes as Rondthril sliced open the neck of the closest guard. Red blood jetted across the room.

Rauglir, wearing Baleron's body, leapt forward and skewered the sorcerer, this time through the front. The tip of the sword entered the mage's body from just below the ribcage and angled upwards, ripping through the lungs and tender flesh. It found the heart and drove through it, cleaving it in two.

Logran's brown eyes went wide, then dimmed, and his body went limp in Rauglir's embrace. He let out a final shuddering breath and was still.

The Archmage was dead.

The room trembled with his passing, and the wind roared

loudly, stirring the scattered papers in the room. The flames in the fireplace leapt higher and turned blue, then green, then red, then black, before returning to normal.

Rauglir dropped the dead sorcerer and whirled about to face the guards, who were upon him in an instant. The demon was not a thing of nature, and neither was Rondthril, and together they moved Baleron's body in ways he never could have. It leapt and spun and dodged with blinding speed.

The Fanged Blade stabbed, hacked and sliced. It jabbed one guard in the throat, another in the belly, one it gave a slash across the face to distract it while it pierced the side of another, then went back to the one with the ruined face and cut off his head.

When they were all dead, their bodies all bleeding into the carpet, Rauglir howled at the ceiling.

He knelt over the body of the sorcerer. A hand rifled through Logran's robes and came away with a strange artifact, an elvish source of power, a gift from Elethris to Logran. It resembled a single flower made entirely of light, and it rested in a thin glass tube; Logran had carried it close to his heart.

"So pretty, so fragile," Rauglir breathed.

He threw the glass on the floor. It shattered.

Snarling, he reached down and snatched the Flower up; it burned his fingers, but he ignored the pain.

"Oh, you're powerful," he breathed. "If I eat you ... yes. Yes, I think—"

He bit off its head. Pain shot all the way through his borrowed body, and he sank to his knees, screaming. He felt the flesh of Baleron's mouth burn and hiss. He pushed past the agony and forced himself to his feet. He swallowed the Flower's head, the pain traveling to his belly, and flung the stem into the fire. The flames flared brightly, burning with white light, then died.

Through a grimace of pain he grinned. He knew that that cursed Flower had given Logran the ability to power the magical shields that protected the city, and now it was gone and so was the only sorcerer in Glorifel powerful enough to wield it. Rauglir's job was complete.

Almost.

Drenched in blood, racked by pain, he carried himself onto the balcony and sniffed the smoky air. Borchstoggish war drums rolled across the land. *Doom boom doom.*

Below, in the courtyard, a large coach had been brought to the main stairs leading into the palace and was awaiting the king's arrival. Rauglir knew it would bear Lord Grothgar to the city walls, where he would direct the fighting and mayhap even fight some Borchstogs himself.

Overhead, the sky rippled with strange lights and someone shouted, "The shields! The shields are failing!"

Rauglir looked up at the pretty colors and smiled. It was working! The Borchstogs were attacking right when the shields were failing: Gilgaroth's will at work. Now Ungier could marshal the entirety of his forces and send them pouring over the walls— dragons and glarumri, as well.

Rauglir wondered if the other sorcerers could stabilize the shields in time. Now that Logran was dead, the energies he focused were removed, and Rauglir found it unlikely that any of the Archmage's students, or anyone else for that matter, would be powerful enough to raise the shields again—at least, not in time to prevent the city from being sacked utterly—and even if they could, the shields' strength would be paper-thin with the elvish artifact's destruction. This night, Rauglir knew, would see the fall of Glorifel, and the doom of Havensrike.

Below, King Grothgar emerged from the palace and strode down to his waiting coach. He looked grim, but didn't he always?

Rauglir's smile turned hungry. He ignored the lingering pain of the Flower and quit the terrace. The Flower burned, but it would make him stronger. If he hurried, he could reach the coach in time. Perhaps he could bluff his way past the guards and the king's skepticism to get close enough to sink Rondthril in

Albrech's hard heart, or perhaps not. Perhaps the guards would cut him down.

He hated to dispose of Baleron in this fashion. He had a more elaborate plan in mind for the prince's demise, and he'd worked too hard at twisting the young man into near-insanity and complete disgrace to be happy with losing him now before the climax, but his duty was to Gilgaroth and that was that.

The essence of the Flower of Itherin had weakened Rauglir and Baleron's Doom temporarily; in time Rauglir might absorb its energies and be made stronger, but for the moment he was vulnerable ... while at the same time the Flower had strengthened Baleron.

The prince shoved that icy tendril back, slamming the door behind it.

As Rauglir walked again through Logran's suite and passed the gaggle of dead bodies, Baleron's spirit—watching through his eyes, seeing the torn body of Logran—stirred in anger, and that anger made him even stronger. He gained just enough control of his body in that one instant to release the fingers of his right hand, dropping Rondthril to the floor. That broke the union between the Fanged Blade and the demon. After that, it was easy.

Rauglir screamed, but to no avail. Baleron overwhelmed the demon and shoved him aside, forced his evil spirit down his left arm, down and down and down ...

There! The demon was confined to the hand.

Baleron sank to his knees, grabbed a sword out of a dead guard's stiff grip, and held it high. The spirit of Rauglir squirmed, and angry growls echoed through Baleron's mind.

"Die, you bastard!" Baleron shouted. *"Just die!"*

He brought the sword down on his extended left arm and cut the hand off at the wrist, right at the scar. Pain flowered inside him. He screamed. He felt the blood ooze out of him, felt the life drain from him, and he dragged himself over to the fireplace, as blood gushed everywhere; the world heaved and turned and dimmed. Cringing, he stuck his bleeding, spurting stump into the hot coals, held it there a moment, and wrenched out the blackened remains with a gasp.

Darkness came over him. For the first time in weeks, he didn't dream of wolves chasing him through the blackness.

He awoke among the littered bodies and body parts, groggy and disoriented. He propped himself up and, noting his feet were uncomfortably hot and too close to the fire, dragged himself away from the flames.

He also noticed a burning pain in his mouth and remembered watching helplessly as Rauglir ate the Flower's head. Ah, well. His flesh would heal. The Flower didn't pain him now that the demon was gone. He wondered if eating it would do anything to him. To have *swallowed* such a thing! He'd have to be careful.

He surveyed the carnage, hardly able to believe it, staring at the body of Logran for a long time.

Logran, dead! And by my own hand! The old man really had been like a father to him. *Rauglir, I hope you burn.*

How could this have happened? The magical defenses of the city had fallen. Already Ungier would have his necromancers ripping at the failing shields, and soon he'd send his Worms and glarumri and other monsters to ravage the city. Baleron knew the men could not repel them this time.

Glorifel was doomed.

And his father, proud Lord Grothgar, was heading right into the heart of the battle. He would be killed, along with everyone else, or kept alive for torture.

But ... it did not have to be that way. Perhaps Baleron could *undo* some of the evil committed in his name.

He had to reach his father. Had to bear him to safety. Even if the city fell, the Enemy could not declare a complete victory if the king still lived. As long as the monarch survived and was free, he could summon the remaining free peoples of Havensrike to him, could marshal a resistance, or barter with the other countries in the fractured Union for aid.

This desperate plan began to form in the prince's mind, and he seized on it like a drowning man to a soggy bank. No longer did he want to throw himself on the swords and spears of the Borchstogs. No longer did he want to seek a noble death in battle. He wanted—needed—to save the king. No matter how much the king resisted.

As he prepared to depart the room, some instinct made him turn. He narrowed his eyes and swore.

The hand, his wicked left hand, had gone.

A chill ran up his spine, and his eyes darted all about. Rauglir could be anywhere. Even now, creeping up on him from behind ...

He whirled.

Nothing.

He breathed a sigh of relief. But then he heard a sound, a clattering off to his side, and spun around again. Still nothing. He growled in frustration.

"Why won't you just die!"

He retrieved Rondthril and sheathed it so that it hung at his waist, then selected a dagger from one of the guards and strapped it about his chest; he might need another weapon should Rondthril betray him again.

Two sorcerers, who must have felt Logran's death, entered the suite, an urgent look in their eyes. Having spied them through a doorway before they could see him, Baleron pressed himself against the wall next to the door and held his breath. He couldn't afford to be caught, not now. He was a fugitive.

As soon as they stopped in shock over the piled bodies, Baleron sprang from behind and struck them each on the head with the handle of his dagger. They crumpled to the floor wordlessly. Just to be sure they didn't go anywhere too soon, Baleron tied them up and gagged them so they couldn't mutter any spells after him, then crept down one corridor after the other. Bells tolled throughout the city, and all was organized chaos within the palace. Though scared, the people here had drilled for this and knew their places, and they rushed to and fro breathlessly. They seemed to sense the end was coming, judging by their pale, tightly-drawn faces.

Without the Flower's shields to ward off the worst of the onslaught, Baleron knew the rule of Men in Glorifel was over. It was only a matter of time now.

The bloody left hand crept out from behind an overturned chair.

Sensing the two semi-conscious sorcerers, Rauglir turned himself into an armored black scorpion, poison oozing from his tail, scuttled over to the waking forms and jumped upon the nearest one. The mage struggled and cried out into his gag, but Rauglir merely scuttled up to the mage's face and stung him on the cheek. Even as the toxins traveled through the sorcerer's bloodstream, the convulsions began.

Rauglir did not wait to see the results, but jumped to the second sorcerer. After stinging this one, too, he turned himself into the form of a small black snake, slipped under the door of the suite and into the hall.

His forked tongue tasted the air. Where had *ul Ravast* gone?

Chapter Seven

Lightning cracked above, and the floor under Baleron's feet shook with the fury of thunder.

He made for the servants' wing. There he found a loading dock where several coaches were drawn up, emptied of their wares and, as far as he could see, their riders. Only one coach had horses and a driver who seemed to be waiting for something, perhaps a crew to take to the walls. Baleron didn't take the time to find out but leapt up to the driver's bench and punched him on the side of the head. The man went limp. Throwing the driver over his shoulder, Baleron flung him like a sack of spuds into the coach interior.

"You can sit this one out," he said. "Today a prince will be driving *you*."

Baleron took the driver's perch, raised the whip, started to crack it over the horses' heads, but suddenly he hesitated. Frowning, he half-lowered the whip. *What am I DOING?* he wondered. Then, defensively: *I'm going to save the king!*

But the first voice asked, *Oh, really? Then why do I feel ... odd?*

It was his Doom. It must be. There were no signs of it—no

coldness, no darkness. But it was there still, and it was potent despite the Flower.

It wants me to finish my labor. To get close to Father and kill him.

On the other hand, how could Baleron be certain? He wanted to reach the king for his own purposes, after all, to save him, to drag him back to the castle ruins and take him through the secret tunnel ...

Sure, just me, him, Rondthril and my Doom alone in a long dark hall underground ...

He shivered.

Fine, then what? If my Doom's so strong, how can I counter it?

He had no choice, save to let his father die. His Doom be damned. But he would be watchful, oh yes. He took a breath, held it, and nodded to himself. *Go! Waste no more time.*

He cracked the whip over the horses' heads. "Ra!" he shouted. "Ra!"

The horses leapt forward, straining against their harnesses, and the coach was off, charging through the chaotic streets. He yelled and cursed and drove them mercilessly as bells still tolled throughout the city. Glarumri flew above, and several Worms; he knew that could only mean that the shields were well and truly down.

He saw one Worm pass right above him, flame licking its lips, eyes blazing, several dead Havensrike soldiers clutched in each claw, and felt its heat as it passed by. In a second, it was gone.

It quickly became apparent that driving a coach was a skill meant for the two-handed, as a driver needed one hand for the whip and one for the reins, but he made the best of it. He tucked the whip under his left arm and yanked it out when need be. Sometimes he held both whip and reins in his right hand at once.

His blackened stump throbbed, and several times he thought he would black out again, but every time he thought of Rolenya, and persevered.

Rain and wind lashed him, and he was drenched to the skin

and freezing. He made for the South Gate, where his father would most likely be. If he was fast enough, perhaps he could even overtake the king. How long had he been unconscious, anyway?

Too long, apparently.

When he had been amongst Ungier's hordes, he hadn't noticed the Spiders, the *igrith*, but they must have been there somewhere, as they'd already launched their attack. He envisioned Mogra's spawn swarming over the walls as a black tide, too many for the men to resist, and without Logran to coordinate the other sorcerers' energies, the soldiers would've been doomed. Instead of aiding the Borchstogs and the other minions of Gilgaroth, the *igrith* had driven into the city and began wreaking havoc in the streets and buildings of the interior, sowing fear and confusion as they went.

One Spider leapt into the street before Baleron in pursuit of a little girl. The girl made it across, but the creature wasn't so lucky. The hooves of Baleron's horses trod it into mush, and the wheels destroyed what was left.

The *igrith* had not been alone. The others in its group had seen its demise and, enraged, they struck out for their brother's murderer. Some hopped after Baleron in huge leaps that carried them fifty feet at a stretch. Others shot silken strands at tall buildings and swung their way through the air.

One landed atop the coach behind him. He heard the thud of its impact, then spun, throwing down reins and whip.

As Baleron reached for his weapon, he hesitated. If he chose Rondthril and his part in spinning the Dark One's web was over, then the Fanged Blade would obey its Master's will and let the creature kill him. Did he trust that his Doom still followed him, or should he use the dagger instead?

He chose Rondthril.

Unsheathing the Fanged Blade, he half-crouched in the driver's bench, and just in time. The bulbous Spider leapt on him, fangs glistening with venom.

The blade cut through the side of the monster's head, and dark blood sprayed. Where it struck the coach's roof, it smoked like acid.

"It burnssss," hissed the *igrith*, surprising Baleron.

Not bothering to respond, he jumped forwards and drove Rondthril through two of the arachnid's eight black eyes and into its head. Its long, hairy legs shuddered, and the body sagged. Holding his breath (the creature was rank), Baleron kicked the bloated, still-twitching arachnid off his blade and with some effort heaved the corpse from the coach. It smacked the pavement of the road and broke apart, spilling ichor.

More *igrith* pursued him, a score or more of them. He replaced his weapon in its scabbard and turned back to the horses.

They charged through the streets, terror in their wide eyes, froth at their lips. They sensed only too well that if they faltered, the Spiders would not only kill their driver but themselves as well. The sound of their hooves on the cobbled streets echoed loudly.

Wind whipped through Baleron's hair and tore at his face. His blood hummed and he felt more alive than he had in a long time. Lost in the moment, he lifted his head and howled at the night.

The horses swerved onto Kings' Road, which was choked with traffic and pandemonium. When they slowed, Baleron cracked the whip above the stallions' heads. "Ra!"

The animals obediently threaded their way through the chaos. Some coaches were stopped or overturned. More than one was on fire. Bodies littered the ground, some men, some arachnids, and many more species besides. Creatures of all types had made their way inside the walls, it seemed, some singly, some in groups. Baleron wanted to help the people he passed, some of whom were even then engaged in mortal struggles, but he dared not. He pressed his horses on, his wild delight spent. Seeing his home reduced to a war ground shriveled some deep part of him.

The Spiders that had been pursuing them, faced with the

chaos of Kings' Road, had a tough choice to make, and some continued to chase the prince while others went after the owners of the stopped coaches.

Wind carried smoke from the fires that were even then burning down sections of the city, and Baleron wrinkled his nose at the acrid stench. Fire consumed a bakery off to his right, and the heat brought a flush to his skin. *My home ...*

Hate and horror welled up inside him. The walls were closer now.

Rain soaked him. Ahead a flaming bridge stretched over a dark rushing river—the Nagradim. A score of Borchstogs stood on this side of the bridge. Half seemed to be archers, and the other half helped the archers light their arrows. As Baleron watched, a flaming volley arced into a watermill on the bank of the Nagradim, and the Borchstogs cheered as the building caught fire. One of them saw Baleron and launched a javelin at him. It struck, quivering, in the wooden back of the bench beside him.

"Ra!" he shouted at the horses, who were wavering, not wanting to charge through the line of Borchstogs and over the flaming bridge. "Go on, damn you!" He cracked the whip again, and the horses plowed ahead. Borchstogs scattered. The coach's wheels crunched over the disintegrating span and dark water rushed beneath. A loose, burning plank fell into it, disappearing without a trace. Unlit arrows flew after them, *thunk*ing into the coach harmlessly. Flames from the bridge leapt all about, and the horses whinnied nervously.

Another *igrith*, one of those still pursuing Baleron, jumped onto the roof, and Baleron turned to deal with it. The coach rocked beneath his feet and the smoke-filled wind tore at his eyes and nose.

Unsheathing Rondthril, he said, "Come on!"

The Spider came, snapping its mandibles.

Baleron hacked off one of its forelegs. Black ichor smoked on the coach roof. The Spider cried out in a high-pitched whistle.

"That sword!" it cried, and Baleron was no longer surprised to hear such a thing speak; they were Mogra's spawn, after all, just as Ungier was, if not as powerful, not mere beasts. "That's ... " Its eight eyes regarded Baleron strangely. "You're *him*."

Baleron drove his sword at the monster's head, but it dodged aside. Coiling its legs, it lunged at him and bore him to the roof so that he was crushed under its bloated, armored belly.

"Borchstogs may worship you, but the Children of Queen Mogra don't. No one will ever know I killed you."

"That's right," he grunted, unable to draw air, "because you won't," and drove Rondthril up through the brittle armor into the Spider's bowels.

It shrieked and convulsed wildly atop him, its many legs kicking and beating on the coach top. Its dark ichor smoked and gurgled where it struck him, and he gasped, kicking the heavy monster off of him. It was then that he saw a strange thing. From one of the many cuts on his body, blood had poured onto the Spider.

And his blood ... *smoked* where it touched the monster.

The Flower! "Damn you, Rauglir. What did you do to me?"

Shoving with all his strength, he managed to throw the body off the roof and into the river below, where it disappeared with a splash. Then the coach was over the bridge and the river receding behind him. The bridge, succumbing to the flames, began to collapse, and the Borchstogs cheered.

Baleron took up the reins once more.

He considered what it meant that Rondthril still worked for him, that he was still fulfilling his Doom. He hadn't been sure till now. *And the Flower ...*

The horses threaded their way through the chaos of the broad, tree-lined avenue that was King's Road, many of the trees on fire, as were several of the buildings that lined the Road. There were even more overturned and abandoned coaches on this side of the river, and even more monsters. A corrupted Giant, thrice or more the size of a Troll, walked down a side street swinging a terrible mace, people impaled to the spiked end of the weapon, not all of them dead. The Giant whipped it back and forth across the street, killing as it went.

Havensrike archers shot at its head, but its skull was too thick for the arrows to penetrate. Others aimed at its throat. Blood trickled down it, but Baleron knew it would take a lake of lost blood to fell that behemoth. It no longer looked humane at all, having four arms, clawed feet and a reptilian tail. Its teeth were long and sharp, and its flesh was slick, green and hairless.

The Giant threw back its head and roared, smashing the weapon into a nearby spire. Cracks spread at the impact. The Giant struck it again. The top half of the building listed and fell, smashing into another, smaller building as it went and crushing a score of people in the streets.

Suddenly the Giant stepped right in the middle of King's Road, blocking Baleron's way, and the horses whinnied in fear.

"On, you cravens!" Baleron shouted, cracking his whip.

The Giant loomed above them. Nearer and nearer. Rain dripped off its glistening dark-green skin in sheets.

Baleron would shoot right between its legs!

But then its awful mace came back around, some of the bodies impaled on it still moving. It swung at them.

Baleron ducked. The horses bolted forward.

BOOM! The mace missed them, hitting a building. Bricks exploded, one sailing past Baleron's head, nearly decapitating him.

He guided the coach right between the Giant's legs and past him. Baleron wished he had time to stop and assist the archers, but there was no time, and he had no bow anyway. Desperate, he cracked his whip over his horses' heads, guiding them through the war-torn roads, and they plunged onwards into the chaos. The giant roared at their backs, but thunder drowned it out.

Overhead Baleron saw a fleet of glarumri pass by, raining flaming arrows into the courthouse, where a mass of Havensri had gathered to form a resistance. The Havensri scattered, and fires began to consume the courthouse. Unable to do anything else, Baleron charged on.

Glorifel was a hilly city, and many of the streets passed through tunnels under the green rolling hills. Kings' Road was no exception. Ahead gaped the Sadram Tunnel, and Baleron cringed at what might have made a home in there in the chaos. Maybe he should try to go around the hill, he thought, to avoid the darkness beneath it.

Something blotted out the storm clouds above, and he was in shadow—a great, winged shadow. Something huge flew above, breathing fire.

He made for the tunnel.

To his surprise, Sadram's entrance was guarded by fifty or so men hunkering down behind a barricade of overturned coaches and debris—a makeshift refuge of the townspeople! He was heartened to see they weren't all overrun.

The men saw him coming, and their archers took aim but didn't fire. After studying him for a few moments, a group pushed one of the coaches aside, allowing him in. Grateful, he slowed his horses as they passed within the barricade, then drew rein. The men pushed the coach back into position behind him, grunting with the effort. It felt good to have a roof over his head again.

Above, a Darkworm spewed a column of fire, torching several buildings all in one fiery breath.

"My wife!" one of the men said, tears in his eyes.

"I'm sorry," Baleron said. "Thank you all. I owe you."

"Then will you stay and help us fight?" another asked.

"I can't, I'm sorry. I'm Prince Baleron, and I've got to find my father."

They looked him up and down, and a large man grinned. "Why, it *is* the prince!"

Another exclaimed, "The Dueling Dandy himself! Look at him!"

The big man said, "Why, you dog! He's Baleron of Baleron's Fighting Five Hundred—speak ill of him at your peril!"

A third man asked, "What happened to his hand?"

"It's Baleron!" said another, just arriving. "Prince Baleron!"

Baleron looked ahead to the far end of the tunnel. Between here and there were hundreds of people—men, women, children, soldiers and civilians—all desperate, all scared. Torches lined the walls, and their smoke was carried away by the tunnel's ventilation system. Just the same, the tunnel was gloomy and full of shadows, and it gave him an uneasy feeling.

"Indeed it is," said a familiar voice from the darkness.

A stout, medium-sized man with a royal bearing emerged, hard blue eyes as penetrating as ever. His crown, stained with blood, glinted in the torchlight.

"Father!" said Baleron.

Albrech carried a broadsword crusted with Borchstoggish viscera. He wore only rudimentary armor, including a bloody breastplate, apparently not having taken the time to don more. Baleron knew that this spoke to his burning love of Glorifel and his desire to helm its defense even at his own expense. Five guards flanked him.

"Son," said the king, his voice grave.

Lightning split the night sky beyond the tunnel, and thunder rolled across the city.

Well, Baleron supposed, his search was over, but it looked as though his mission had only just begun. For they were trapped under a hill in an overrun city, with countless horrors all around. He didn't know how he could get the king to safety, or if the king would even want to go.

Chapter Eight

L eaping down from the driver's bench, Baleron strode over to Albrech. "Why aren't you at the wall?" he said, meaning to embrace his father—he never got that close.

Albrech pointed his sword at his throat and said, "Stop right there."

Baleron closed his eyes and took a breath. When he opened them again, the king was studying the red stains on Baleron's clothes.

"That's not Borchstog blood," Albrech said. "Guards!"

Instantly, a ring of sharp steel surrounded the prince.

Albrech narrowed his eyes suspiciously. "To answer your question, we never made it to the wall. It was overrun just as soon as the shields collapsed. Dragons and glarumri broke our defenses. My company and those we gathered to us sought refuge here ... and the shields' failing can mean only one thing: Logran is dead." He paused. "*Interesting* that that happened just as soon as I sent you *to* him."

"Father, I can explain."

"You have an explanation for everything, don't you?" Albrech grimaced in distaste. "Just the same, it *was* I that sent you to him. I suppose I'm to blame, too."

Baleron hung his head. *Steady, Bal,* he thought. *Stay on course.*

Slowly, he lifted the stump of his left arm. It was a blackened ruin. Where it wasn't black, the skin looked as though it had melted, and the whole thing was an inflamed, reddened mass of tortured tissue. The king actually started upon seeing it.

"Rauglir is gone," Baleron told him steadily. "The demon is gone. It did kill Logran ... but it cannot harm anyone else."

Thunder cracked again, and rain began to fall from the dark clouds Gilgaroth had thrown over the city. A chill breeze gusted through the tunnel.

Albrech eyed Baleron skeptically. "This is the same demon that pretended to be Rolenya?" the king said.

"The very one."

A beat passed. Albrech reached his decision. "We need all the men we can muster, I suppose. General Kavradnum is dead. I don't think the Enemy knows I'm here, otherwise they would have overrun us already. But we need every able-bodied man and woman to take up arms. I don't know if I can consider you able-bodied, but ... you do have a sword." He studied the Fanged Blade. "Is that ... your old sword? The cursed one?"

"Rondthril, yes. The last thing Logran said was that I should keep it."

Albrech nodded slowly. "Yes, you did wield it well, if I remember. When it wasn't betraying you. And me. Just the same, perhaps with it you could still prove of help to us—if you can resist the urge to murder any more of your fellow countrymen."

Baleron hadn't thought the jest humorous when Logran told it, and it hadn't improved since. "Father, staying here is suicide. No matter how long you hold out, they'll come for you eventually." He paused significantly, then said, "Glorifel has fallen."

The king glared at him. "You weakling. Coward. How *dare* you say that!"

"It's true, Father. I've been out there. I've seen it. Our only hope—Havensrike's only hope—is for you to live and somehow marshal a resistance in the north."

"I won't abandon my people!"

"You said yourself the city was doomed. If you don't leave now ... right now ... you will die. Then you truly *will* abandon them."

"I will not stand here and listen to your bile. Either take up your sword and fight the Borchstogs, or be damned! I'll put an end to you myself!"

Baleron gritted his teeth. *Patience, Bal.* "Very well, Father. Borchstogs it is."

Turning to one of the men, Albrech said, "Put him on the north barricade. And keep an eye on him."

"I can't keep eyes on him and the Borchstogs both," said the captain of the assigned barricade. "I need men I can trust."

"That's ill for you," spat the king. "You've got him instead."

He stalked off, leaving Baleron with the captain.

"Where do you want me?" Baleron said.

The captain placed him at a spot on the barricade, and Baleron settled in with the others to watch the rain-thrashed city succumb to the horrors of Oslog. Gloom began to dig its way into him. The eyes of the other soldiers were glazed and dull and hopeless, and he knew if he stayed here long enough his would be the same. The terrible part was that the soldiers were right to think as they did; they *were* doomed.

Baleron tried to talk sense into the captain, whose name was Marz Sider, a colonel under General Kavradnum: "My father will die if he stays here. You must help me get him to safety. I know a way. It's the only chance for Havensrike."

Marz Sider shook his head—"You *are* craven"—and marched away. Baleron decided to bide his time until the moment was right, then steal the king away himself, somehow or other.

As things happened, that didn't prove necessary. About an

hour after Baleron's arrival, a wave of Borchstogs swarmed across the bridge and broke against the barricade, howling and calling for blood. The men fought back with everything they had, women and children picking up arms beside them. Many died, but ultimately they drove the Borchstogs back—at least temporarily. The enemy would return.

Bleeding from a cut on his arm, Marz Sider drew Baleron aside. The captain looked haggard and frightened, but Baleron knew it wasn't for himself; the king had been forced to draw his sword during the fighting, and he'd been wounded—only a shallow cut along one cheek, but it had evidently been enough to convince Sider of something.

"You were right, Baleron," he said without preamble. "The King *will* die if he stays here."

Baleron waited.

"You seemed to think there was a way to get him safely out of the city," Sider went on. "Is there?"

"Yes. It's an old family secret, but I guess it doesn't matter now. Beneath the ruins of Castle Grothgar there's a tunnel. It will take us beyond the city, assuming we can find it under the rubble."

"An old escape tunnel for the king," mused Sider. "You'll need men."

"How many can you provide?"

Sider thought it over. "Maybe nine or ten."

"It's not quite my old five hundred, but it will have to do. Get them ready immediately. We'll need help to kidnap the king."

For as long as he could remember, Baleron had wanted one thing above all else—his father's love and respect—but he knew that if he did this thing, if he took the king away from the fight here at what Albrech must think of as the bitter end, his father would not thank him, would in fact never forgive him, and Baleron would lose any chance he ever had of making up with him. To save the man, Baleron must give up his dream. If nothing else, the prince could not have asked for a better partner. Marz Sider was well respected and an able fighter.

To accomplish the plan they'd need to go up Kings' Road yet again, and it was in worse shape now than before; at least one bridge was out that Baleron knew of, and the Omkar knew how many creatures lurked in the dark, not to mention the hordes of Borchstogs that had brought them ... and, of course, the dragons and glarumri.

Baleron watched himself closely. He waited to feel a stab of ice in his breast, or a swell of shadow, or some other sign of his Doom. Nothing. Still, he remained wary.

At length, Sider returned to him. "The men are ready, sir."

The king was giving a speech to a group of perhaps fifty soldiers and civilians, trying to rally their spirits. All looked grim and weary, most especially Lord Grothgar. "We will fight and we will die," Albrech was saying, "but, Illiana help us, we'll take as many of them down with us as we can. We'll weaken them so much that our allies will be able to wipe them from the earth. Our sacrifice *will save the world!*"

The troops cheered raggedly, though Baleron doubted many believed the bold words. Baleron just felt sick. *He* was the reason for their deaths, and he didn't forget that for a moment.

As the gathering broke up, he approached his father, who appraised him coldly and said, "Yes?"

"I've something to talk to you about ... privately."

"Oh?" Albrech did not budge.

"It's about Rolenya."

The king arched an eyebrow. "What about her?"

"It's something I don't feel comfortable talking about here. Come."

Reluctantly, Albrech followed him into the shadows in the center of the tunnel, the farthest place from the torches, right next to the coach Baleron had stolen from the palace. It had been drawn up by one of Sider's men, and father and son huddled next to it conspiratorially.

"What is it?" asked the king.

"She lives," said the prince.

It was the signal.

All at once three soldiers rushed around from the other side of the coach, one shoving a gag over the king's mouth. The largest wrapped his muscular arms about his lord and held him while the third slugged the king in the face to subdue him; the man looked frightened even as his fist landed, but it worked, and some of the fight went out of Albrech, though by no means all.

Colonel Marz Sider jumped into the driver's bench and another, bearing a longbow and a full quiver, joined him.

Baleron opened the door and they prepared to fling the king inside.

The prince had forgotten about the unconscious driver.

The man still lay in the cab, even more still than before. Blood coated his throat and chest and face. Flies buzzed all about, and a stench of decay and death filled the tight space. All those gathered before it gasped and recoiled at the sight.

A long, dark form rose from the dead man's chest—where it had been coiled inside one of the wounds, within the man's very body—and reared its scaly head at kidnappers and king.

Its hood flared.

Albrech screamed into his gag, his eyes bulging. Baleron reached for Rondthril. Chose the dagger instead.

Rauglir, a serpent now, coated with blood, struck at Albrech, but the distance was too great and Baleron leapt in between them, dagger flashing. Rauglir retreated into the darkness of the cab.

All over the tunnel, people shouted and pointed towards the coach.

"Hells!" snapped Sider. "Hurry, boy!"

The first three kidnappers dragged the kicking, thrashing king back a few feet, while Baleron leapt into the coach, growling in desperation—the others in the tunnel would be upon them soon —and slashed at the snake, again and again, but Rauglir was too quick. Hissing, the serpent vanished into the shadows.

The shouts and screams and commotion drew closer. Louder. In seconds Baleron and the rest of the kidnappers would be caught and killed.

He heard a sound and flung the dagger at it. The blade quivered in the wood floor, catching nothing. Damn!

Rauglir flew at the prince's face.

Baleron barely had time to reach up and grab the snake by the neck. Rauglir, slippery with blood, twisted in his grasp, but Baleron held firm. The snake tried to bite him, but Baleron avoided his fangs. Frustrated, Rauglir began changing forms—first to a scorpion, then a left hand, then a spider. Working quickly, Baleron evaded his mandibles and stinger and kept his grip, until finally, exhausted, Rauglir returned to his snake form.

Hearing the noise outside, Baleron knew he had to do something fast and bitterly lamented the loss of his left hand. He threw the black snake at the wall and pinned him there with his boot.

"Get comfortable," he said.

He jerked his dagger out of the floor and ran Rauglir through, right to the hilt, impaling the demon to the cab wall; the blade passed right below the snake's head; he did not want the snake dead, as that would just free Rauglir's spirit to cause further mischief in a new form.

To the kidnappers, he shouted over his shoulder, "In! Now!"

The three leapt inside, dragging their captive with them, and with a crack of Sider's whip the coach was off. The dead body of the coachman was flung unceremoniously outside.

Marz Sider had recruited several of the men along the barricade, and they shoved a coach out of the way so that the king's vehicle would have an opening to break out of. They'd begun shoving the overturned vehicle out of alignment with the others the second their captain had jumped into the driver's bench, and by the time Sider lashed the horses into action the way was open.

The coach shot out of the tunnel, and not a second too soon. In an instant an angry mob was swarming out after them, but fortunately none were mounted, and the king and his kidnappers were safely off.

Looking out the rear window, Baleron watched as the angry mob turned their venom on the men that had breached the barricade, and a swell of shame rose in him. Yet more deaths on his conscience.

"Go to the Lights of Sifril," he whispered. "And thank you."

Rain slashed down at the charging coach, and lightning struck the ground. The once-fair city was now a place of horrors. Ghouls and goblins and demons walked the streets. Darkworms, aided by glarumri, eliminated all organized resistance from above, while foul spirits possessed the living, and an evil army burned the town down around them.

Baleron and the kidnappers raced through the streets. Borchstoggish arrows riddled the vehicle and beasts gave chase. Once a Serpent bearing many Borchstog archers pursued them for a while, and Sider had to drive the horses through twisting dark alleys to elude the creature. Just the same, some of the archers managed to hit the coach with flaming arrows. The rain put out the blaze.

Three bridges had burned down between Sadram Tunnel and the ruins of Grothgar Castle, and Sider had to take them the long way around, finding alternate routes where he could.

All the while, Rauglir hissed and taunted those in the cab in a strangled, gurgling snake-voice. "Fools!" he hissed. "You will all be killed, if you're lucky."

The king's gag had been removed and, once he'd stopped struggling, his bonds had also been taken away. At first he'd denounced them all as cowards and traitors, but he seemed to have resigned himself to his capture and possible survival. Baleron had told him of their destination, and he'd just grunted. Now, glaring at Rauglir, he said softly to Baleron, "So ... that's the thing that ... possessed Rolenya ... and you."

"Yes."

Albrech's eyes hardened. "That's the thing that killed my sons, my wife, my sorcerer ... *doomed my city* ..."

Lightning split the skies and illuminated the war zone beyond the coach, which its inhabitants could see through the windows; their little black drapes were pulled to, but wind tore them aside. Rain and cold wind ravished the inside, and all were shivering and wet. *At least we're not as bad off as Sider and his archer*, thought Baleron.

Lord Grothgar rose to his feet and put his face as close to Rauglir's as he dared.

"A little clossser," hissed the snake.

"Demon!"

"Yessss."

The king was winding himself up into a fine fit of rage, Baleron saw. "Don't kill Rauglir," he warned. "Don't free him from that body. That's just what he wants."

"Oh, I won't kill it. I have better plans than that."

Albrech tore the drapes off the largest window and jerked the string out. Acting quickly, he yanked the dagger out of the wall, Rauglir still wriggling on it like meat on a spit, shook the serpent loose and dumped it into the sack created by the drapes, tying the ends off with the string. Rauglir thrashed and struggled, but he couldn't tear his way out of the sack, not right away. The cloth was thick and heavy.

"There you are," Albrech said, holding up his prize. "Now I can take you anywhere."

"That won't hold him for long," Baleron said. "Better to bind him and leave him."

The king tossed Baleron the bloody dagger, then, with sudden violence, smashed the sack against a wall.

Rauglir hissed in pain. Hidden coils writhed furiously from within the sack. Albrech, a mad light in his eyes, smashed again, and again. And again. Sweat flew off his brow, and he swore and cursed viciously with every strike. Baleron, who hated Rauglir above all others, didn't stop him. Part of him wished he was the one wielding the sack.

"This is what you get!" the king shouted. "This is what you get, you filthy demon, for all your wickedness and deceit!"

Rauglir hissed and squirmed, but his struggles were growing feebler.

"This!" shouted the king, striking again. "This!"

Baleron still had the dagger in his hand.

The king's back was to him.

Suddenly a throb of ice exploded in his chest and a freezing tendril shot into his mind.

He was waiting.

All this time he'd been thinking of his blood smoking on the Spider's corpse, thinking of the Flower of Itherin, trying to feel it inside him. Now he did. He called on it, clumsily, but it heeded his call. Strength surged through him, and he forced that icy limb down, down and away. *Not this time, you bastard.*

Baleron didn't know how long the Flower would stay in his system, but prayed it lasted long enough time to get his father to safety. To the horses, he thought, *May the gods give you wings.*

He sheathed the dagger.

When they finally reached the blackened ruins of the castle,

Baleron was shocked to see just how large the mound of rubble was; the castle had been massive, certainly, but it was *still* massive, and the fact that it sat on a hill made the ruins look even more impressive, even ominous. Lightning backlit the jagged, black-ened thrusts of the mound, and thunder shook the earth.

Baleron jumped down from the coach and the others followed him. One of the soldiers had taken Rauglir from the king, so Albrech's hands were free, and, surprising Baleron, he clapped one on the prince's shoulder.

"Our old home," sighed Albrech, his eyes gazing up sadly at the dark ruins.

What is this? Baleron wondered. *Has he forgiven me?* Aloud, he said, "And our way out."

He led the way into the desolation, and they began searching. His greatest fear was that the opening would be covered by debris too heavy to move. As it happened, most of the entrances into the lower levels of the castle—the dungeons, wine cellars and arcane libraries, all underground—were indeed blocked, but two were still accessible. Baleron picked one and they all congregated around it.

"We'll need a torch," he said. "Some light."

They looked at each other blankly. None had brought anything.

The king shook his head wearily, grimly amused. "Rauglir was right: I've been kidnapped by fools."

"Foolsss," agreed Rauglir from the sack, now wet with his blood.

Just then, a great shadow blotted out the lightning-torn clouds above, and everyone looked up. Baleron's jaw dropped open, but it immediately closed tightly, clenching. His eyes narrowed.

For, flying his great scaly bulk across the charcoal-colored sky was the greatest dragon he had ever seen. Vast wings spread like dark clouds. Flame licked his lips. Smoke issued from his nostrils and trailed behind him like a black tail. He spiraled above the ruins of the castle, his spiral drawing tighter and tighter as he descended from the heavens.

"Throgmar," breathed Albrech.

"He's coming," whispered Baleron.

Chapter Nine

Rolenya stood at the balcony of her suite at Krogbur and gazed longingly at the horizon. Wind whipped her black hair in streamers to one side, and billowed her white dress in a ghostly fashion.

She'd asked for the illusion of the snow-capped mountains of Illistriv to be stripped away, tired of deception—no matter how ugly, she needed to face the truth—and Gilgaroth had complied. That in itself was unsettling.

Below her, beyond the terrible Inferno that wreathed the tower's lower half, stretched his foul hordes—Borchstogs and worse, monsters great and small, spawned by Gilgaroth and Mogra. Rolenya felt queasy at the sight: should Baleron decide not to fulfill his labor, she would be thrown down ... *to them*. The thought made her tremble and even wish there was some way she could kill herself, but there was not; should she try, Gilgaroth would simply bring her back.

Just the same, she hoped Baleron would find a way to save their father, as that's still very much how she thought of Albrech Grothgar. He had been her father all her life, and she could not think anything different of him now. Strange that she could think differently of Baleron.

Someone knocked on the door.

"Come in," she said. It always surprised her that the fell Men who served the Beast bothered to ask her permission, but they did. She'd requested that Men attend to her rather than Borchstogs, for the Borchstogs had somehow found out about her possible fate and they constantly leered at her and made obscene gestures, indicating what they would do to her when she was their plaything.

A tall man entered: Hierghast, swarthy and always regally poised, as though he'd been a king prior to coming here, and perhaps he had; it was an *honor* to serve in Krogbur. He bowed politely. "The Master awaits your presence in the Feasting Hall, my lady."

"Will he have me sing again tonight?"

"I make it my business never to predict my Lord's desires."

"A wise policy, I'm sure."

He gestured toward the door. "If you'll allow me to escort you?"

She dismissed whatever resentment she felt at being a slave—she'd had plenty of experience at that in Gulrothrog, after all—and allowed Hierghast to escort her from her suite and up the halls and tunnels. The Feasting Hall was packed tonight, she saw, and full of restlessness. The Borchstog chiefs wanted to be on the attack already, tired of camping outside the Black Tower, though Rolenya knew they appreciated its dark energies and reveled in the sense of power the place emanated. A fight was going on in the pit below: three titans battled a Grudremorqen. One titan was a large reptilian creature, one was wooly and tusked but stood on two legs, and the third was a writhing mass of fungus-like tendrils. The Grudremorqen fought them all with a sword of flame.

On the other side of the arena sat the Dark One on his black throne, and this night a new throne sat next to his, as Mogra in her more humane form lounged beside him. With her six arms, she fingered the rubies and pearls and jewels that adorned her otherwise naked body. A golden clasp bound her thick dark hair, and her violet eyes, only two of them, sparkled in amusement above a slightly smirking mouth. When she opened it, two fangs glistened in the torchlight.

When her eyes fell on the princess, she frowned slightly. One of her hands had been on Gilgaroth's armored arm, but now she removed it and began fingering one of her dripping necklaces that fell between her full high breasts.

Rolenya, afraid to match the Spider Queen's gaze, averted her eyes and allowed Hierghast to escort her down the stairs to the first row, where he seated her, then took position just behind her —her servant, protector, and, she was all too aware, captor.

Borchstogs brought her steaming food on golden platters and slopping goblets of wine. She ate and drank conservatively, and she tried not to watch the bloody fights, though bellows and roars pierced the air. She also tried to avoid looking at either Mogra or Gilgaroth. For the most part, she kept her eyes on her food, which if nothing else agreed with her. Gilgaroth kept her well.

She thought of Baleron, as she often did. She wished he would arrive right now and wrap her in his arms, take her away from this awful place. It would be so wonderful to be with him again.

On the other hand, she dreaded to see him, for it would mean he had completed his task—had murdered Albrech, murdered Logran, and consigned Havensrike to the fires of the Wolf. Racked by conflicting emotions, Rolenya felt tears well behind her eyes, and only with a sudden surge of will did she force them away.

Eventually the tentacled horror entangled the Grudremorqen, and the other two, who were by then mortally wounded, were able to destroy it. It died, but they soon followed it into darkness, and the tentacled creature succumbed to the burns the Grudremorqen had dealt it, leaving no victors at all.

As the bodies were carted away, Gilgaroth rose from his throne. Rolenya steeled herself as his black voice rang out, as she knew it would:

"Sing for us, my dove."

Even with the Spider Goddess here, she sang for him nearly every night, and, though it pained Rolenya, she was glad to do it, as with every song she sang she drew her own web about him—a web of Light and Grace, to be sure, but a web nonetheless. She sought to bind him to her, to ensnare him in love for her. Surely if she succeeded he could not throw her to the Borchstogs, or visit any other tortures on her for that matter. And ... if her spells were powerful enough ... perhaps she could even seek to influence his actions, to bend him to *her* will.

Of course, it was risky. Very risky.

But, as she saw it, she had precious little to lose. She only hoped that her songs were working. She suspected they were. Why else would Mogra be glaring at her if the Mistress of Shadows did not suspect something amiss? She would be unlikely to feel simple jealousy, Rolenya felt sure.

Quelling her doubts, the princess stepped down into the arena, still avoiding Mogra's eyes, and took her position in its center. She actually looked forward to singing; it was the only time lately when she felt whole.

All the Borchstogs fell silent, and a hush descended upon the room. Even the terrible wraiths hiding above the smoke that wreathed the ceiling ceased stirring.

She cleared her throat and looked Gilgaroth in his burning eyes. She no longer had to look away from him. His eyes held no evil for her. Indeed, quite disturbingly, the opposite was true.

Thus, gazing at him openly, she began to sing. She opened up the gates of Light and Grace within herself and let them pour into him through her voice.

Mogra's eyes narrowed.

Rolenya tried to ignore the Shadow-Weaver. With ever greater power, she let her voice ring out.

Gilgaroth's expression was difficult to make out on his shadow-wreathed face, but she saw it, and it warmed her. She was beginning to feel almost ... kindly ... towards him. It was her songs, she knew. They worked both ways.

She thought it strange, even *profane*, to think of, but she'd discovered Gilgaroth to possess other facets to his being than the one he normally showed, even, possibly, a facet that knew love. Perhaps—

She sang on.

The Leviathan tucked his wings behind him and dove, flame licking his lips.

"TASTE THE FIRE OF *UL MRUNGONA*!" he roared, and shot a burning lance as he dove for the tunnel entrance.

"Quickly!" shouted Baleron. "Inside!"

He ran into the dark opening, rebounded against a wall, nearly breaking his nose, and ran on. The others followed quickly behind. Once they rounded a few corners he felt safer, but Throgmar's fire still chased their heels, immolating the ruins around the opening and sending fire deep into the tunnel itself. Its heat reflected off the wall and up the bend, singeing the kidnappers but not roasting them.

"Damn!" said Sider, fingering his burned eyebrows and soot-streaked face. "I hate dragons."

"I hate *that* dragon," said Lord Grothgar.

Baleron said nothing. He'd suffered months of torture just for the chance of slaying Throgmar, and he still harbored that enmity deep within him, but his hatred was mixed with satisfaction now; he'd already had his revenge.

Fires flickered from wreckage further up the tunnel, and the smoke stung at his eyes. Outside, Throgmar roared loudly, then Baleron heard the sound of the dragon landing.

"THINK YOU CAN HIDE FROM ME IN THERE?" the Leviathan said. "I'LL UNEARTH YOU LIKE A BIRD OF PREY UNEARTHS A GRUB!"

The tunnel began to rock. Baleron could imagine the Worm ripping at the mountain of debris with his mighty claws, tossing huge chunks of rock and masonry aside. The reverberations of his excavation shook the corridor, and the kidnappers looked at each other nervously.

"HOW DOES IT *FEEL* TO BE A GRUB?" shouted the Worm. "ARE YOU PALE AND WRIGGLING?"

This series of tunnels led to the wine cellars, which was in the direction Baleron desired to go, and unlit torches lined the walls at regular intervals. He plucked one from the wall and stabbed it into one of the fires left by Throgmar's rage.

"Here," he said, passing the torch to Sider. "Lead on. My father knows how to get to the escape tunnel."

Albrech grunted. "Escape! What a lot I've fallen into."

"It's not for you," Baleron snapped. "It's for the Union. You're going to survive, damn it, whether you like it or not, and you're going to lead whatever forces you can summon against Gilgaroth, and you're going to defeat him."

He glared at Albrech hotly until the king, shockingly, looked away. Baleron felt a surge of triumph.

"Go," he said. "I'll delay the dragon."

"You're mad," said Sider. "You don't stand a chance, and anyway I doubt one human could delay such a beast for long in any case."

"Let him," Albrech said dully.

Baleron did not take offense at Albrech's tone. Finally, after all he'd been through, he felt unconcerned about his father's judgment. It was about damned time, he thought.

The tunnel shook, and dust rained down from the ceiling.

"Hurry," Baleron said.

"Good luck," said Sider.

Wait! came a voice in the prince's head. *How can you let your father go off with this rabble? How can you let them take him through miles of subterranean passages? They look a shifty lot, and that Sider has a queer look in his eye.*

Baleron merely smiled and ignored the voice.

Sider hurried off into the darkness, the torch lighting the way, and the others followed close at his heels. The king paused, lingering behind. Surprisingly, he squeezed Baleron's shoulder, for the second time that night.

"This is farewell, then," Albrech said, and Baleron did not argue. "I never thought *you* would sacrifice yourself for *me*."

"I'm not," Baleron said. "And it's for Havensrike, if I am, not you. Now hurry."

Albrech did not move. He stared Baleron in the eye. "You're my last," he said, and his voice was thick. "I never told you this, but I ... I ..."

Baleron waited. He had waited his whole life for this. Despite himself, he found that he was holding his breath.

But then another roar shook the hall, and Albrech's gaze wavered. "I ..."

"Yes?"

Albrech looked back into his eyes. "I ... " Clarity returned. "I never did like you."

Baleron just stared at him. Then, unable to stop it, he laughed. "I never liked you either."

Albrech nodded to himself, as if he'd settled something, gave his son's shoulder one last squeeze, gave the Heir's blue eyes one last looking-into, then hurried off into the darkness, chasing that pinprick of light. Baleron watched him go until his father had rounded a bend and was gone. He knew he would never see the king again. Then he squared his shoulders, set his jaw and strode outside.

The air out here stank of smoke, burnt stone and metal—and death. Smoke still rose from the spot Throgmar had torched, and the ground was hot underfoot.

Just the same, there was a chill wind blowing, along with the constant drizzle, and Baleron was instantly just as cold and wet as he had been before.

He squinted up at the towering figure of the Betrayer.

A many-forked tongue of lightning licked the ground and sent out a peel of thunder, and for a moment the mighty Throgmar was backlit, a massive, horned silhouette against the sky. Fire seethed from his mouth, lapping at his scaly lips but not burning them. He was a creature of fire and his own fires had no effect.

His amber, reptilian eyes narrowed at seeing the prince, and his whiskered mouth drew into a pained expression.

"YOU," he said.

"Me," Baleron affirmed. With a *snick*, he drew out Rondthril. He did not know what Gilgaroth's will was, and he did not care; he only knew that his dagger would have little effect on the Worm.

"I WONDERED IF I MIGHT MEET YOU HERE, PRINCE."

"How?"

"OH, OUR SPIES FOUND OUT ABOUT THE SECRET TUNNEL LONG AGO, AND I TASKED MYSELF WITH GUARDING IT. I COULD NOT ALLOW YOU TO FLEE."

"You knew I'd left Krogbur?"

"OF COURSE. I WAS SENT TO RETRIEVE YOU— AFTER YOU'D COMPLETED YOUR LABOR."

"Well, it's not complete, and it won't be, not if I have anything to say about it."

"*WHAT* IS THIS? *DEFIANCE*? HA! THE CITY'S FALLEN! THE ARCHMAGE IS DEAD! YOUR PEOPLE ARE LOST AND OVERRUN. WHAT FEW SURVIVE SHALL

ONLY LIVE AS CATTLE LIVE, AS SLAVES TO MY FATHER'S WILL."

Baleron returned sneer for sneer. "Like you?"

Smoke plumed from the dragon's nose. *"WHAT DID YOU SAY?"*

"You're a coward!" Baleron raged. "A yellow, stinking, pus-bag of fear and shame! I'm surprised Gilgaroth even suffers you to live!"

"YOU GO TOO FAR."

Baleron lunged forward and slashed the dragon across one of his clawed fingers, between plates of armor, drawing blood. Throgmar's sharp intake of breath revealed the pain that Rondthril could inflict, even on so mighty a foe.

Kill! Kill! sang the sword. *Blood! Blood!* Baleron could tell it loved the taste of dragon.

"How far have I gone now, Worm?" he said.

The dragon drew back a bit, wary now. "DO YOU WANT TO DIE?"

"May be!"

Evidently impatient with this foolishness, Throgmar shot out a claw and pinned Baleron to the ground. A huge lead weight was on Baleron's chest, crushing the life out of him, Rondthril wedged between two enormous fingers. Baleron was being ground into the mud and rubble, and he could not get enough air to talk. Is this how his life would end?

Throgmar brought his huge horned head close to the prince's. "MURDERER," he snarled. "I HAVE NOT FORGOTTEN YOUR CRIME. TEMPT ME, AND I *WILL* BE TEMPTED."

Baleron wondered if he had delayed the Leviathan long enough. Would his father have gotten to safety yet? He hoped so. If he provoked the Betrayer any more, he would not be around to delay him any longer.

Throgmar narrowed his eyes, seeing something revealed in the prince's face, or perhaps in his mind.

"A TRICK," the dragon seethed, understanding. "YOU SEEK TO SLOW ME." He snorted flame. "VERY WELL. THEN LET US END THIS NOW." He paused. "YET BEFORE I DEVOUR YOU, LET ME JUST SAY THAT YOU ARE A FOOL IN THE GRANDEST TRADITION IMAGINABLE. YOU WERE ON THE CUSP OF EVERYTHING; I WOULD HAVE DELIVERED YOU TO KROGBUR, WHERE ROLENYA AWAITS YOU, AND TOGETHER YOU COULD HAVE LIVED OUT YOUR LIVES AS THE RULERS OF SOME DISTANT LAND. YET YOU PROVOKE ME AND AID YOUR FATHER IN HIS FLIGHT, WHEN HE IS DOOMED REGARDLESS."

He wrapped his claws about Baleron and held the prince aloft in a giant, scaly fist. The dragon shook him, not gently, but just enough to hurt and jar him, and to make him release his grip on Rondthril; the Fanged Blade spun to the earth and embedded itself blade down, quivering, sinking slowly into the wet ground.

"FOOL!" Throgmar spat.

He unclenched his fist and with the other foreleg grabbed Baleron by a boot and hoisted him high overhead. The Great Worm opened his terrible mouth so that Baleron, dangling, stared down at the dragon's red, fleshy mouth and ivory-colored, gleaming teeth, which were all long and sharp and glistening. The red tongue squirmed between them. Baleron knew he was facing his end.

"THIS IS FOR FELESTRATA," announced the dragon.

Strangely, fear did not fill Baleron. He would die, he supposed, and the king would live, and as long as the king lived, so would hope. That was enough for him.

Just the same, he would go down fighting. He pulled out the dagger. Dangling by a foot over a chasm of fangs and a flashing red tongue and a hellish gullet, when all his attention was focused on those massive jaws and teeth, a strange voice stopped the Worm from releasing Baleron's boot and plunging him, slashing, into that cavernous maw.

"Sssspare him," pleaded a small voice from below.

Irritated, Throgmar clamped his mouth shut and craned his long neck to see just who the speaker was.

To Baleron's shock, it was none other than Rauglir.

The demon had escaped! Baleron had *known* this would happen. Hadn't he warned his father? Damn the man's stubbornness, his need for revenge! Smashing the sack against the wall had torn a hole in it, or perhaps the demon had gotten out on his own.

Still in his serpent form, Rauglir had evidently stuck around to watch the spectacle, but this eating of the prince was too much for him to sit idly through.

"WHAT?" asked Throgmar.

"I will take care of the king," promised the snake. "It issss why I was sssent."

Something about the reptile forced recognition on the dragon. "RAUGLIR," he said. "I SHOULD'VE KNOWN YOU'D TURN UP."

"The bad onesss alwaysss do." Rauglir flicked his head to the still-dangling prince. "I've worked too hard to twissst that one to see you ssssimply *eat* him. Besides, he *is* The Ssssavior."

"THEN WHAT WOULD YOU SUGGEST, DEMON?"

"His Doom hasss delivered him and hisss father into our ... handssss. You were sent to retrieve him. Retrieve him. The king ... isss mine!"

Now dread did begin to build up in Baleron. Rauglir was right. Baleron had tried to master his Doom, but his Doom had won. It had prompted him to seek out and kidnap the king and bring it to where its Master's agents were waiting.

But what other choice did I have? It was a good plan. A worthy one. Unfortunately it had been the Enemy's, also, and now his father would die; Baleron knew without a doubt that Rauglir could easily catch up with Albrech and his kidnappers. If Rauglir went after them, they were dead men. Somehow he had to stop the demon.

"No!" he shouted. He hurled his dagger into Throgmar's eye.

It worked better than he'd hoped. Throgmar grunted in annoyance and dropped Baleron to the ground. He struck hard, the breath driven from him. Forcing himself not to pause, he rolled aside.

Throgmar plucked the comparatively tiny dagger from his eye and tossed it aside. It had done very little damage. A bass rumble issued from his throat, and fire licked his lips.

Off to the side, Rauglir just chuckled.

"Take him to the Massster," hissed the demon.

"YES," agreed the Leviathan. "HIS TORMENT SHALL CONTINUE. YOU'RE RIGHT; IT IS THE BETTER WAY."

"Yesss." The serpent regarded Baleron. "Goodbye, lover. I will give your regardsss to your father."

Baleron lunged at him, meaning to crush the life from him with his one hand, but the snake darted aside.

The prince gave chase—crippled, soaked to the skin, wide—eyed and desperate, hair pasted to his skull, stumbling frantically in the mud and rain after the skillfully-slithering serpent towards a half-blocked opening in an immense ruin that had once been the seat of government in the mightiest nation of the Crescent—but Rauglir was quicker than he and in an instant the demon had disappeared into the shadows of the tunnel.

Baleron charged after him, all his thought bent on stopping the snake, but a huge scaly claw suddenly blocked the tunnel, and Baleron slammed into it. Bounced off. Flailing, he reeled backward, stumbling in the mud and debris, then fell.

Throgmar loomed above him.

Baleron saw Rondthril sticking from the earth, shining in the darkness, and, leaping to his feet, he wrenched it loose from the wet ground and turned to confront the Worm.

Chuckling, Throgmar said, "PUT THAT AWAY."

A cloud descended on Baleron's mind, and he had no choice but to comply. He sheathed Rondthril. It would have been useless, anyway.

"SO YOU ARE MINE NOW. AGAIN."

The cloud departed, replaced by a claw. Throgmar picked him up. Baleron screamed and thrashed in the dragon's grip, but Throgmar gave no heed.

"NOW YOUR MISSION IS FULFILLED. SO IS MINE. BUT THERE IS SOMETHING *ELSE* I MUST DO. ONE LAST THING, AND THEN IT IS DONE BETWEEN US."

"What?" Baleron demanded. *"What?"*

But Throgmar did not answer.

The dragon launched himself into the sky, his great wings mastering the air. Still carrying Baleron in his armored fist, the terrible Worm began to climb the storm-tossed heavens, and the fallen city began to recede below. Borchstogs and worse continued to ravage it, which despite the rain was half in flame and half in shadow.

Tears running freely down his face, Baleron desperately watched the tunnel entrance diminish below—hoping, praying, that the king would miraculously stumble out, clutching the beheaded body of Rauglir and laughing victoriously in the rain—but knowing that within minutes his father would be dead, and there was nothing he could do to stop it. The king would die, Havensrike would fall, and the Shadow would lengthen, consuming all in its path, when its path was the world entire.

The Dark One had won.

Baleron's Doom had been fulfilled, and his web was complete ... or so he supposed. He prayed to Illiana that it was. What more could *ul Ravast* possibly do?

He still had one hope, though, fragile and treacherous a thing as it was—Rondthril. Both Logran and Elethris had seen something in it, and in Baleron's wielding of it, that would indicate some high cause could be served.

But, of course, something had to happen first. Had it happened already, perhaps? Baleron wondered where Ungier was at that moment.

Ungier, commander of the gathered host, watched the sacking of Glorifel with great pride. His chest swelled as his eyes drank in the slaughter. It was glorious.

Ringed by his royal guard of trolls, the Vampire King strode up and through the very Gates of the City. This was the proudest night of his life. Borchstogs looted and raped and slew mercilessly all around him. Darkworms flew overhead, setting fire to great portions of the metropolis. Gaurocks wallowed in the rivers. Igrith sowed terror into the hearts of the surviving Men. Beasts and vampires and monsters of all sorts prowled the alleys.

In a certain courtyard Ungier came upon a wide tangle of dead bodies, some human, some Borchstog, some other, and with his power he raised the corpses from their slumber and instilled wicked spirits in them. The walking dead then stalked off to do his bidding, and he laughed.

He saw a gang of Borchstogs pursuing a teary maiden and stayed their assault. His eyes transfixed the girl, and she went to him, thinking in her delusion that he would offer sanctuary. Instead, he wrapped her in his arms and sank his fangs into her neck. Hot blood spurted the back of his throat, and he gulped it hungrily. He drained the very life from her, and then threw back his blood-spattered face and howled joyously. Tonight was the best night of his long life.

Chapter Ten

Glorifel succumbed to the evil of Ungier. Baleron watched it happen.

The area about the city was hilly, and Throgmar set down on a high point to the south. From there the two watched in silence as flames and terror washed across the capital of Havensrike. Baleron let the tears fall without restraint. He sank to his knees and wept. Throgmar watched him, seeming to bask in his horror and grief.

Finally Baleron turned to the dragon angrily. "You must think this is all very amusing, you bastard."

"WATCH YOUR TONGUE, MORTAL."

"And if I don't? Will you kill me?"

"PROVOKE ME AND WE SHALL SEE."

Baleron spat at the dragon's clawed feet. "There!"

"DO YOU WANT TO DIE?"

"Yes!"

Throgmar's eyes glittered. "GOOD."

They said no more to each other. In the morning, Throgmar bore him down from the mountain and over the city. Baleron saw that half of it had been burnt to the ground, but the other half still stood, if scorched and ugly. Ungier did not intend to raze it utterly, then; he wanted a place to *rule*, something with which to replace Gulrothrog.

Public squares had been turned into places of horror. Scaffolds and racks and machinery had been erected, and men and women and children alike were undergoing torture to the delight of the Borchstogs. But some humans had been kept from that fate; Borchstogs were herding groups of enslaved Glorifelans through the streets, gathering them in King's Square. It was there that Throgmar sat down, upon the very ruins of Grothgar Castle. The stifling air stank of smoke and death and the rot of Borchstogs. Ungier stood on a platform built before the statue of King Grothgar I, where Albrech had given his speech upon returning from Larenthi. The statue's king as well as horse had been decapitated. No, *decapitated* was not exactly the right word, Baleron saw; the heads had been switched.

The Vampire King surveyed the chained and huddled masses of the human survivors as his Borchstogs finished rounding them up. Most were women and children, Baleron saw, and all were dirty, soot-streaked and terrified. It hurt him to look upon them, and he could not meet their gazes when they turned to see just what manner of man had been flown in by a Great Worm. When they were all gathered, he did a rough count. There were less than four thousand of them. *Four thousand!*

Of course, doubtlessly some had fled into the hills and others were still being rounded up, but it was still staggering.

He wondered if Amrelain were among them, but did not see her. Surely the Borchstogs would not have killed one so beautiful. Perhaps she had been among those to escape.

He saw many undead things stirring about the city, and he recognized a few of them. Some had been members of the Five Hundred. Halthus was there, lurching and moaning, most of his chest gone. Blood spattered his mouth, and flies buzzed about him. Baleron shuddered. Would Glorifel become a city of demons and the living dead? At the thought, bile burned into the back of his throat.

Ungier spoke, his words directed at his prisoners, and he wore a gloating sneer as he shouted, "Welcome! Greetings from Oksilith! From Oslog!" A few women wailed in fear. "Thank you all for joining in the rebirth of your fair city, for that is what it shall be: a new beginning." He took a breath. "Let me tell you a story. *My* story. I was birthed of an egg made of dead flesh, the flesh of my Master's finest fallen warriors. Out of their demise came my life, and so it shall be here. Your city is dead, but from its rotting corpse will come a new day, a new world, and it shall be glorious, just as I am. You will see. You will grow used to the whip and the lash. You will grow used to the blood-letting. You will grow used to your friends disappearing in the night. Sometimes they will return to you. Sometimes they will be whole. Other times they may be ... altered." He smiled. "For *I have come*, and I am your master now. Your first task will be to build me a Palace, then a Temple."

Another woman wailed.

"You monster!" shouted one, striding forward. "You beast!"

"That's right," he said. "That's what I am. I am a monster. I am a beast. *And I will be your god.* I will rename the city Ungoroth, and you will bow before me. You will live in one quarter of Ungoroth while Borchstogs and others inhabit the rest. Yours will be the slave quarter."

"We will not be slaves!" said the woman.

Unimpressed by her bravery, he motioned to one of his Trolls, who stepped forward and picked her up.

"Release her!" Baleron shouted, stepping out from the shadow of Throgmar. "Release her now! Your Savior commands it!"

Ungier's black eyes swiveled across the gathering to him. "Baleron ..."

Baleron marched across the square to the platform of the statue and glared up angrily at the vampire.

"Let her go," he said.

Ungier looked at the Troll. "Our Savior makes a good point. Why *don't* we release her from the city? Let her go free?"

The Troll grinned. "It would be my pleasure, m'lord."

With no further ado, he drew back his arm and flung her as high and far as he could. Baleron gasped. Her body flew through the air for a good ways, but it did not make it anywhere near the Wall. Instead, she fell, screaming, and Baleron shouted in rage as she hit the ground.

"Pity," Ungier said, shaking his head. "She didn't make it. The next one, perhaps."

Baleron, his fury overcoming his good sense, pushed past the cordon of Borchstogs before the stage and leapt on the platform. No one immediately stopped him, perhaps because he was *ul Ravast*.

He punched the vampire right in his skeletal nose.

Ungier stumbled back, surprised. He merely raised his leathery palm and Baleron flew backwards as if struck by a fierce wind. He landed amidst the gathered survivors, and pain flared through his back. The survivors made space for him, and one even helped him to his feet. Groaning, he stood.

"Thank you," she whispered.

A Troll, the same one that had thrown the girl to her death, picked him up in its huge hand and squeezed him painfully, but not hard enough to kill.

"What shall I do with him, m'lord?" it asked Ungier.

Baleron grunted, trying to pry its fingers from him. He thought there was something familiar about its cruel smile.

The Vampire King appraised the prince thoughtfully. "I don't know. Shall we release him, too? It would be fun, I think, to give him a sporting chance. Perhaps he's learned to fly in his time away from Gulrothrog. Perhaps he's been trying to emulate me."

"I would rather immolate you," Baleron said, wheezing.

"DO NOT HARM HIM," Throgmar said. "HE IS *UL RAVAST*. I MUST TAKE HIM TO KROGBUR."

"Krogbur ..." said Ungier, somewhat dreamily. "I confess I would like to see it. Is it as grand as I have heard?"

"RELEASE HIM." Throgmar sounded impatient. Smoke rose from his nostrils. The air about him shimmered. "NOW."

"Oh, very well." Ungier motioned to the Troll, who opened his hand. Baleron gladly slipped out of it. To Throgmar, the Vampire King asked, "Why did you bring him here if not to let me have some sport with him?"

"I WANTED HIM TO SEE THE DEVASTATION OF HIS CITY AND THE ENSLAVEMENT OF HIS PEOPLE. I WANTED HIM TO SEE WHAT HIS VENGEANCE HAS WROUGHT."

"*I* didn't do this," Baleron said. "My Doom had a hand, but you can't lay this all on me."

"I CAN. I DO. FOR, IF YOU HAD NEVER SLAIN FELESTRATA, I WOULD NEVER HAVE TAKEN YOU TO KROGBUR AND YOU WOULD NOT HAVE BEEN DISPATCHED TO BRING ABOUT THIS RUIN. IF YOU HAD ONLY SLAIN ME INSTEAD, AN HONEST REVENGE, GLORIFEL WOULD STILL BE STANDING."

The women and children glared at him as if he were a traitor, and he turned his face away.

Suddenly, Ungier raised his hand and Rondthril flew from Baleron's scabbard into the vampire's grasp.

The Lord of Ungoroth examined the weapon thoughtfully. "I think I'll take this now." To Baleron, he added, "Thank you for returning it. I am glad I was wrong and that we did indeed meet again, Baleron the One-Handed." He tapped his chin thought-fully. "What more new titles have you now? Let's see. Shield-tearer, perhaps. Kinslayer, most definitely. Servant of Doom. Spreader of Shadows. Wolf-hand. Spinner of the Web Unseen—at least to you. For, little spider, I do see it—glistening in the morning dew, its fruit little white shrouds holding Havensrike and Larenthi. I most enjoy it."

"Then I hope you rot in it! Usurper—that's *your* new title. Lackey! Wretch! Craven!" Baleron's eyes blazed. "Now I know why you enjoy holding slaves so much. Because it's the only way you can feel higher than others. For you're a slave, too, though you don't seem to realize it. You think Gilgaroth will let you keep this city? Keep this country? You're a fool. He sees you as the little bug you are."

Ungier smiled calmly, and it infuriated Baleron.

"I enjoy your attempts to rattle me," said the vampire. "They tell me how desperate you truly are, and to me your desperation is like the finest of wines, mixed with the finest of bloods. It is the nectar that I have been longing for, and I will be sad to see it pass from my lips so soon." His eyes went to Throgmar. "Brother mine, traitor to my House though you are, you are welcome here, for you bring your redemption in this mortal."

"I DO NOT SEEK REDEMPTION. NOT FROM YOU."

Ungier smiled indulgently. "Very well. But we were a mighty trio once, you, me and Grudremorq. The Flame, the Shepherd, and the Guardian. You broke that alliance."

"SO I DID." Throgmar did not offer an apology.

"And yet I will forgive you now, if you allow me but a bit of sport with your charge. Honored Worm, will you not stay for dinner? It will be a feast like no other."

Throgmar hesitated. He clearly wanted to be away, but he also seemed to know that every second Baleron spent here was a hell for the prince. In the end, he chose to prolong the prince's suffering:

"WE WILL STAY."

"Good. *Ul Ravast* will be the guest of honor. *Roschk ul Ravast!*"

The Trolls and Borchstogs repeated it: *"Roschk ul Ravast!"* *"Roschk ul Ravast!"*

Baleron threw back his head and roared. He felt lower than

he'd ever felt, and he knew that unless he could get Rondthril back, and unless he could slay Ungier, there really was no hope.

Baleron simply glowered as he was seated at one end of the long banquet table. He glowered as Borchstogs and vampires and even some Men took their seats. He glowered as Throgmar was given a whole side unto himself.

It was nighttime, true nighttime, not the false night spread by the clouds, and torches lit the palace's rear garden. The table was at least a hundred feet long. This was the manor of the Esgralins, much of it still intact. Baleron had attended many social functions here over the years. Were the Esgralins all dead now? Were some slaves, or upon the racks in the public squares? Or did they perhaps flee into the hills? He wondered which was the better fate.

At last the Vampire King himself arrived and sat at the other end of the table. Baleron glared at him but said nothing. Ungier just gave a small, self-satisfied smile, and shouted, "Let the feast begin!"

The surviving Glorifelans, the slaves, set about bringing out large platters of food, roast hog and potatoes and gravy and many sweet pies. The slave woman who placed the butter near Baleron actually spit on him as she did so. It was the same woman who'd helped him up earlier, before she knew of his complicity in the city's fall. Shame burned within him.

Instantly, two Borchstog guards seized her and threw her to the ground. "You dare touch *ul Ravast*!" one shouted. "Die!" They were about to start kicking her to death, but Baleron leapt up and shoved them away from her.

"Leave her!"

They bowed deferentially. *"Roschk ul Ravast!"*

She looked up angrily at him and said, "Too little too late, you devil! I always knew you were rotten."

"I am not rotten," he insisted.

She just spat again, on the ground this time, and scurried away.

"Want we should go after her?" asked one of the Borchstogs. "We'll hold her down for you. Or we could bring her to your tent ... for later." He grinned nastily.

Baleron snarled, "Shut your filthy mouths and get out of my way!"

He sat back down, feeling deflated. Throgmar watched him dispassionately.

Ungier, as usual, leered. "Everyone!" he shouted when all the food had been presented. "Eat your fill and rejoice!" To Throgmar, he added, "Except you. *You* be more conservative."

"I HUNGER," replied the dragon.

"Help yourself to anyone here."

Some of his guests looked at him nervously.

"I WONDER ... HOW DOES *VAMPIRE* MEAT TASTE?"

Ungier scowled. "I am the god-king of Ungoroth, brother, and I will not tolerate your insolence. You are a vagabond, a houseless beggar chained to your penance."

"AS YOU ARE TO YOURS." The Leviathan grinned cruelly. "YES, I KNOW OF YOUR BETRAYAL TO FATHER. YOU WERE NOT *SUPPOSED* TO SEND ME AFTER BALERON. FOR THAT YOUR HOME *AND MINE* WAS DESTROYED. I WAS JUST A TOOL, I SEE THAT NOW. I ALSO KNOW HOW YOU TRIED TO HIDE ROLENYA ... FROM *HIM*."

Ungier stared daggers at Throgmar, and the dragon returned the look. Smoke trailed up from the Leviathan's nostrils and Baleron could feel him grow hotter; the air grew hazy around him. A hateful light burned in his huge amber eyes.

The dinner guests looked nervously from their host to *ul Mrungona*. They did not touch their food.

Ungier broke the tension. In a surprisingly low voice, he said, "What I did I did for love. I sent you to kill this *mortal* because

he slew my Firstborn. I hid Rolenya away to save her from possession. In both things, I failed." This thought seemed to sadden
him, but with an effort he rallied himself. "I have a new start here.
Ungoroth will be great. And it is only the beginning of my empire.
Oh, I will have glory! Such glory!" He looked around at his dinner
guests. "Eat!"

The haze around Throgmar faded, and the hateful light faded
from his eyes.

The dinner guests, all presumably heads of their legions, some
perhaps even dignitaries from foreign (southern) lands, began to
do as their host had bid, and the Borchstogs especially ate with
fervor. The roast hog was not roasted very thoroughly, Baleron
discovered, and its blood ran everywhere. The Borchstogs ate it
greedily, sometimes fighting over it. After the first course, the
slaves brought out the second. The serving platters were large,
and when the silver domes were removed Baleron saw they
contained the dismembered remains of Glorifelans, some cooked,
some raw.

He rose and began to stagger away, sick to his stomach.

"No!" shouted Ungier. "You will stay!"

Borchstogs blocked his path and forced him back into his
chair. "*Ul Ravast* must sit."

"You are the guest of honor," said Ungier with a smile. "It
would not do for you to leave." He raised his blood-and-wine-
filled goblet. Its jewels twinkled in the torchlight. "To *ul Ravast*!"

All the guests save Baleron and Throgmar raised their glasses
and said, "To *ul Ravast*!", then drank.

Baleron glowered murderously at the Vampire King, but said
nothing. The dinner continued. Baleron refused to eat what he
was served, but he did drink some wine to steady his nerves.

He tried to ignore the others' conversations, but soon something caught his ear: Ungier said, "It is *Rolenya*? You are *certain*
of this?"

He was speaking to one of his daughters, Serengorthis, one of the messengers that went constantly back and forth between Glorifel, Clevaris and Krogbur.

She nodded. "It is her, Sire. The Master has brought her back. Ask *him*." She indicated Baleron. "He knows."

Ungier narrowed his eyes at the prince. "Is this true?"

Baleron would not answer.

"Is this true?" Ungier repeated.

Baleron said nothing.

"And she *sings* for Him," added Serengorthis.

"Sings?" repeated Ungier.

"Most beautifully, so I've heard. He keeps her caged, letting her out only to please Him with her voice, like a man might keep a bird."

"She never sang for *me* ..." Ungier added, "Of course, I did get some noises out of her ... though I would not count them as *songs*." He smiled at Baleron as he said this. "But they were music to me."

Most at the table laughed, and Ungier looked pleased. But he also wore a contemplative air, as if he were mulling something over, and Baleron did not have to wonder what it might be. Ungier considered Rolenya his. Despite his claims, it was not love, exactly, at least Baleron did not think so, but if nothing else it was pride of possession; she was Ungier's greatest prize, or had been, and now the one who had taken her away from him was enjoying her more than he.

Dark clouds drifted across the vampire's face.

Perhaps in an effort to dismiss them, he called for the entertainment to begin. Borchstog musicians started up an eerie yet merry tune, and Borchstog performers came out, naked and painted red. They wore odd, spiky hats made of rib bones—whether human, elf or borchstog was hard to tell. Yet apparently their appearance was comic, for the dinner guests laughed and hooted.

The performers had brought along many severed heads and

limbs of Glorifelans, and they juggled them. The body parts were often slippery and squirted out of their hands. Much amusement was had as the Borchstogs floundered around on the ground trying to retrieve the parts. Sometimes the performers tossed the limbs and heads to each other, juggling, sometimes they danced as they did it, or stood on their heads, or more, and all the while the musicians continued to play.

One course was served after another, and it seemed a fine old time for the hellspawn. Baleron tried not to look. He noticed that Throgmar seemed ill at ease, as well, and remembered that the dragon had pretenses of goodness. At the thought, he snorted.

At last the Borchstog performers left. Corpses of all sorts were wheeled in next and deposited in the performing area where once Baleron had played croquet with the younger Esgralin daughter.

Ungier raised these corpses and made them dance and perform comic routines to the roaring delight of his guests.

Next live naked prisoners were marched in. The Troll that had earlier flung the woman to her death now stepped forward. He grabbed a trembling Glorifelan in each huge hand ... and began to *juggle* them.

Horrified, Baleron stood up to protest, but his handlers shoved him back down and his protests were ignored.

The Troll continued to juggle. Sometimes he would snatch another screaming prisoner and add him or her to his routine. Occasionally he would drop one. Baleron could not tell if this was accidental or intentional, but whenever it happened he received a guffaw. The dropped prisoner, mewling on the ground with broken bones, would eventually be ground beneath his heels. Baleron had to be forcibly restrained.

All the while, the guests continued to eat and talk and enjoy themselves, as if this were an ordinary high social occasion.

But then the Troll wanted the prisoners set on fire so that he could have something more interesting to juggle, and Throgmar ended it. He blew a column of flame over the Troll's head and said, "*I* WILL GIVE YOU FIRE!"

The Troll glared at him, said nothing.

"I HAVE HAD ENOUGH. END THIS NOW. I DEMAND IT."

Ungier merely laughed. "You are a guest at my table, and it is my duty to oblige your whims, however foolish." He beckoned to the Troll, who reluctantly abandoned his routine and came to stand at the Vampire King's side, bodyguard once more.

More performances followed, and more courses. Finally the entertainment ceased and Ungier ordered the last course to be brought out. All hushed. Flames from the braziers and torches crackled in the silence.

A platter with a silver dome was set before Baleron, but he refused to open it. He had not eaten since the first course, and he was not hungry now. Far from it. He had retched twice and was still nauseous.

With heavy-lidded eyes, Ungier gazed across the table at him. The Vampire King looked suddenly hungry, staring intently at Baleron and the platter. There was a particularly nasty look on his face.

"Open it," bade the Lord of Ungoroth.

"No."

"Open it!"

Baleron shook his head.

Ungier's eyes transfixed him, and he no longer had Shelir's charm to protect him. "*Open it,*" ordered the vampire.

Baleron could not fight it. Against his will, he reached out a hand toward the silver handle, and his fingers trembled despite the fact that Ungier guided his actions. He cringed. What was underneath that dome? What would give Ungier so much pleasure? Dread built in him, and he tried to mash his eyes shut, but Ungier would not let him.

His fingers curled around the handle. He fought against the

vampire's will even more strongly, but Ungier would not be denied. And so, with a shaking hand, Baleron raised the dome, and, horribly slowly, the contents of the platter came into view.

Baleron reeled backwards and toppled out of his chair, a cry in his throat. Ungier's presence withdrew from his mind.

The whole table erupted in evil laughter as Baleron stared agog at the contents of the platter, but he barely heard it. A swell of horror and hate welled up within him, and he shook, as if there were an earthquake inside him. And there was. His hands balled into fists, and he ground his teeth in rage. For, sitting upon the gleaming silver dish, still bloody, was the severed head of Albrech Grothgar. The dead eyes of the Lord of Havensrike stared accusingly at his son.

"Nooo!" Baleron roared, throwing back his head and howling in misery.

Ungier's black eyes glittered hungrily, savoring this.

Baleron sank to his knees before his father's head.

"Father ..."

This was too much. Much too much. Baleron's soul cried out in torment.

The king's dead eyes gazed unblinking. Albrech's mouth was open, as if in surprise, but his eyebrows were locked in a scowl.

So I really did fail you, after all, Baleron thought. *You were right about me all along.*

"I'm so sorry ..."

His shaking hands reached out and picked up the severed head. It was heavier than he thought it would be, pregnant with possibilities that would never be. He lowered the head to his lap and stared down into his father's dark blue eyes.

"*Rauglir*," he growled. Would the demon kill everyone he ever knew?

The true weight of it slowly sank in. Not only was his father dead, but so was the king. There could be no more hope for

Havensrike now, no hope that Albrech could gather the remnants of the kingdom together and marshal a resistance to Ungier.

And more ... this meant that now *Baleron* was King—though the king of what? There was only Ungoroth now, and some scattered cities and towns without central authority, and likely there was little of those left. Baleron was the last of his House, the ruler of a realm that was no more.

He ground his teeth. Sorrow threatened to overwhelm him, but he forced his rage to scour any weakness from him. He could not afford to be overwhelmed. He needed his wits about him.

Ungier still has Rondthril.

The dinner guests continued to laugh and mock him. The wickedness of Ungier and his guests infuriated Baleron, nauseated him, but one particular laugh stood out from the others, and he found himself looking up at the face of the Troll that had picked him up earlier, the one that had flung the woman to her death, the one that had wanted to juggle flaming slaves.

He knew that laugh.

"Rauglir."

The Troll, who had been watching him, smiled, and Baleron recognized that smile. too.

"Yes, my beloved," said the demon, "it is I."

That sent the guests into fresh fits of laughter.

Baleron's mind reeled, and he began to see what must have happened: Rauglir would have approached Ungier after the sack was complete and told him the tidings of Albrech's murder, and afterwards the rithlag had rewarded him with a new body, a powerful one.

Baleron's eyes went from the dead face of his father to the grinning face of the Troll.

"This... was *your* idea, wasn't it?"

The Troll shrugged modestly. "Consider it my dowry."

"You ... you ... "

"How do you like this new form?" asked the Troll. "Do you find it as pleasing as Rolenya's? You loved me then."

Baleron was so full of rage and pain that he could not speak, could not form words. Somewhere he could hear Ungier laughing.

"I hope this doesn't affect your decision to marry me," Rauglir added.

Ungier laughed so hard he nearly fell out of his own chair.

"Wonderful!" cried the vampire. "This is priceless. Throgmar, you're forgiven."

The Leviathan narrowed his eyes.

Baleron looked again to his father's lifeless face. The rest of the world faded away, and he became lost in those dead eyes. *Father, I am so sorry.*

At the far end of the table, a serving girl was refilling Ungier's goblet. It was a young maiden, clearly terrified, and her hands shook as she poured. Her dress was rent and dirty, her eyes hopeless.

Ungier drank up her fear. Just as she was finished, he knocked the goblet over and its contents spilled onto the table and dripped to the ground. "Oh, look what you've gone and done, you clumsy thing," he scolded. "Lick it up."

"Y-yes, m'lord," she said, her voice quavering.

She broke out sobbing before she could begin, and was so racked by tears that she could not summon the focus necessary to clean the mess.

Ungier roughly threw her upon the table. She screamed and tried to roll off, but with his eyes he bound her, mesmerizing her, and she stilled and quieted. The Vampire King tore open her dress, and she did not protest. He sank his fangs into her throat. Blood spurted into his mouth. She cried out but could not move.

By this time, Baleron had replaced his father's severed head on the platter and had been staring, lost, into Albrech's eyes. He had not been paying attention to the girl's plight, but her screams drew him.

Seeing the situation, he bounded to his feet. When the two Borchstog guards tried to shove him back down, he was prepared. He elbowed one in the throat and jabbed the other in the eyes. Then he wrenched loose one of their huge broadswords, leapt on the table and ran down it, howling, jumping over dishes and the clutching hands of the guests.

Ungier was so focused on sucking the girl's blood that he hardly noticed, and when he did it was too late.

Baleron kicked the vampire off her. Ungier fell from the table onto the ground, and the prince was upon him, sword flashing down.

Ungier caught the naked blade in his long-fingered hands and tore it from Baleron's grasp. The blade did not even cut him. Then Rauglir was pulling the prince away.

Ungier rose, eyes narrowed into slits of hate. "How *dare* you!"

"I dare!" Baleron said.

"You will wish you had not."

With a look to the girl, Baleron said to Ungier, "Drink of me instead. Spare her. I'll take her place."

Ungier barked a laugh. "To drink of the Savior? To end the Ender? I would love nothing more." To his guards, he said, "Let her be."

The girl nodded her silent thanks to Baleron, then ran, crying, from the table, holding her tattered clothes about her.

Rauglir lowered Baleron to ground level but did not release him. Only the prince's head and shoulders showed above the Troll's thick fingers.

"Yes," Rauglir said to Ungier. "End it now. My game is ready to go to the next level." To Baleron, he added, "See you in Hell, beloved."

"The one good thing about dying," Baleron reflected, "is that I'll never have to listen to you again."

"Oh, but you will, dear heart, for I will come personally to visit you in Illistriv. *I* will be the one to oversee your eternal torment. You see, my dear—if I may call you that—our game has truly just begun." Rauglir laughed, a great big Troll laugh that shook Baleron up and down, up and down.

Ungier stalked forward, grabbed the prince by his hair and exposed his neck. Baleron smelled the vampire's musk, felt his power, and braced for what would come next.

"NO," said Throgmar suddenly.

Striking swiftly, his horned head lunged forward and his massive jaws snapped closed around Rauglir's throat, biting off the demon's head. A gout of black blood shot up, and the big body toppled. Throgmar crushed the head between his huge teeth and swallowed it.

Baleron, seeing his chance, struggled free of the dead Troll-hand and sprang up. For a moment his eyes lingered on the decapitated creature. It did him good to see the ruin, though he did not relish the thought of Rauglir's spirit on the loose again. At least without a body the demon was powerless for the nonce.

Ungier was so surprised by Throgmar's attack that he raised no hand against the prince as Baleron punched him in his skeletal nose for the second time that day. Ungier's black eyes remained fixed on Throgmar, who loomed above, massive and fiery.

Baleron tore Rondthril from Ungier's scabbard and held it up so that it caught the torchlight. It felt good in his hand.

Ungier wiped black blood from his face. "That blade is mine."

"It *was*," Baleron said. "So was Rolenya. Now they both belong to me." He replaced the Fanged Blade in its scabbard.

Ungier glared at Throgmar, seeking to place blame. "How dare you interfere in my business! This is *my* land now! Begone!"

"YOU SAID I COULD EAT ANYONE HERE. CONSIDER YOURSELF LUCKY THAT I DID NOT CHOOSE YOU."

Baleron's eyes lit up. "Eat him!" he cried, seeing his chance. If Rondthril could not slay its maker, and Ungier could deflect any other weapon, then why not let the Leviathan do Baleron's work for him? "Eat him and you'll be king of Ungoroth! Of Havensrike!"

Ungier's mouth dropped open and his eyes grew round as they stared up at the Worm. In fear, he stumbled backwards, wings fluttering.

Smoke curled up from Throgmar's nose.

"Yes!" Baleron said. "Do it!"

But then the smoke died and Throgmar picked Baleron up in a claw. "I DO NOT WANT TO BE KING. WE LEAVE."

"Good riddance!" Ungier snarled. He straightened and suddenly looked his old haughty self. His gaze found Baleron in a space between two scaly fingers. "But I'll see you again. I too must go to Krogbur."

What was this? Even Throgmar paused to hear the rest.

Ungier smiled, almost serene now, as if causing Baleron consternation had somehow relaxed him. "I've longed to see the Black Tower since Gilgaroth first spoke of his vision to me thousands of years ago. But in the main I go to win back that which was mine—that which you have stolen."

Baleron gave him a hard look. "She will not be yours."

"She shall."

"She is mine."

Ungier raised an eyebrow. "From the sounds of it, she is Gilgaroth's."

"Then he will not give her up to you."

"He must. She will be my prize for conquering your city. Although, I must say, I would have done it for nothing."

"ENOUGH," Throgmar grunted.

He bore Baleron away, flying up into the dark heavens and away from the ruins of Glorifel, and Ungier grew small below.

"THE BLACK TOWER AWAITS," said the Leviathan.

Baleron gripped Rondthril's hilt. Quietly, he said, "Then it waits for its destruction."

Ungier watched the diminishing shape of Throgmar against the night.

Perhaps I can beat them, he thought. Either way, he must go. Glorifel was conquered. Rolenya would be his once more.

His eyes fastened on the decapitated body of Rauglir. He had never liked the demon, not after it had possessed Rolenya, but in this form it had proven an interesting companion. *Ah, well.*

Swiftly Ungier appointed a lieutenant to oversee Ungoroth in his absence, and departed. A squad of glarumri flanked him as he went, cutting a black swath through the night. All others fled before them.

I will win her, he vowed. *I shall make her Vampire Queen of Ungoroth.*

Chapter Eleven

On the second day of their journey, Throgmar set down for a rest. He'd been flying relentlessly, silently, without so much as a word to Baleron, since they had left Glorifel. *Ungoroth.* The prince had watched the land unroll under him with shame and loathing and sadness; the beauty of Havensrike had stretched to its borders and beyond, but now all was burnt and blackened; cities and villages razed and sacked, forests burnt or cut down for lumber. Rivers were poisoned or ran red with blood. Monsters lurked in the lakes, and ravening beasts lived in the hills.

Not despair but hopelessness filled him. He had a plan, yes, if such a thin thing could be called that, but he did not see how it could be achieved. For unless Rondthril could be purified of Ungier's spirit and Baleron given the chance to use it—which seemed impossible at this point—the world was lost.

How could it have come to this? It was a scene out of a nightmare that he'd been dreaming for years, and it had come to its head.

But he was determined to find a way to defeat Gilgaroth. If he did not have that hope, he would go mad—if he was not already. And he *might* be: he often caught himself mumbling incoherently, and sometimes he would see the faces of dear ones floating by: Sophia, Salthrick, Logran, Elethris, Shelir, Albrech, Rolenya ... all dead, or nearly. Was Rolenya still waiting for him? Did she still live? Was it true she now sang for the Wolf like some songbird in a gilded cage?

On the second day, Throgmar set down on the burnt top of a high hill near a muddy brook whose waters were still drinkable, though just barely, and both partook of the moisture with relish.

Afterwards Baleron took the opportunity to stretch his legs, Rondthril sheathed at his side. Cramps seized him, and he tried to work them off. Being in the unwavering grip of a dragon for days on end was a torture on the body, as well as the mind.

Throgmar sat, brooding, by the stream.

"DO NOT STRAY," he warned Baleron.

The prince said nothing.

In a while a group of Borchstogs who had seen them alight on the hill approached. They were mounted on murmeksa, but they swung down from the shaggy backs of the creatures and bowed low to the Worm, and their leader spouted obsequious words that turned Baleron's stomach.

The Borchstog offered their steeds to Throgmar for sustenance, and Throgmar took one look at the huge, tusked hog-like creatures with long rat tails, dark fur and cloven hooves—and said, "LEAVE THEM."

"Yes, your Greatness," said the leader in Oslogon. "Is there anything else we can do to ease your time?"

"WHAT CAN YOU DO TO AMUSE ME?"

The Borchstog thought a moment. "We have been trained in the festive arts. We can sing and dance for your pleasure. We can juggle, do tricks."

"NO MORE JUGGLING."

"Yes, Great One, as you say. Well, at our camp we have some captives you can devour or entertain your Greatness with, if you desire. There are some human women. If you can change your shape you can have them."

Throgmar snorted. "I HAVE NO INTEREST IN MORTALS OR IN IDLE PLEASURES OF THE FLESH."

"Truly?" The Borchstog's curiosity overcame his good sense, and he asked, "Then how do you enjoy yourself, my lord? You've lived for thousands of years and will live for eons to come, surely. How do you get through each day?"

Throgmar stared at him with an evil expression until the Borchstog chief quailed and cast his gaze down.

"Forgive me, your worship," he said. "I have overstepped my place."

"INDEED. LEAVE ME THESE MOUNTS OF YOURS AND BE OFF."

He snorted flame, and the Borchstogs hurried away. Left alone with the dragon, the great hogs shuffled nervously. Throgmar watched the Borchstogs go and, when they were out of sight down the hill, he spat a column of flame that roasted the ten tusked steeds where they stood. Then, without a word to Baleron, he ate them. After two days with no food, the cooked pork smelled delicious to the prince-king? Heir, at least—but he refused to beg the dragon for scraps.

When the Worm had had his fill—eight murmeksa—he slunk over to the brook and slaked his thirst, then folded his wings about himself like a blanket and lay down, making his camp for the night.

Using Rondthril, Baleron hacked off a chunk of hog, and the Worm did not stop him. He sheathed the Fanged Blade and ambled over to the Leviathan. Cautiously, he sat beside Throgmar cross-legged as he munched on his meat. Though overdone, it was actually not as bad as he'd feared.

Tilting back his head a bit, he stared up at the stars. Despite everything, it was a pleasant night, not too cool, not too hot, with a gentle breeze that blew across the hill with a feminine sigh. There was even the faint scent of flowers in the air.

It was good to see the stars again. Both at Krogbur and at Glorifel, a screen of dark clouds had blocked out the sky, and their merry twinkle lifted his spirits more than they would have.

He looked over to the vast mound of the Leviathan. The dragon's eyes were closed, but he doubted Throgmar slept.

"So," he said slowly, "am I returning to Krogbur as a prisoner because I failed to complete my task, or a hero because I did?"

"THAT IS FOR *HIM* TO DETERMINE. I AM JUST THE DELIVERER."

"You do not have to be. You could have simply killed me outright. You were about to."

"PERHAPS GILGAROTH WILL PROLONG YOUR SUFFERING. I HOPE SO. IF HE DOES, IT WILL BE SWEETER FOR ME THAN YOUR MERE FLESH."

"That's right, you don't like mere pleasures of the flesh."

Now both amber eyes were open, and they narrowed to slits of hate. "YOU SLEW THE ONE BEING I COULD ENJOY THEM WITH."

Baleron knew he was treading on brittle ice, and he did not think it wise to continue this leg of the conversation, yet he was, as he'd been told often enough recently, both foolish and rash, and so he marshaled his resolve to say, "You deserved it. You torched my city, and burned my home. You killed thousands."

"YES, *I* DESERVED IT. DID *SHE*?"

Baleron did not know how to answer that. He had actually given the matter much thought over the months of his imprisonment, and it haunted him still. Felestrata's murder had bothered him, and he supposed it would continue to do so; he had killed a helpless, reasoning being who had done him no harm.

However, he was also disturbed by the memory of the she-Worm changing into the form of Rolenya before his eyes. What could it mean?

He turned it over and over in his mind, playing with it as though it were a puzzle. Someone had wanted him to hurt. Someone had known he would slay her—after all, he'd been fulfilling his Doom—and had prepared for it. Throgmar had dismissed her transformation as a mere trick, and it was. But what kind of trick, and played by whom? Throgmar surely blamed his father, and there could be no doubt that it bore his signature. Yet ...

Turning again to the dragon, he said, "Just how long did you know her?"

Throgmar, who'd closed his eyes, opened them again. "FELESTRATA?"

"Yes."

"NOT LONG. A YEAR, PERHAPS. SHE CAME TO ME IN THE CAVERNS OF OKSIL, HAVING HEARD THAT I WAS THE LAST SURVIVING DRAGON OF THE FIRST BROOD, THAT I HAD SIRED A THIRD OF ALL THE DRAGONS THAT FOLLOWED OF THAT LINE, AND THAT I WAS ALONE AND HAD REBELLED AGAINST OUR MASTER. SHE CAME TO SUCCOR ME, AND TO LEARN FROM ME. WE GREW VERY CLOSE IN A SHORT TIME, AND THEN ..." His voice hardened, and dripped with hatred. "THEN YOU TOOK HER FROM ME."

Baleron wisely stayed silent for a while. During the silence, he thought on the dragon's words and was reminded of the time the Wolf had sent him Rolenya in his pit, then stolen her from him. Suddenly, it came to him. As if out of a vision, the truth of what must have happened coalesced in his mind, and it was crystal clear, though no less monstrous because of it.

He was on the verge of revealing what he'd determined when the dragon's hatred gave him pause. In telling what he knew, or thought he knew, he might just be spelling his end, right here and now.

Throgmar seemed to sense his thoughts and said, as if despite himself, "WHAT TROUBLES YOU?"

"Nothing." Baleron turned his face away.

"NOT NOTHING. I CAN READ YOUR FACE ONLY TOO WELL, MORTAL. I CAN FEEL YOUR FEAR. TELL ME, OR I WILL RIP IT OUT OF YOUR MIND."

Baleron resolved to himself that he would not. He had too much to accomplish; he could not afford to die.

"LOOK AT ME."

The dragon exerted his will. Baleron struggled with it, but it was a losing battle and he knew it. He looked.

Throgmar's amber eyes began to glow. Without the aid of a protective amulet, Baleron felt drawn in. Amber surrounded him, drowning him in seas of gold, and he was lost in the dragon's power.

"TELL ME," bade the dragon.

"It ... was Mogra. Felestrata ... she was Mogra."

A long pause, then:

"NO. IT COULD NOT BE."

"Yes, it could. It was. Ask yourself why she was in the region of Worthrick just at that exact moment. Don't you see? He sent her to you in that form to lure you, to tempt you, to seduce you. He did it so that he could take her away from you—that so-called potion of his—so he'd have a tool he could use against you. *Her*. You'd do anything for her, even betray your own mind. That is why she was in those mountains, how she came to us so quickly. And that is why she left before we had been set free, so that she could return to Worthrick and assume Felestrata's form once more."

Throgmar shook his head in denial. "NO. IT COULD NOT BE."

"Oh, yes it could." Baleron tried to stop himself but couldn't. The Worm's compulsion was still upon him. "It's just like him. It's exactly what he would do, and you know it. But he never had any intention of giving her back to you. He and Mogra knew what I'd do, that I was following you ... that I'd kill her. They stole her from you, and used me to do it. But they were clumsy. Finally, they made a mistake. Don't you see? *Because they tried to make it painful for me, too.* Mogra, pretending to be a dead Felestrata, changed into Rolenya, trying to wound me, to make me think I killed her. In accomplishing my revenge I would destroy my greatest treasure. They love to cause pain. You know they do. They feed on it like vampires feed on blood."

Throgmar was shaking his horned head. "NO. IT'S NOT POSSIBLE. MOGRA ... IS MY MOTHER."

"She's a mother to Gilgaroth also, and you know how close they are."

Seething, Throgmar snorted flame, almost killing Baleron. Thankfully, he was not looking straight at the prince, and the flame plumed to his side. Still, Baleron was singed a bit, and he shrank back a few feet. The pain shook him from Throgmar's power, and he could master his own mind.

Yet he did not stop.

Throgmar looked horrified. "IT CANNOT BE. NO ..."

Taking a perverse delight in it, Baleron said, "But it is. *There was no Felestrata.*"

"NO ..."

"They used you, Throgmar." It was the first time he'd called the dragon by name that he could remember. "You knew they were using you. You just didn't know how much, and to what lengths they would go. Remember, the only reason they had to use you at all is because *through you* they could get access to Glorifel. And why? Because you had helped me, as they knew you would." His voice took on a tone of defiance and hope. "Help me again, Throgmar. Help me like you did back then. Together, maybe we can strike at Him. Maybe we can—"

"NO!" roared the dragon, rising to his feet. "NO, I WON'T HEAR IT. YOU AND YOUR KIND ARE FULL OF LIES.

YOU'RE OF THE FALLEN RACE, AND I WON'T SIT
HERE AND LET YOU CORRUPT ME WITH YOUR FILTH.
I PRESERVE THE PURITY OF FIRE. YOU WOULD TAINT
ME WITH YOUR WORDS, BUT I WILL NOT STAND
ANOTHER SECOND OF IT."

So saying, he scooped up Baleron in a mighty claw, squeezing
him tightly, and took to the skies, evidently too worked up to
sleep. Baleron just breathed shallowly, as he couldn't expand his
chest enough for a deep breath, and hoped for the fit to
pass soon.

It didn't.

The dragon flew for two more days straight through without
stopping. And when he did stop, Baleron tried to bring it up
again, risking his fire. The Betrayer, however, would have none of
it. He mesmerized Baleron with his eyes and forbade the prince
from ever mentioning it to him again.

They flew on.

If nothing else, Baleron thought, at least he would see Rolenya
again. For, with every beat of Throgmar's wings, the Black Tower
drew closer.

A trail of red smoke neared the rearing tower of Krogbur, deep in
the dark center of Oslog. Shaped like a great crimson serpent, the
tongue of smoke approached the screen of dragons that
constantly circled the tower. Below the Inferno licked the tower's
sides, millions of screaming souls swimming through it, pursued
as ever by demons. The Worms of the aerial moat eyed the red
smoke and knew it for what it was—Lord Ungier—and even if
they'd wanted to stop him, they could not, not in this form. He
was taking no chances tonight.

The formation of glarumri that escorted him hung back as
he neared the tower and began circling it ... at a good distance
from the dragons. Ungier slipped through the scaly moat of

Worms and made his way up toward the black and lightning-lit clouds, ascending towards the highest terrace reserved for the most important visitors. Who could be more important than he?

Still, he marveled at the wonder of Krogbur as he climbed. It was mighty. It was beautiful. It pulsed with power, like the great black heart it was. Just passing through its air he felt strengthened. Revitalized. His father had outdone himself this time.

Ungier coalesced into his tall, batwinged form as he alit on the highest terrace, his all-black eyes glaring imperiously, and drew his wings about himself like a cape. Who was here to greet him? He saw no one.

However, before he could become offended, a huge shadowy shape stalked out of the depths of the interior. Eight long, segmented legs clicked on the slick hard surface, and Ungier swallowed as the being's bulbous body came to loom over him. Lightning flickered, reflecting off its glistening carapace, black with traces of flowing purple. A strange, intoxicating musk radiated off it, and Ungier shivered, half in terror, half in delight, as eight unblinking red eyes gazed down at him speculatively.

He had not expected this. He would not have been surprised if Gilgaroth had come to greet him personally, or if he had sent some high servant, but to have sent the Spider Goddess—their Mother ...

This was an ill portent, and Ungier began to wonder if Gilgaroth suspected the reason he'd come. Suspected—and resented. It was with great fear and trepidation that he looked up into the Spider Queen's many blazing eyes. He inclined his head to her slightly, a small bow.

"My Queen," he said. "My Mother."

"My son." Her voice, as always, was heavy with meaning, yet beautiful, and her words well shaped. "*Why* have you left your escort out beyond the dragon-moat?"

"I ..." He could not say he feared rebuke for coming here; that would display weakness. But if he lied, she would know. "I'll bring them in directly."

"Why have you come?" she asked. What did she know? Did she suspect? "Surely you have not yet conquered the whole of Havensrike so swiftly."

"No. But," he hasted to add, "Glorifel is taken, as is the southern third of the country, and its armies are broken. For all intents and purposes, it is defeated."

She paused, letting him worry, then: "I know." Nothing more. She was waiting for him, playing with him like a wolf with a hare. He did not like it, and it made him edgy.

"I have come to claim my prize," he said, with perhaps too much boldness.

Another pause, calculating. "No prize was offered you."

"Let me take it up with Him."

She studied him. Her spider-face was impossible to read. "What prize do you require?"

"Rolenya."

"He will not part with her. If you ask him for this, you will regret it."

"For her, I would risk anything."

Again she studied him. "Here," she said, tapping a foot, and two Borchstogs emerged from the tower holding something between them. It rippled in the wind, glimmering darkly. The Borchstogs knelt and proffered the item to him.

He accepted it hesitantly, warily. It was a cape made of Spider-silk.

"I spun that for you myself," Mogra told him.

"Why?" he asked, unable to keep the note of suspicion from his voice.

"A mother needs no reason to gift her son. But know this. With this I commemorate your return to your Father's goodwill. Yet I fear that his favor will be fleeting, for you have come as a swaggering victor, not a supplicant—and as a thief."

"I am no thief. Rolenya is rightfully mine—awarded me by my Father for being the spider's custodian. I had her for three years. I would have *married* her."

"Argue not with me and mine."

"But I am yours. Come now, Mother, perhaps we can arrange a deal. You wish to be rid of her, surely, and I wish to take her. Perhaps we can arrange an alliance ..."

She drew herself up, and Ungier felt himself shrink. Her shadow danced and swelled, and seemed to grow deeper. He suddenly felt icy cold and shivered beneath her majesty. Her eight eyes blazed redly in the darkness.

"Fool!" she said, and the floor quaked beneath Ungier. "What madness has gripped you that you would plot treachery against your Father?" Seething, she added, "It is that *thing*! That *elf*! Why are you and he so drawn to her?" She let out a growl, a spidery trill of frustration.

She started to turn about, then hesitated. Not facing him, she said, "When we sensed your coming, my Lord expressed his desire that you should attend his sending-off of the gathered army." One of her legs gestured outwards and downwards to the huge host of Borchstogs and others that had massed at Krogbur's roots beyond the encircling flame. "He shall order them to begin their assault a few nights hence. You shall attend the ceremony."

He nodded shakily. "O-of course."

She wheeled about, and the darkness withdrew. Ungier, gasping, looked around to find himself lying on the terrace clutching the cape, which fluttered ghostly in the wind. Shakily, he rose and entered the tower, probing the shadows for ambush as he went.

He wondered if he had beaten Baleron here.

After her meeting with Ungier, Mogra, in agitation, visited Gilgaroth. He was in the Well of Krogbur, that great dark shaft in the tower's core, where he communed with the powers under his command, issuing orders to generals prosecuting his War and listening to the prayers of those who made sacrifices to him in his temples. She waited, and at last he finished the business of the moment and turned to regard her.

"Ungier is come," she said.

He waited, sensing that she had more to say, so she added, "He has conquered Havensrike and desires a reward. An excuse to ask a favor of you, more like. He wants the elf girl."

She could feel Gilgaroth stir, and his darkness hummed with thought and energy, yet he said nothing.

She must plead with him, she saw, if she was to save Ungier—and him, too, perhaps. "Why not give him what he seeks?" she asked. "Why sour your bond with him just when it is renewed?"

At last Gilgaroth spoke, and his words held dark meaning: *"He does not care. He would sour that bond. He would dissolve it. And all to take away my songbird. He would rather cause me pain than be a son to me. He would rather have my treasure for himself than have my love."* She could feel the sadness, the regret, the bitterness, radiating from him like smoke from a fissure.

"No," she said. "He knows not what he does. He is blinded by her light. She is an enchantress, my Lord."

He regarded her coldly. *"You fear she enchants even me."*

She nodded wretchedly. "She drives you and Ungier apart, and I sense that is a dangerous thing. The webs of fate are strange and nebulous, yet I can sense them like few can, for I am a spider. I sense that your thread is bound to his, and that if his should be cut, yours will as well."

"Begone. I have things that need tending. War is like a delicate flower. It needs constant pruning, watering, and caring. Leave me to do it."

And so, troubled in her deep heart, Mogra left.

Just beyond the entrance to the Well, she met Ungier, who approached the archway wearing, she was glad to see, his new cape. Perhaps that meant he had decided to accept his parents' favor and leave off the subject of Rolenya.

Instead he told her, "I've come to discuss my prize."

In that instant she wanted to crush him. "If that is why you have come, then wait," he said. "Now is not the time."

"I must see Him."

She was blocking his way. "Turn back, my son. He is in no mood to receive you."

This clearly frustrated Ungier, but he seemed to sense that she meant what she said, and, not wanting to anger his father, he bowed, turned about and withdrew. Sadly, she watched him go.

Chapter Twelve

Things were getting strange in Krogbur, Rolenya decided. She did not know where he had come from, but Lord Ungier was attending the festivities that evening at the Feasting Hall. Attended by several sycophants wearing the armor of glarumri, he marched down the aisle looking tall and powerful and commanding. He wore a cape made of fine Spider-silk, and when he moved it trailed him like a glimmering shadow.

Rolenya was already seated—on the first row, as usual—and when he saw her he actually stopped in his tracks. His black eyes grew round, he appeared to steel himself, then strode boldly over to her and took her hand in his, bent and kissed it. She had endured his kisses too many times to shudder now.

"Good evening, my love," he said, his eyes staring openly into hers.

"There is little good about it," she answered, trying to suppress the quaver in her voice.

He stroked her cheek with a long, leathery finger, and she twisted away.

"Don't touch me," she said. "I'm not yours anymore."

"That will change," he said, and there was a throatiness in his voice and a strange urgency in his tone.

Nervously, she said, "What do you mean?"

"Havensrike is mine," he said.

She gasped, feeling horror rise up inside her.

"Fear not," he said. "You will be my queen, and together we will remake it."

"Never!"

"We will see."

He took his seat across the aisle from hers, and his sycophants gathered about him. The games began, and despite the spectacles of the arena he often diverted his attention to shoot her strange looks. She tried to ignore him, but it was difficult; she feared him, and despised him.

There was more to it than that, of course. She had not forgotten all their nights together. True, she had been his unwilling slave, but he had not been without his charms, and when he wore a human façade he was devilishly handsome. Over her three years of confinement at Gulrothrog, she had, despite herself, often been attracted to him, though she had been careful never to let him or anyone else (especially Baleron) know. Of all his concubines, and of all the women in his harem—for they were separate and distinct, the concubines and the harem—she had been his prize. They had almost ... *almost* ... wed. She would have been his ninth still-living wife, if living his wives could be called.

But the Wolf had changed all that. Gilgaroth had appeared unannounced at Gulrothrog and slipped past the Vampire King's defenses. The Dark One had found Rolenya in one of the huge bathing rooms of the harem, where she had been washing herself in a steaming pool of water, assisted by her handmaidens. Suddenly *he* appeared and the handmaidens fled. Rolenya would have, as well, but he'd bound her with his will, then removed the armor from one of his hands, exposing his naked flesh. With it, he had touched her, and his touch alone had been enough to steal the life from her body, and her soul. It was said that all he touched died save that which he created, which is why his hands were always armored, though Rolenya didn't know if this was true. It was further said that if you died in any of the lands where his influence was strongest that your soul would be sucked toward him and consumed, then cast into the Second Hell. In that way, to enter Oslog was to risk one's soul.

He had slain her, stolen her spirit and consigned it to the gardens of Illistriv. There she had mourned for Baleron and their father, for the Crescent itself. Despite the deceivingly beautiful surroundings, she had known only despair.

Now, watching Ungier, she doubted he had ever forgiven his sire for that theft—though he had not known about it till afterward—so it was strange to see that, despite his natural arrogance and aloofness, the Vampire King was fearful, not angry. His wide black eyes often probed the shadows around him, and he was constantly on edge.

Fortunately, his nervousness was tempered by his seeming love of the fights. He cheered and whistled and laughed as the combatants toiled away below, blood and sweat flying in equal measure.

The Borchstogs, naturally, gambled on the fights, and he joined in—though, Rolenya noted, there was much grumbling about this among the Borchstog circles; he had too much power and money to bet at their level. Yet they let him, out of fear of his wrath if they didn't.

Mogra, meanwhile, eyed Rolenya cattishly.

She knows, Rolenya thought. *Gods help me, but she knows.*

Rolenya tried to focus on her songs to come, and her spells. Gilgaroth would ask her to sing, as he always did, and she knew she had little choice but to comply. She was interrupted when Ungier, in the grip of some nervous tension, apparently could not stand merely *watching* the fights any longer. In the break between two bouts, he leapt to his clawed feet and shouted, "I'm next!"

Drunk on wine and immensely powerful, he had no fear. He

tore the table aside and jumped down into the arena, cape and wings billowing, with a howl of savage glee. Was he mad?

The Borchstogs cheered lustily, loving it.

A frown twisted Mogra's lips, and she leaned back, fingering (worriedly?) a strand of jewels that cascaded from her black hair down over a naked breast. Her violet eyes twinkled, and the many rings that adorned her six hands sparkled of gold and diamonds and pearls.

The Dark One regarded Ungier with flaming eyes.

"You seek sport, do you, my son?"

Ungier laughed. "I do, my Lord. I seek to spill some blood tonight!"

The Borchstogs cheered, and Ungier encouraged them.

"But even more, Father, Mother, I ask a boon of you. Hear me. I have conquered Glorifel. Havensrike is mine—ours. My first act as ruler of Ungoroth will be to build you both great temples, and your shadows will grow long indeed. All I ask in return is one thing." He looked over his shoulder, right at Rolenya, and pointed a finger. "Her."

"I will be no prize," she stated loudly. Still, her voice sounded small in the huge chamber.

"You will be *silent*," Ungier admonished indulgently.

"No," spoke Gilgaroth calmly, and all turned to him. *"She is mine, and she will be mine, and she will not be silent."*

"But I have toppled the mightiest pillar of the Crescent!" said Ungier. "Surely that deserves some prize."

"How DARE you demand a reward for doing my will! I did not hire you to do this thing. I asked you, as a father to a son. Do you not see? For ages you have denied me, have turned your back on me. I gave you a chance to return to my good graces. I gave you an army. I gave you a worthy labor. And what do I receive in return for these gifts? DEMANDS?" He paused, letting the tension build, and said, very deliberately, very coldly, *"You err."*

JACK CONNER

Ungier suddenly looked very small. "But the mastering of Glorifel ..."

"Is a feat I accomplished when I Doomed Baleron, when I sent Rauglir to destroy Logran's Flower. Thus I earn the reward, if a reward is to be earned." He shook his head ruefully. *"And to ask such a boon! Your gall is to be admired, if not your wit. I would have given you anything, my son, anything at all. Except ... her. Had you come to me and asked for a thing, I would have given it to you. A kingdom, a castle, a creature. But instead you come to me and DEMAND a prize, and you choose the one prize I would not have given you had you begged."* His black laugh was chilling, and Ungier shrank even further.

Mogra said, "Indeed you are a fool, Ungier."

The vampire hung his head. "How so, Mother?"

"Do you not realize that many of those that fight here are of my loins? Just like you. Many of them have died right where you're standing, and I have watched them go to their deaths with a smile. You think *you're* any different?"

"I am powerful," he boasted.

"Indeed," agreed Gilgaroth. *"For we did not make you as a creature, but as a son. Yet in Gulrothrog you were too long away from us, and your mind has grown weak. It needs sharpening."* He snapped his armored fingers. *"Thorg!"*

The terrible wolf rose and leapt into the arena, snarling angrily.

"My Lord, wait," said Mogra. Her harshness was gone, replaced with worry for her son.

"No," answered Gilgaroth. *"This vulgar display must end."*

Ungier looked up to his father with worry, obviously surprised at this turn of events. "I only wanted some sport," he protested. "I only wanted my woman back. I did not want death."

He bowed tentatively to show his subservience, but his father continued to regard him with disdain.

Thorg charged, jaws wide.

All eyes were on the arena. No one was watching the tall hooded figure standing in the shadow of an archway leading out of the hall, spying with interest on the action unraveling below. Baleron had arrived earlier that day and was still sore from Throgmar's handling, but all his aches and pains faded now.

He smiled as he realized what was going on down in the arena. This was beyond his wildest hopes. *Ungier may not get his prize, but I might.*

If Ungier died, it would solve a good half of Baleron's problems. Thank the Omkarathons for Rolenya's ability to inspire love, or at least emotion, even in creatures so vile. She shone brightly below, close to the arena, a white thorn amidst the darkness, and Baleron was joyous to see her, to know she was safe and whole, but at present his attention was fixed—hopefully—on the vampire courting death in the pit.

Rolenya watched breathlessly as Ungier easily dodged aside. Thorg wheeled about, fires licking the back of his throat.

Ungier laughed mockingly. "You don't scare me, dog."

"I will grind your bones between my jaws," returned Thorg.

He charged again. Ungier whipped off his glimmering cape and waved it before the charging beast, taunting him. Thorg tore through the cape, fangs flashing, but did not even wound the vampire.

Ungier, however, raked his claws across the beast's passing flank, drawing blood, then licked his dripping fingers.

"Tasty," he said as the wolf turned around again.

Thorg belched fire at Ungier, but the flames parted around the powerful vampire as if an invisible shield protected him, and Ungier gave a thin smile.

Thorg's eyes burned, his gaze burrowing into his foe. He would try to *hypnotize* the Vampire King! Amazed, Rolenya found herself favoring Ungier. She still remembered her time in the arena with that same cuerdrig all too well, while Ungier, for all his faults, loved her.

The vampire merely laughed. His own black eyes seemed to grow wider, and the two combatants stared at each other, each trying to enthrall the other. Rolenya looked up to the Dark One and his bride to see them watching the battle tensely. Mogra looked nervous.

When the contest of wills between vampire and cuerdrig ended, Thorg lowered his head and said, "I serve you, Lord Ungier."

Ungier turned a sneer up at his father. "There!"

Gilgaroth snapped his fingers again. *"Slorch!"*

The second wolf sprang down into the arena and, before Rolenya could catch her breath, Slorch charged Ungier. The vampire leapt into the air, wings pumping, and landed behind the monster.

Having enthralled Thorg, Ungier used him to assault Slorch, while the lone cuerdrig raged, bitter at having to fight his brother.

Rolenya was shocked. It seemed to her that Gilgaroth was really trying to *kill* Ungier ... and the Dark One was willing to sacrifice his favorite pets to do it! Ungier must have sinned greatly in his eyes.

Below, the vampire had his puppet Thorg charge his brother, and while Slorch wrapped his jaws about the other wolf's throat, Ungier used his claws to slash Slorch's own jugular, and Slorch fell, blood pooling around him. Thorg, though wounded, survived.

Rolenya sat back and tried to calm down. She felt like she would be ill.

Mogra, looking dull, perhaps sad, also leaned back, sighing.

Gilgaroth's expression, as always, was nearly impossible to read. His flaming eyes simmered.

Ungier knelt over the still-warm carcass and drank Slorch's hot blood, lapping it up with his tongue, then looked up to the thrones with a bloody, defiant smile.

"Have I passed the test, Father?"

Gilgaroth said nothing.

Ungier turned to the Borchstogs of the audience and raised his blood-drenched arms. "Have I not won?" he shouted to them.

They roared in approval, beating on the tabletops. This was likely the best, most significant, most unexpected fight they had ever seen.

Triumphant, Ungier turned again to Gilgaroth. "I have earned my prize, Father."

"No."

"But, Father, I—"

"NO."

Ungier's face screwed up in anger. "You just want her for yourself!"

The Borchstogs gasped, muttering to each other. They loved a victor, but they hated anyone who went against their Lord.

Mogra's mouth twitched.

"That's right, isn't it, Father?" Ungier continued. "You won't give me the prize that I have earned because it is *you* who covets her. Why don't you come down here, Father? Why don't *we* do battle here, right now, in the arena? The winner takes Rolenya. That's what you really want, isn't it? Let me oblige you. It will be a bout to be remembered for all times. Our war shall shake the heavens!"

Rolenya was taken aback. Ungier must truly have gone mad! Even the Borchstogs fell silent, awed by the challenge.

Mogra said, "You go too far, my son."

"Do I?" he asked. "Perhaps I have not gone far enough." He looked to Thorg, then to Gilgaroth. His black eyes were serious and deadly. "Thorg, *slay your maker.*"

Baleron stifled his laughter only with great effort. *Ungier had gone insane!* Surely Gilgaroth would kill him in due course and Rond-thril would be released from the sway of the dark powers.

He expected it to happen any minute. Any second.

For once, fate was on his side.

The cuerdrig looked from the Vampire King to the Dark One and could not seem to make up its mind. Infuriated, Gilgaroth wrenched the sword that was embedded in the side of his throne out and hurled it at the beast. His blade, in proportion with his giant stature, skewered the mighty Thorg to the ground, and smoking blood pooled across the sand, which drank it up greedily. The cuerdrig was dead.

"You err," Gilgaroth said again, this time almost sadly. Looking up to the masked ceiling, he shouted, *"Descend!"*

The host of wraiths that inhabited the upper reaches of the smoke-filled room descended into the arena and swirled about Ungier, a swarm of living shadows. They howled and shrieked and created such an unholy din that the Borchstogs, shivering in fear, closed their eyes and clamped hands over their ears.

Rolenya remembered when she had been at the center of a similar vortex, and the sight—and the memory—chilled her to the bone.

The ghosts ripped at the Vampire King with insubstantial hands and claws and teeth and worse, and Ungier screamed in agony. They tore his soul loose from his body, and his body slumped lifelessly to the floor.

His soul, visible in this place of power, was a shadow blacker than theirs, and it twisted and fought against them, but they were too many. Shrieking, they bore him up to their Master, who rose to his feet and removed the armor from one hand.

Mogra shifted uncomfortably.

With the hand that was still encased in armor, the Dark One seized the squirming soul of Ungier and stared mercilessly at the shadowy thing, and it trembled beneath the weight of his judgment.

Gilgaroth raised his naked hand and pressed it close to Ungier, who knew that the touch of that hand meant instant death, the demise of his very soul. He tried to twist away, but his father's iron grip was too strong.

"I can slay you at any time I choose," said Gilgaroth. *"More, I can prolong your torment for eons. Even now I have enemies locked in the dungeons of this very tower that I have been torturing for thousands of years. I transferred them here from Ghrastigor so that I would not be without my favorite playthings. Do you think I would hesitate to add you to that collection? Or ..."* He twitched his dark fingers. *"... I could simply touch your naked soul now, or at any time henceforth, and kill it utterly so that you will never know agony, or peace, again. Only oblivion."*

The soul of Ungier shook.

"Do you now understand the depth of your folly?" asked Gilgaroth. *"I hope so. I will not be so forgiving a second time."*

He flung the soul down into the pit, right into the inert body of the Vampire King, and the body stirred. Rolenya, who had not realized she had been holding her breath, took a deep one.

———

Baleron gnashed his teeth in frustration.

He'd come so close!

"Damn it all!" he hissed.

Gasping, Ungier sat up, rubbing his throat as though it could be sore when it was his soul his father had been grasping. He was so unsteady that Borchstogs had to help him up. He stretched his arms out and regarded his own body in a strange, frightened manner.

"My powers ..." he whispered. His head snapped up. "You've stolen my powers!"

"*I gave them to you,*" Gilgaroth replied. "*They were mine to take away.*"

Ungier made pathetic little noises, but he was wise enough to choke down his words. Rolenya was shocked to see that he was crying in mute rage, frustration, and impotence; his tears were black drops of blood leaked from all-black eyes, though, and it was not a sight to endear him to her.

The Dark One's attention fell on her, and all else washed from her mind.

"*Erase this ugly scene, little one,*" he said. "*Come. Sing for me, my dove.*"

Mogra tapped her armrest in agitation, eyeing the tattered remains of the shadow-cape sadly.

Borchstogs removed the bodies of Thorg and Slorch, and a group of them lugged the heavy sword back up to its Master, who replaced it in his throne. He watched the bodies of his prized cuerdrigs go with an inscrutable expression, though Rolenya did note that the fires of his eyes seemed to dim, just slightly.

Ungier dusted himself off and flew up out of the arena. He paused at the overturned table, casting Rolenya a sidelong look.

"I would have liked to have heard you sing," he said.

"Then you should not have been such an ass!" she snapped.

He fled up the stairs, minus his cape. On his way out, he shot a wary glance up toward the hidden ceiling, where the wraiths had returned, and seemed to shudder. Wordlessly, he left.

"*Please,*" Gilgaroth said, his eyes on Rolenya, and gestured toward the now-empty arena.

Sighing, she gathered herself and descended.

"Don't," protested Mogra, laying a caressing hand on his arm. He had replaced the armor on his other hand. "She weaves spells with her songs; she casts a net over you. Send her away—to Clevaris, as planned."

From the tone of her voice it was plain that she had voiced this objection before. Rolenya was surprised she would speak so before the Borchstogs, but, then, they loved their Father and Mother with such devotion that a little bickering between the Two would go unnoticed.

"Nonsense," Gilgaroth said. *"You are merely jealous. She is but a slip of a girl. What power can she have over me?"*

"She can harness Light and Grace, the gifts of Brunril to the Elves, and funnel them into her songs. Close your ears to them, my Lord. Deny her the chance to bind you to her. Don't you see? That is her plan."

Gilgaroth regarded his bride for a long moment, then turned his gaze on Rolenya. The princess trembled. Would Gilgaroth destroy her? The moment stretched, and stretched, and Rolenya tried not to look guilty.

At last, Gilgaroth threw back his head and laughed. The candles dimmed, and so did the torches and urns. Rolenya had to fight the urge to wrap her arms about herself, feeling cold all of a sudden; gooseflesh covered her.

The laughter died.

"Let her sing. Let her weave her little spells. I have enough darkness in me to counter any light."

Mogra glared at Rolenya, bearing her teeth in a most horrid smile. The Spider Queen's fangs were very sharp, and Rolenya was reminded that Gilgaroth was not the only one she had to fear.

Baleron watched Ungier depart the room, broken and humiliated. He enjoyed the vampire's discomfort, but he knew that was not enough.

Ungier needed to die.

The Lord of Ungoroth vanished through a door several aisles over from the archway in which Baleron hid, and, when the vampire was gone, the prince took a deep breath and quit the hall. He hated to miss Rolenya's songs, but this was more important.

He found himself in a long, curved corridor, and headed right, the direction Ungier had taken. Killing the vampire should be easier now that Gilgaroth had removed the fiend's powers, or at least some of them, Baleron reflected.

As he made his way along, he heard Rolenya begin singing; her voice carried far and could even be heard out here. As always, her voice was lovely, and the song beautiful. It seemed surreal to him that such angelic notes should provide the backdrop for his mission of murder.

He stalked up the high black hall, and shadows leapt and swayed to scant torchlight, almost in time to the song. He kept his footfalls soft, kept his breathing quiet and steady.

There! Ungier lingered in an archway leading into the hall. It seemed he had thrown away all pride and dignity and was even then pressing a bat-like ear to the door, an enchanted smile on his face.

Baleron grunted with amusement.

Ungier heard. He spun about to find Baleron already descending on him, having snatched a torch from its bracket and bringing the fiery end down on the vampire's head.

Ungier caught Baleron's wrist and stopped the torch's descent. Had Baleron two hands, he would have punched the vampire in the throat or nose with his free fist, but it was Ungier who still had two hands, and they were both tipped with long claws.

His free hand drove toward the Heir of Havensrike's face, meaning to impale his eyes. Baleron broke away. The torch clattered to the floor.

The two combatants crouched, circling each other warily.

Fury blazed in the vampire's face. "You!"

"Me," Baleron agreed.

There would be no fancy exchange of mock titles this time.

They were down to the end of it, now, and both sensed that the time for games had passed.

"Alone at last," Ungier said.

"And you without your powers. Pity."

The Vampire King eyed the length of Rondthril at Baleron's side. "I think I'll have that back now."

"Come and get it."

The fiend flew at him, and they grappled with each other, at last rolling about on the floor. Baleron wrapped his one hand about the vampire's throat and tried to crush his enemy's windpipe, while Ungier sought purchase on Baleron's face to pluck out his eyes and drive his sharp thumbs into his brain.

Baleron used his stump as a bludgeon. It hurt every time he struck with it, but it was worth it to hear the sounds of impact on the vampire's chest and head.

Baleron had one advantage, and that was that he was trained in hand-to-hand combat and Ungier was not. All his long life, Ungier had relied on his godly powers, but now they had deserted him.

Baleron had to thrash and writhe and kick and buck to avoid the vampire's claws and fangs, as the fiend had the longer reach, and with all that motion Baleron could not find a solid enough hold to crush Ungier's throat. And even if he could, he doubted Ungier could be killed that way: god or not, the vampire was still an undead *thing*.

Infuriated, Ungier at last kicked away and stood, wiping a trickle of blood from his cheek. Baleron stood, too.

"*Rolling about on the floor like a pig!*" Ungier said, his voice dripping disgust. "Is this how mortals fight? It is beneath me. I refuse to continue this farce. I may be weakened, but—" (as if to confirm Baleron's fears) "—I am no *mortal*." He fairly spat the word.

Baleron forced a smile. "Then will you let a crippled one chase you off?"

The vampire bared his fangs.

Several Borchstogs wearing the armor of glarumri emerged from the Feasting Hall. Their wolf-head helms were long and were inset with red rubies for eyes. The Borchstogs half-bowed to Ungier.

"My loyal troops," he said, half mocking.

"My lord," said their leader, his eyes going from Ungier to Baleron. "Please accept our apologies. We stayed a minute to listen to the she-elf. We beg your pardon."

Ungier turned a nasty look to Baleron. "No godhood, perhaps, but I still possess authority." To the glarumri, he said, "Kill him!"

The glarumri gasped. "But, my lord, he is *ul Ravast!*"

Baleron nearly smiled to hear the growl that issued from Ungier's throat at that moment. The Vampire King shook off his rage and said to the Borchstogs, *"Look into my eyes."* Apparently he still had some power.

Baleron ran.

Chapter Thirteen

fter she had sung and was allowed to leave the Feasting Hall, Rolenya returned to her suite to bathe in one of the hot, steaming pools created by the stream that ran through her rooms. She felt dirty and soiled by the smoke of the Hall—the smoke and the blood, and the evil that hung there as palpably as grease in the air.

She had three attendants that appeared to be elf maids, though she doubted their appearances and thought it more likely they were Borchstogs given elvish form. Spies. They rarely spoke, but they obeyed her instructions well enough. One was sponging her back when there came a knock on the door.

"See who that is," Rolenya said, and a handmaiden complied.

In a moment she returned. Curtsying, she said, "'tis Lord Ungier."

Rolenya's mouth dropped open. She started to say something, rethought it, and started over again. Composing herself, she turned to the third handmaiden and said, "Fetch me a towel." To the second one, she said, "Show him in, but don't let him wander."

"Yes, my lady."

Minutes later, Rolenya was clad in a bathrobe and preparing

herself to meet the vampire. It would be the first time she'd seen him in an intimate circumstance since Gulrothrog. Still, her body was warm and freshly scrubbed, and perfumed with the scent of flowers. She felt good and had consumed more than her fair share of wine. She was feeling bold.

She strode into the main living room, where Ungier warmed himself beside the fire. Tall and regally poised, he wore his spider-silk cape, which one of his servants must have retrieved from the arena—or perhaps his mother, to make up for recent unpleasantness? Its rents had mended, as if of the cape's own accord.

Rolenya had half expected him in human guise, but of course he was not; Gilgaroth had stolen his godhood.

"Good evening, Lord Ungier," she said, trying to stay formal.

"Likewise, fair Rolenya."

He took a moment to drink her in, and something about her seemed to relax him. He took a deep breath and sighed.

Too, something about her seemed to quicken him, as his eyes grew larger and his expression more determined.

"You smell lovely," he told her.

"Why, thank you."

"I enjoyed your singing tonight." He glided about the room, beginning to circle her. "Though I had to put my ear to the door to hear it. You have a most beautiful voice. It sounds like crystal bells over a pure running stream."

"Not so pure," she said, reminding him of how he'd stolen her maidenhood, how he'd destroyed her innocence.

He did not have the decency to look abashed. Quite the reverse: he seemed to smile fondly at the memory. "Indeed," he said, and his voice was heavy with desire.

"Enough!" she snapped. So much for formality.

He stopped circling and spun to face her. "You know why I have come."

"Yes."

He strode closer to her. His steps were quick and urgent and full of power, like those of a jungle cat.

Lightly, she stepped backwards. "It's not to be," she said.

"Oh, but it is."

He reached her and wrapped her in his rough embrace. Pressing himself against her, he crushed his leathery lips to hers. She struggled and pushed at him, but even with his powers diminished he was mighty, and she couldn't tear away from his grasp.

"Maids!" she shouted, wrenching her lips from his. "Help me!"

But they cowered in fear on the edges of the room, looking at each other worriedly, and none had the courage to assist her.

"Go!" snarled the First Vampire. "Leave us!"

They fled the room.

"You are at my mercy," Ungier said, his need evident. "You are *mine*."

"No. Never again." She beat at his chest. In his vampire form, he was not at all attractive, though it would not have mattered anyway. "Never!"

He grinned evilly. "You were nearly my bride—my Queen—and I shall make it so again."

"I think not," said a voice from behind.

Ungier turned his battish head in time to see the fireplace poker swinging down at him. If he hadn't been so consumed by lust, he probably would've heard the intruder, or smelled him, but he was too late. The iron poker slammed down on the crown of his head, his black eyes rolled up in his head, and he slumped to the ground lifelessly.

Baleron, fireplace poker in hand, stared down at him and said, "Finally."

His eyes found her.

"Baleron!"

She flung herself into his arms, peppering him with kisses and hugging him tightly. He felt so good and strong and she wanted to bury herself in him.

"Oh, Baleron," she cried, and she was not a bit embarrassed when tears leaked from her eyes. Pulling herself away, she looked up into his face and was startled by how old he looked: gray hair ran through his dark waves, and his blue eyes looked ancient. Grooves lined his face, and he looked bowed by a great weight: his Doom. Of course. He was still handsome, but his boyishness was gone.

"It's so good to see you," she told him.

He kissed her and stepped back. Looking down at the body of the Vampire King, he said, "I need to kill him."

"*What?* You'll bring the wrath of Gilgaroth down on us!"

He patted Rondthril's hilt with his one remaining hand. *His one remaining hand!* She stared at his stump in dismay.

"My blade—" he said, then stopped. "I'll tell you later." He looked to the fireplace, seeming to study its dimensions, then to the balcony. Wind gusted the drapes. "There," he said. "We'll throw him over. Grab his feet."

She hesitated. "No, Bal. We can't. It's—"

He half smiled. "What? Foolish? Rash? I'm beyond that now. Let's just do it."

He knelt down and picked up Ungier's upper half, awkward with his one hand and stump, and, reluctantly, Rolenya grabbed Ungier's clawed feet. On the count of three, and against her better judgment, they hefted the body up and carted it out to the terrace. Wind gusted coldly, and she shivered. Once they were fully outside, she began to tremble.

"Baleron, are you sure this is wise?"

He laughed recklessly. "Not at all."

He began to tilt the inert body over the railing.

"Now!" he said.

The body would tumble down a long, long ways, she saw. It would fall into the very fires of the Second Hell and be consumed, if such fires could consume Ungier, and she thought they could. Nothing would be left of him, save his spirit, which would hopefully be trapped in the Inferno. She prepared to tilt Ungier's lower half and release it to the abyss—

Two flaming discs opened in the darkness.

Gilgaroth in his Worm form, hovering outside her suite and cloaked in the darkness which he emanated, said, *"Drop him and you'll burn in the fires of Illistriv forever more."*

Baleron nearly jumped out of his skin. As it was, he almost dropped Ungier over the side out of sheer fright. He hadn't been this fearful when Ungier's glarumri were pursuing him; luckily for him they were less adept on their feet than in the air. It was only with great control that he carefully lowered the vampire to the stone of the terrace. Ungier did not stir. *Damn it all! That's THREE TIMES he could've been killed tonight. Why won't he just die?*

"How long have you been spying on my sister?" Baleron demanded.

"She is not your sister, spider," Gilgaroth said. *"She is more my flesh than yours. I made her. In a way, she is my daughter."*

"No!" said the princess. "I am *not* your daughter. My real father is dead, *murdered by my very body*—which *you* stole from me. And I won't forget it!"

Baleron felt a swell of pride at her defiance. Kicking Ungier's ribs, he said to the Dark One, "What'll we do with him?"

Fire licked the back of Gilgaroth's throat, and his long, sinuous body writhed behind him. *"Borchstogs will come for him. They are already on their way."*

In a small voice, Rolenya said, "Did you see what he tried to do?"

"I saw." Gilgaroth's voice sounded patient—almost, to Baleron's horror, fatherly. *"I would not have let him."*

"He's an animal—a beast!"

"He shall be dealt with soon enough."

Baleron liked the sound of that. He liked it less when Gilgaroth turned his eyes on him.

"Throgmar tells me that your labor was completed. Good."

"Is that all he told you?"

"He told me that Glorifel has fallen. The King and the Archmage are dead. All is as it should be, except for Clevaris. I'd hoped your brother Jered would prove as able as you at spinning my web, but it was not to be. Before he could complete his first task, he was slain. You, however, have proven most worthy—whether you were willing or no. Such efficiency will be rewarded."

"Why ... why did you come to my window?" Rolenya asked.

"It is not your window. It is mine."

Without another word, Gilgaroth slipped away into the darkness.

"Damn him!" Baleron said. Almost growling, he cast his gaze down to the inert form of Ungier. "So, we're alone, are we? Perhaps things aren't so black, after all. I think I'll just ..."

Borchstogs burst through the door of the suite.

"Roschk ul Ravast!" they chanted.

There were six of them, and they bowed and scraped as they neared him and lifted the Vampire King onto their shoulders. Baleron and Rolenya turned to each other.

Gilgaroth and Mogra met on the top of the tower. It seemed they stood in a strange world all to themselves, as Krogbur's tip pierced the dark clouds of the sky and there was nothing else to be seen. A howling wind tore across the two, bringing with it rain and thunder, but they were unmoved.

Gilgaroth strode to the edge and waved his hand, and the cloud parted to reveal the innumerable bonfires of the Great Army. Mogra stood by him and together they gazed down on the host that would ensure their victory, not over just the Crescent, but the world.

"*We will send them out on the morrow,*" said Gilgaroth.

"Has the time come so soon?" Mogra asked in wonder. "I did not think it would be so soon."

"*It is not soon to me. I have awaited this for ages.*"

"Ever since your Vision."

He said nothing.

She smiled. "I'm so happy. It's even better that all this is a surprise to me, just as you said. I *have* enjoyed the thrill of it, the shock of it, and it is grand."

He turned his head to her bright face. "*And I enjoy it through you.*"

"I'm honored to be the eyes through which you see it. Tell me of it again, my love. Tell me about your Vision. I so love to hear it."

"*You know the story well.*"

"Just let me hear the words."

He made a fist, and twenty tongues of lightning broke around the tower, to punctuate the beginning of his tale. "*Long ages ago, when first the Crescent rose to oppose me, I put myself to slumber. I cast my soul out into the black and treacherous waters of Time, what few have dared to do. Those waters harbor dangers beyond reckoning, and most who journey there are lost. Yet I braved those depths, and they parted before me, folding away like warm virgin flesh, and before me I saw a great inferno and out of it rose the Black Tower, and it was the very Heart of the World. All bowed down before it, and I was its Lord—the very Lord of the Earth. Seeing this, I knew what I could become, that I could indeed overthrow my enemies and achieve my Desire. I had only to discover how. And so I did, and here we stand, and the world is laid bare at our feet. Naked, it quivers before us, gasping, awaiting only our bold touch. And here,*" he gestured at the Army, and the Hell-Worms, "*is our hand outstretched, ready to seize it, to make it ours.*"

He made another fist, and forty tongues of lightning blasted around them. Mogra trembled against him.

"Oh, my love! I knew this day would come, but now that it is here I am afraid."

"What frightens you, my bride?"

"When the world is ours, and you have grown strong enough to re-forge it, when Lorg-jilaad is with us again ..."

A gleam came into his fiery eyes. *"Then our war on the Omkar of Light shall begin, and we shall prevail. Only then may our war on each other begin."* He looked at her, and in his gaze was love. *"But you worry for yourself."*

"No, I worry for you, and for him. I will put myself to sleep, and only the Victor shall be able to rouse me. I will be the prize. But I fear for the Loser. Never will I look on him again. Never will I feel his hot embrace! He will be destroyed, gone from the world utterly."

"It is the way it must be. You know this. We will not share you."

"Yes, my Son. I know. But I can't bear the thought of losing you, or of losing Him." She pressed herself to him and ran her six hands over his body, and he took her in his arms and kissed her.

"Let me ease your mind," he said.

Wind howled and thunder roared. Darkness grew once more about the tower's tip, and of what unholy sights transpired there, none can tell, but it is said that at one point all the rain that fell on the gathered host below turned to drops of warm blood, and the lightning made strange shapes in the sky.

Baleron, realizing he and Rolenya were finally alone, kissed her passionately.

"It's been too long," she murmured.

"Wait," he said, separating himself. He hadn't had a chance to bathe since his arrival, and the sight of the steaming baths demanded his attention. "The last wash I had was two days ago in some mountain stream cold enough to freeze me solid in a few places, or nearly enough. Some might still be frozen."

She smiled, though it was strained. She still seemed tense, and he didn't wonder why. The sight of him must be a mixture of good and bad news for her. She would not be simply glad to see him, as she knew that if he'd returned he must have completed his labor. She was half-watching him with the eyes of one who fears that she gazes upon the murderer of her adopted father, the traitor that doomed her adopted kingdom.

He took her hands and said, "I did not kill him, Rolenya. Our father, I did not ..."

Something seemed to go out of her, some burden, and tears sprang to her eyes. "Tell me, Bal! What *happened?* I must know what happened!"

He sat her down, and slowly told her his strange, sad tale. When he reached the part about Rauglir possessing his hand and how he'd had to chop it off, she cried and kissed his stump. He told her everything, or nearly everything, omitting only the most hurtful parts, such as the image of their father's severed head on a silver platter at Ungier's banquet. When he described the sack of Glorifel, she burst into sobs and did not stop for a long time, no matter how much he stroked her hair or patted her back. He let her cry.

At last he finished, and he was heartened to see that she no longer looked at him as though he were a murderer. She looked on him as she had before, but with even greater love, and greater sadness.

He moved off to the baths, and she helped him.

"How did you find me at the Inferno?" he asked when he was neck-deep in the hot soapy water and she was scrubbing his back.

"When I returned here and you were gone, I was scared. I guessed at the only other thing that could interest you here: Salthrick. So I went down to the lower levels. I've wandered the halls here a great deal since you left, and I know them well. I knew what lay beyond that archway—one of the Gates of Hell, I call them—and so I went there. Well, not at first. It's one of several, and it's the second one I went to." She shivered. "What a horrible place! But I'm glad I found you in time."

"Why? I could have defeated Rauglir."

She did not answer for a moment. "No, Baleron. I don't think you could. He may play at swords for sheer amusement, but even if you could defeat him that way—he is not human, Bal."

"Not anymore," he agreed.

"He's powerful. Don't take him lightly."

He felt his face harden. "Oh, I don't. I would never take *him* lightly. But ... let's think of other things."

The water was delightful, and he began to feel his old self again, despite everything.

Once she paused in her scrubbing and said, as if just remembering, "You say you ... *ate* ... this Flower of Itherin?"

"*I* didn't. Rauglir did. And just the bloom. But yes."

She frowned. "And you say your blood *smoked* when it struck the igrith?"

"Yes? What?" She seemed excited about something.

She sat the scrub-brush down. "Baleron, bite your hand."

"*What?*"

"Bite your hand or I'll do it for you. We just need one drop of blood."

Curious, he punctured his palm enough for a little blood to well up, and as she directed he positioned it away from the bath and let a red drop fall to a section of the black floor not covered in hides. Instantly, smoke rose up from the spot where the blood had struck.

He laughed, more startled than anything else. "What does this mean? My blood has turned to acid?"

He craned his head back to see her smile in satisfaction. She said, "It means that for however long the Flower of Itherin's power flows through you, your blood is harmful to enemies of the Light."

"I'd rather keep my blood where it is." He mulled it over.

"There's another way it helps. I forgot to tell you, but the Flower helped me master my Doom at one point. It didn't save Father, but it gave him a little while longer."

"Can it destroy your curse?"

"My Doom is the stronger, I can feel it. But at least it's weaker now, with the Flower. I think. Anyway, it's good to know that we're not in this completely alone. The Gods of the Light haven't done much to help us so far, but maybe, just maybe, this means that the fates don't favor evil." Ruefully, he added, "Still, I hate to put our new weapon to the test."

She nodded gravely. "So do I."

That night, they found comfort in each other's arms, but it was a cold comfort, for she knew as he did: unless a miracle occurred, the Dark One had truly won. Just the same, Baleron found that even in Rolenya's tears she seemed somehow resolved, determined to come out the other side of this thing. She whispered to him of her strategy for the future: if Gilgaroth truly did give them a distant realm to rule, they would rule it wisely, bringing enlightenment and goodness to their people, even if they were Borchstogs, and in due course they would grow powerful and challenge Gilgaroth for his Throne. Baleron very much doubted such a thing could be accomplished, but he pretended to go along with it for her sake.

She fell asleep in his arms, and he stayed awake to enjoy the feel of her body against his, of her smooth skin rubbing against him. He stroked her hair and inhaled the scent of her deep into his lungs, and at last he too drifted off to slumber.

Harsh knocking woke them.

It was Ustagrot, the Borchstog necromancer and high priest to Gilgaroth. To Baleron's surprise, he was dressed in his most formal robes and wore a sweeping hat of Eastern style. In a gnarled hand he held a long, intricately carved staff with a sinister-looking demon head on top. He did not wait for the door to be answered but used his powers to swing it open before him so that it banged loudly against the wall, startling those inside. Striding in purposefully, he made his way to the bedroom, where a naked Rolenya scrambled to pull the covers over herself and Baleron.

"They don't teach manners very well in Oslog!" she protested.

"Get dressed!" snapped Ustagrot. "In a short while, the Master will address His army and send the host north. It will destroy what's left of your Union."

"I take it he wants us to attend this speech," Baleron said.

"He has something special planned for you," said Ustagrot, and Baleron wondered if this were the final element of his Doom, as Mogra had intimated. "Besides, you've been instrumental in achieving His ends. You deserve to see the fruits of your labor come to pass."

"I'm fine as I am. Really."

The Borchstog sneered. "You have no choice, *Ravast-ru*. We can force your cooperation, should that prove necessary. Get dressed. Make yourselves presentable. I'll come for you in an hour."

Baleron and Rolenya looked at each other when he had gone, and as one they glanced away.

Baleron still had *some* hope, though. His eyes inched to Rond-thril, which hung in its scabbard from a nearby chair. *Yes*, he told it silently. *It's time. It must be, though I don't know how; Ungier has proven lucky so far.*

Rolenya saw his expression. "What?" she asked. "What is it?"

Should he tell her? He hesitated.

"Spit it out, Bal!"

He almost smiled. "I'm going to do something," he said. "Something mad. This is it. Our last chance. If that army goes north, it's all over for us, for the Crescent, for the world. We can't allow that to happen."

"But what can we do?"

"I'll tell you in a minute. I don't even know if it's possible, but it might be. At least we have a chance. Elethris hinted at it. So did

Logran. So did Vilana." He squeezed her hand. "There's hope, Rolenya." Frowning, he added, "But if we act now, there's no going back. There will be no distant realm for us to rule, no eventual uprising. Nothing. If we fail, we'll burn in the Second Hell forevermore until our souls are used up, far apart, and that's if he doesn't just destroy them outright. Either way, he'll still send his army north. The world will still fall. So ... the risk is high. The chance of success, slim. But it's the only hope I see." He held his breath. "I need to know—are you with me?"

She stared into his eyes.

"Of course I'm with you, Baleron Grothgar," she said. "If I have to, I'll follow you into the very fires of Illistriv. The pain they can inflict is not nearly so terrible as the prospect of a world ruled by the Shadow, a world without Light or Grace, a world of darkness where love has no place, except the love of power and dark things." She clasped his hand tightly. "So of course I'm with you, Baleron. For ever and always, I'm yours. What do we have to do?"

Chapter Fourteen

H e and Rolenya were dressed and ready to go when Ustagrot returned an hour later. Escorted by a full dozen elite troops, the Heir to Havensrike and the Princess of Larenthi left their suite for the last time and followed the high priest through the labyrinth of Krogbur.

They wound along hallways and ascended several long flights of stairs, seeing many terrible things along the way—wraiths in groups or alone, unnatural creatures skulking down tunnels, grim sculptures of demons and beasts, and more. Though this place, this tower, was new, it seemed to be expanding rapidly. Just a few months ago it had seemed much emptier, much more hollow. Now it was crammed full of life, or un-life. Baleron thought it large enough to contain several vast cities, and he shuddered at what horrors might live in its most lightless chambers.

As he walked along, he fingered Rondthril's pommel. It was amazing to him that they'd let him have it. Why would they allow him any sword at all, much less this one? Of course, all the Borch-stogs were armed, and he was of a higher station than they. Weapons were an intrinsic part of their culture. Yet he was a prisoner. Unless, of course, the Dark One was fool enough to trust him, which he surely was not.

It must be that Gilgaroth did not fear Rondthril. The Heir had tried to slay him with it once and failed, so why *should* he fear it? After all, it was loyal to the dark powers. The Fanged Blade was impotent.

Kill! it chanted in his head, as always. *Blood!*

Hungry, but impotent.

That was why only Rondthril would serve his purpose, he realized. If Vilana or Elethris had gifted him with a sword imbued with Light, it would immediately have been taken from him upon his capture, as then it truly would be dangerous to Gilgaroth. But Rondthril was a weapon of darkness, so they trusted it.

Were Elethris and Logran and Vilana right? *Could* Baleron wield it for some high cause? He had to trust their instincts. Otherwise, there really was no hope.

He glanced sideways at Rolenya. She walked with calm and poise, but he could see that she was just as nervous as he was, and scared and racked with guilt, besides, for she would live, but unless they succeeded in their mad plan (if plan it could be called), her kingdoms—both of them—would fall. But despite it all there was a strength in her, a fortitude, and at first it puzzled him, but then he thought he understood: she was righteous, and in her righteousness she was powerful. Her eyes were clear and her face untroubled. She had faith—faith in him, in them, and in Light itself.

He wished he had such faith. All he had was determination— determination that if the opportunity to use Rondthril presented itself, he would act on the instant, heedless of the cost to his own life or soul or even Rolenya's. All he had was the will to destroy Gilgaroth, consequences be damned, and it would have to be enough.

Gone were his days of wine and leisure and women. He knew he would never enjoy such luxury again. Life for him now was hard and sharp, full of darkness and blood. Just the same, he no longer felt empty. Before he'd found Rolenya again, he had been a mere shell of a creature, a machine working on clockwork, surviving just to survive. She had filled the emptiness in him.

He squeezed her hand and held it as they made their way through the tower, and at last they emerged into what he thought of as the Main Hall, the one that led from Gilgaroth's giant Throne Room down the endless flight of black stairs to the largest and highest terrace. They were very near where Baleron had crouched that day, after dispatching the two Borchstog guards, when he'd spied on the meeting between Throgmar and his father. That seemed very long ago, a lifetime, before he'd slain Felestrata and lost whatever innocence he'd still possessed, before his months of torture, before the fall of his city and the death of his father.

He felt a stirring in his blood, a quickening. Taking a deep breath, he urged himself to be calm, to stay collected and focused.

They stepped into the wide, high corridor and made their way to the end of the short hall, where the terrace began. Ustagrot stopped, and so did the procession behind him.

"We will wait here," the high priest whispered to Baleron and Rolenya, "until we are invited to do otherwise."

Brother and sister shifted uncomfortably. Dimly, he could hear rhythmic chanting from below, from the very earth at Krogbur's feet: the Borchstogs were sounding out. It was a great, dark swell of noise, primal and harsh. They were calling for their Master.

If Baleron could hear it from here, just below the roof of clouds, the sound must be awesome indeed. It must shake the earth.

The night was the color of charcoal, laced with violet-tinged edges of clouds, and here and there lightning flickered and cut the gloom. Thunder rolled.

Queen Mogra descended the stairs. In her humane form, she was naked and defiant and at least twenty feet tall, jewelry winking on her six arms. More jewelry adorned her body and clasped the thick, dark hair that fell past her shoulders. She seemed to sparkle when she moved. Her full high breasts jutted proudly from her chest, and the hair of her pubis was oiled and combed. Baleron was taken by her raw sensuality; she exuded sex and lust and power, and when she walked down those endless black stairs her hips rocked back and forth. She strutted down to the level floor and sauntered past Baleron and the rest of his group, teasing them with the scent of her heady and intoxicating perfume, if perfume it was. Smiling, Mogra stepped out onto the large terrace and made her way to its edge.

She lifted all six arms in a dramatic gesture, and the Borch-stogs far below roared lustily.

"Do you love me?" she shouted.

They roared even louder.

She half turned and motioned to Ustagrot and his charges. One jewel-laden hand beckoned them.

The high priest and necromancer, obviously proud at sharing this moment with his goddess, led the way onto the balcony; the prince and princess, and their guards, followed. The air was brisk and cold, and there was a slight spray from the clouds just above. Mogra's tawny body gleamed.

As always, hundreds of dragons circled the upper reaches of Krogbur, serving as an aerial moat and a constant watch. They did not fly quite this high, but circled about the tower somewhat further down. Baleron supposed they would be sent off with the Army upon its departure; after all, that was one of Krogbur's main functions: to serve as a doorway by which the Hell-Worms could cross over.

Baleron gasped when he glimpsed the army below. Beyond the bright reach of the Inferno, it stretched from the Black Tower's roots all the way to the foothills of the distant mountains. Bonfires glittered like the stars. The host was endless. It was comprised of many races, he knew, from Borchstog to Man, from

Spider to Troll to corrupted Giant, and many others, besides. There were even a few hulking Colossi standing about. The titans shielded large numbers of soldiers from the rain. There must be millions of troops, Baleron thought. No resource of the Crescent —or the world—could resist it.

Mogra had conjured several images of herself down below; larger than life, she stood a hundred or more feet tall in various places amongst the army; Baleron saw that these images rose from bonfires and were made of flame. Sparks danced high, and smoke seemed to rise from her gold-flecked heads.

The Borchstogs looked both at her real form, far above, and at these images, which showed her exactly as she was, but taller and forged of fire. Some Borchstogs were on their hands and knees in worship. Some tossed bound sacrifices atop the pyres. Some leapt atop the fires themselves.

"Do you love me?" Mogra shouted again.

The roar that followed staggered Baleron.

Mogra smiled wider, enjoying this, basking in their worship.

"You are my children!" she said. "Each and every one of you. And it is you, my children, who will bring down our enemies and unleash us from this prison!"

They roared so savagely that Rolenya cast a worried glance at her brother. "*This* is the shape of the future?" she asked in a whisper. "*These* are the ones to inherit the earth?" She shook her head bitterly, wincing at the thought.

The Spider Goddess's hearing was excellent.

"You don't like my children?" she asked, breaking off from her speech and half turning.

Rolenya visibly summoned her courage, tilting her chin up. "As a matter of fact, I do not."

"Good. I will keep that in mind, and if in the future you misbehave I will destroy that pretty new body of yours, as slowly as I care to, and slip your quivering little soul into the body of a Borchstog, or something you find even fouler." She paused, delighting in the repulsed expression on Rolenya's face. "A Spider, perhaps," she added with a wink to Baleron before returning her attention back to her cheering throng. So did her hundred-feet-high images.

"I am Mother to you all," she said. "Love me. Worship me. With every life you take, Man or Elf or Dwarf or other, you honor me. With every town you burn and every field you raze, you give me a gift. I am with you at every turn, and everything you do, you do for me, as well as your Sire. We made you as you are to be the best of the races, the strongest, the most fearsome, and you are. Embrace this. Your Master wove your souls out of his shadow, and I ask you now—no, I demand you—to fling his shadow to all quarters of the world!"

They roared.

"Now your Lord Sire would like to address you. *Are you ready?*"

They clenched their fists above their heads and roared.

She raised her arms again, then stepped back away from the front edge of the terrace and assumed a waiting posture.

The great black figure of Gilgaroth himself strode down the long stairs that led up to his Throne Room, moving with power. Darkness swelled around him, and from it his eyes of fire smoldered. In one hand he carried his long staff. A dark cape fluttered behind him, and a dark helmet masked his head, concealing all save his burning eyes, which seared everything they looked upon. He was even taller than Mogra.

He marched out onto the terrace, right past Baleron—who felt himself unconsciously drawing back and shielding Rolenya with his body—and took up the position Mogra had just vacated. He inclined his head downwards, surveying his army harshly. The Borchstogs exploded, roaring out their love for him, beating on their breasts and pumping their weapons over their heads. The other various beasts and monsters joined in. Baleron could not see all the details, but he could imagine them.

Something at the corner of his eye caught his attention.

Down and to his right was another terrace, not as large, and on it stood none other than the Leviathan. *Ul Mrungona* saw him. They regarded each other warily, smoke issuing from the dragon's nostrils. His wet scales flickered in the lightning-rent night.

I should've known he'd be here, Baleron thought. *Gilgaroth wanted Rolenya and I here—he wanted the chance to gloat—and he wants Throgmar here for the same reason. I'll teach him the price for his arrogance.*

Wordlessly, Throgmar averted his amber eyes from Baleron. He looked from Gilgaroth to Mogra, and Baleron could see dark wheels turning in the Leviathan's mind. *Good*, thought Baleron, then returned his own attention to Gilgaroth, his hand unconsciously clenching into a fist at his side. Almost of their own volition his fingers inched toward Rondthril's handle.

Kill! Kill!

Taking a deep breath, he stilled the troublesome digits and let his right arm hang limply at his side. Rain stung him, and he shivered, suddenly realizing how small and frail he was next to the likes of Gilgaroth.

"My army," said the Dark One. His image too appeared in the bonfires below, looming over the Borchstogs, who would be gazing up at him reverentially. *"You should see yourselves, my sons, my daughters. You look STRONG. Mighty. Stout as stone. Nothing can stand against you. You are the wave that will erode the last bastions of Light. Your purity of essence will be my enemies' undoing. You will go north and crush the siege at Clevaris. You will burn and blacken the Elvish gardens of Larenthi and spread my wrath throughout the kingdoms of the Crescent. Then you will go into the northlands and make them mine at last. We are partly of the same flesh—YOU HAVE MY BLOOD IN YOUR VEINS!—and you will now be the instrument of my ultimate will. And that will is Ruin!"*

They bellowed loudly, gnashing their teeth.

"The Union has kept me pinned behind the walls of my Black Shield for thousands of years, and it shall be you who sets me free. Be proud! Be

strong! Be bold! Strike fear into the hearts of all who do not bow before me. Make this tower the very Heart of the World!"

He clenched a fist and a thousand tongues of lightning flickered out of the clouds and a terrible *boom*! nearly knocked Baleron to his knees. The Borchstogs were so awed they fell silent.

"You will need a leader," Gilgaroth continued in the silence. *"Someone worthy to march you to victory. I must stay here to oversee my various hosts, and to sustain this very tower until it is strong."*

He gestured to the shadows within the Main Hall and a batwinged form materialized from the darkness.

Cautiously, Ungier, former Lord of Gulrothrog, Father of Vampires, late Shepherd of the Flame, stepped onto the terrace. He looked hunched and nervous. His all-black eyes darted here and there in suspicion. They found Baleron and he sneered nastily. Then they shifted to Rolenya, and a strangely sweet smile crossed his face, though he acted no less nervously. He seemed to sense something amiss.

Hope fluttered in Baleron's chest at the vampire's unease, but he tried not to let it rise too high. Rolenya clasped his hand, her grip tighter than she probably intended. She was getting anxious.

Giving her an encouraging look, he slowly disengaged his hand so that it would be free.

Gilgaroth held out his own hand and the Vampire King made his way past prince, princess, Borchstogs and mother to his Master's side. He stood there uncomfortably, gazing down on the endless rows of troops.

"This is Ungier," said Gilgaroth to his army. *"One of my favorite and most powerful sons."*

The Borchstogs started to cheer the Lord of Ungoroth, and Ungier smiled hesitantly. The meager hope in Baleron's chest began to die.

But then Gilgaroth swept his arm flatly and the Borchstogs fell silent. Ungier's smile withered.

"I gave him an order—to take Havensrike in my name," Gilgaroth

said. *"And so he captured Glorifel, the shining jewel of Man. But in his arrogance he sought REWARD for his labors. More than this, he asked the one gift that I could not give. And when I would not give it, he in secret tried to take it by force."* His voice grew gravelly with rage. *"For that he shall suffer, and YOU shall bear witness to the working of my justice."*

Ungier's face turned gray. Judging from the expression, he had half suspected something like this was going to happen.

Mogra looked surprised, even fearful. Her mouth opened, as if about to say something, but then she closed it.

"It was a mistake!" Ungier cried. He pointed an accusing, trembling finger at Rolenya. "She ensnared me! She's a witch! She's ensnared you, too, Sire. Don't you understand? Shut your ears to her. Do not listen to her songs. Cast her aside!"

Gilgaroth regarded him stonily. *"And ... give her to YOU?"*

Ungier swallowed. "Not necessarily, no. But maybe. Perhaps if—"

"Silence!"

The vampire looked to Mogra for aid. "Mother, help!"

She looked regretful. "I would aid you, if I could, Ungier, but for one thing: you challenged your Father in combat. You would have slain him if you could, and for what—*her*? I'm sorry, my son, but I cannot save you this time."

Finally! thought Baleron. Though rejoicing at Ungier's downfall, however, he almost pitied the vampire. To have risen so high and to have fallen so low, and for a love that Baleron could understand—

With sudden movement, Gilgaroth wrapped an armored hand about Ungier's waist and hefted him high off the rain-soaked balcony. Ungier's claw-tipped feet scratched at the empty air, and his batwings flapped uselessly.

"You erred, Ungier," Gilgaroth said. *"Once at Gulrothrog, when you jeopardized my most important spider—"* (his helmeted head indicated Baleron) *"—and again by asking me to give you my most treasured posses-*

sion as a reward for a task whose only reward was my love. My love was not enough, so now you will be cast out of it forevermore."

Ungier struggled in his father's grip, but his powers had been removed and he was helpless. "Forgive me!" he pleaded. "She's a witch! She mesmerized me! She's mesmerized you! Mogra, save me!"

But Mogra kept silent. She may have hated Rolenya, and she may have suspected the princess had some hold over her sons, but she was loyal to Gilgaroth and would not speak against him in this, no matter her private misgivings.

Shaking, Ungier cried, "Father, forgive me! Please!"

"Forgive?"

"Mercy!" Ungier's battish face screwed up in misery. His all-black eyes looked very large. "Mercy, Father!"

"What IS this ... 'mercy'?"

The Dark One pinched one of the vampire's wings with his free hand. He paused, savoring his son's fear, then he tore the leathery wing loose with a spray of blood. Ungier cried out in agony.

Rolenya gasped and turned her face away.

"No!" shouted Ungier, writhing, leaking black blood.

"Yes," said Gilgaroth, flicking the batwing away; it drifted on the wind and was soon snatched up by a passing dragon. The Lord of the Tower nodded to the throng below. *"You have drunk the blood of many over the centuries, my son. Now it is time to give back."*

"Don't do this!" screamed the vampire.

It was too late. Gilgaroth drew back his arm and, with a mighty heave, flung the godling from the terrace. The Vampire King spun end over end, howling as he fell. It seemed to Baleron that for a moment time seemed to slow, and Ungier's all-black eyes glared briefly at him for the last time, then passed on to Rolenya. His eyes lingered on her lovingly before his face twisted in terror at the fall to come, and he disappeared over the side.

JACK CONNER

Baleron, and everyone else on the terrace save Gilgaroth, leaned over the edge to see what would become of him.

With his one wing, Ungier tried to master the air. He spiraled down, down and around, flapping that one appendage pitifully.

He would not go easily. As he fell, the vampire passed various prominences that jutted out from the tower overlooking the Great Inferno, and on some dragons lounged. Others were mere decorative spikes. Desperately, almost comically, Ungier flapped his wing, angling himself toward one of these prominences.

He nearly missed it. As it was, his long arms reached out and just barely grabbed hold of a nightmarish gargoyle with his nimble claws, jerking him to a halt. Visibly trembling, he huddled there, safe for the moment.

The Borchstogs roared in thwarted bloodlust.

"The fool!" hissed Mogra. "Can he not even die with dignity?"

Ungier hugged the prominence, trembling, trying to fold himself up and merge with the brooding architecture. He looked down into the bright flames of the Inferno, then up at the terrace high above, then around him.

He issued a high-pitched whistle.

A nearby terrace held the nests of a brood of glarums, and one rose and took wing, flying toward the Vampire King. Ungier might actually escape!

Baleron glanced toward the towering shadow that was Gilgaroth, but Gilgaroth did not move. *He's letting Ungier go.* Baleron, unable to believe this, ground his teeth.

The glarum approached Ungier's prominence. In another few seconds, the vampire would be away.

"I think not," said Baleron.

He wrenched a crossbow loose from one of his guards and aimed at the dark, small, lanky figure of Ungier. The vampire was a long way down, through rain and night, but Baleron did not hesitate. He sighted along the lethal bolt and fired.

The shaft flew. Just as the glarum neared the prominence to

which Ungier hung, the bolt struck the pitiful figure in the side, and the speck that was Ungier lost its hold and fell toward the hungry flames. The glarum veered away and returned to its roost.

The Borchstog reclaimed its crossbow with a snarl, raising its hand as if to strike Baleron but seeming to think better of it.

Ungier, clutching the bolt that protruded from his ribs, still flapping that one wing, head thrown back in a scream, plummeted toward his doom, and Rolenya clung so tightly to Baleron's arm that her fingers dug painfully into his flesh. Baleron watched Ungier's plummet with grim satisfaction, feeling a swell of pride— not pride for himself or his marksmanship, but pride for Rolenya. He had tried and failed many times to kill Ungier; Elvish sorcerers and a queen had been unable to tame Rondthril; the Archmage of Havensrike had likewise failed. It had taken Rolenya to destroy the vampire, and that without even trying.

"There!" shouted Gilgaroth to his army as Ungier sailed down, as if Ungier being shot had been of his doing. *"THERE is my gift to you! His blood—and his example! Do not fail me as he did, or suffer his fate you will."*

At long last, Ungier passed into the fires of Illistriv and burst into flames. He screamed, audible for miles around. Shrouded in fire, screaming hideously, he disappeared into the depths of the Second Hell, never to be seen again.

Baleron's heart sang with joy.

He instantly felt a change in Rondthril; the Fanged Blade seemed to sigh, as if with release.

The time has come.

Below, Borchstogs cheered the execution.

Mogra smiled lovingly. "Eager, aren't they?"

Baleron was just about to pull Rondthril from its scabbard when suddenly Gilgaroth turned and did something unaccountably odd: he reached out a hand and ... beckoned ... to Baleron.

Shocked, the prince just looked at Gilgaroth. What was this?

"Come," said the Dark One.

Was Baleron to meet the same fate as Ungier? Is this how his own labors would be rewarded? Rolenya shot him a worried look, and he tried to put on a brave face for her.

"It will be fine," he told her.

She didn't seem able to bring herself to speak.

Again Gilgaroth beckoned for him to come to his right side, and Baleron did so, immediately feeling the heat that radiated off *ul Kunraggog*. Gilgaroth's smell was overpowering, even more so than Mogra's—the musk of the Great Wolf mixed with brimstone and burning coal. Gilgaroth's living shadow billowed and ebbed, Baleron could *feel* it, cold and hot at once, oily, *penetrating* ... He felt befouled by it, and powerless under its influence.

He stood at the right side of Gilgaroth, Breaker of the World, Prince of Darkness, Lord of Hell, and stared down at the Inferno of the world-bound Illistriv and at the bonfires of the Borchstog hordes that would help the Inferno spread. Wind whipped him, and he shivered. His image appeared in the fires below. He looked very small next to Gilgaroth. *What am I doing here?*

To the horde, Gilgaroth said, *"THIS, children, is my Deliverer. My Savior. My Champion. My Spider—he whom I laid a Doom upon years ago. I planted a seed then, and now it has arisen into a mighty oak and gives me shelter. With his Doom Baleron has helped destroy his country's own army and that of the Larenth. He helped me fell the White Tower of Celievsti. Thus was I able to both raise Krogbur and breach the Wall of Spires. He has helped me kill Felias and Elethris and the Archmage of Glorifel—even King Grothgar, his own father. And his Doom is not yet complete, not while I live. For his web shall CONTINUE to grow, and it shall be more glorious yet."*

He paused, and Baleron felt his insides wrench. *No,* he thought desperately. *Let it be over!*

"Ungier was not fit to lead you," Gilgaroth said to his horde. *"He*

was not worthy." He paused dramatically. "*It shall be BALERON who leads you!* Ul Ravast"

Baleron gasped. Rolenya did likewise.

Below, the Borchstogs cheered. Some took up the chant, "RA-VAST! RA-VAST!"

"*Ten thousand years ago I foresaw that one from among the Fallen Race would deliver me my freedom, would serve as the general to lead my armies in the Final War. That time has come. It shall be HE whom I make General tonight. HE will lead you north to crush Clevaris and Larenthi, and then he will drive you onwards, and under his rule you shall raze the Crescent entire. And then go north, darkening all in your path, to the very Tower of the Sun.*"

Baleron's blood ran cold. Throgmar was right: Gilgaroth truly lived only to cause pain and suffering. Oh, he was evil! He would take the one who hated him most and force that one to spread his evil for him.

Suddenly Baleron decided that he would take no more.

Speaking past the knot in his throat, he said, "I will *not.*"

Gilgaroth looked down at him, curious.

Baleron fingered Rondthril. Could he be quick enough? Unlikely. Not when those eyes of fire were upon him. Not while that shadow was touching him.

"*You WILL,*" the Dark One said. "*And you will do it well. For your Doom still binds you, and it is entwined about your very soul. It will give you no choice. It will prompt you to carry out my will, even when you are unwilling or unaware.*" He paused. "*You thought to shake it when you went to the White Tower, but that only furthered my designs. You thought to rid yourself of it when you hacked off your hand and went to rescue your father, but that only freed Rauglir and brought him within striking distance of the King. You thought to fight me at every turn, but I was ready. I have planned this for Ages, Baleron. Every step and counter-step. There is nothing you can do to thwart me. You are mine. And I look forward to seeing you spread my shadow.*" He breathed contentedly. "*Yes, I will send you out to do my will, and I will keep Rolenya here to await your return. Rolenya, my little songbird. She will amuse me in your absence.*"

Baleron trembled in rage. "You have whole kingdoms at your disposal, and this is the only way you can amuse yourself? You're mad! Mad!" He breathed heavily. He felt his face flush with rage.

Gilgaroth said nothing. He seemed to be enjoying this.

"But fine!" Baleron said. "Give me control of your largest, most fearsome army. Give *me* your legions of Borchstogs, your Colossi, your dragons. Give me all your weapons and power, and then we will have us a show. If it's amusement you want, Gilgaroth, then I can amuse. Will you find your death amusing? Will you find Mogra's? What about the fall of this tower? Will you be laughing then? I will. Oh, yes. I think it's a fine idea. A fine idea indeed. Give me this army. Give it to me now! I demand it!"

Gilgaroth's flaming eyes were smiling. *"Such rage in one so small! There is life in you yet. Good. You will make better sport that way."*

"Sport? I can give you sport. If that's all you wanted, I wish you'd told me years ago."

"I enjoy a challenge. Yet it would go easier for you if you realized the place of Man in this world. You belong at my side, Baleron, not before me in the ranks of my enemies. No. Men are my creatures. Do you not see? You are animals, and base. You have no Grace. You have no purpose, save to follow your whims, to find food and shelter. You are like rats, vermin. You are Fallen, and you are beasts. You have no purpose. There is no reason to your being. You ... do not matter."

"If we're so base, why do you want us at your side?"

"Because it does not have to be that way. You can CHOOSE to have a purpose. You can fulfill your potential. You can fight for me. You CAN matter."

"Then it seems to me that we can matter by standing against you."

"And aid the Elves? Why? To prop up their weakness so that they can survive my wrath and continue standing in the Light while you stand

outside them in the Dark, shivering and cold, hungry and empty? Why? Why, when you can stand with ME and have the world at your mercy?"

"You have no mercy! I think you've demonstrated that very clearly."

"I can give you power and purpose and meaning. You, Baleron, you are in a unique position, to take up my offer and raise your kind out of the mire. You are now the King of Havensrike, or you can be if I allow Havensrike to endure. All kingdoms of Men can be united under your rule. You can be the King of Men, and you can lead your people under my banner. You will have purpose. Your race will have meaning. How does that sound, Spider?"

Baleron scowled up at Gilgaroth. He felt the Beast's influence on his mind, but Gilgaroth did not seem to be tampering with his thoughts, only monitoring them. He wanted Baleron to reach the obvious conclusion on his own.

Gilgaroth's offer was tempting, but Baleron would have been surprised if it were not. That was the Dark One's game, after all.

Baleron shook his head.

"The thing about having no purpose," he said, "no reason for being, is that we must make our own. That is our gift, and our curse. *I* have made it my purpose to destroy you and your evil, and I'd rather exist without purpose than to have it be to serve your ends, you cancer." He looked all about him. "See these dragons flying about? They're the flies that buzz around a hill of dung, and this tower is that dunghill, and those demons down there chanting your name, they're the little maggots that thrive on excrement, and that's what you are, you monster—the Lord of Excrement!"

Mogra, a scream on her lips, stalked towards him, but Gilgaroth laid an arm across her way and said, *"No. He has made his decision, my Queen, and in so doing he has damned his race to serve as slaves and food and sport for our own children. He has ensured that Man will fall even further, and eventually cease to exist."*

"He has insulted us!" she said.

"*No. He has insulted himself by speaking such folly. I gave him the chance to raise men up from the muck of their existence, and he chose to spit on my hand instead. Let him live. Let him see the results of his choice first-hand, even as he drives the engine of our victory himself, a slave, just like the rest of his people will soon become.*"

She nodded, still breathing hard, and relaxed.

To Baleron, Gilgaroth said, "*Return to your place, you fool.*"

Steaming in fury, Baleron returned to the ranks of Borchstogs and to his sister's side. Ustagrot was glaring at him, and Rolenya was looking at him with wide eyes.

"Are you all right?" she whispered.

"Oh, I'm just fine," he answered, but he could hear his voice and it sounded anything but fine.

"Baleron. I'm ... I'm so proud of you. You were strong."

He wasn't so proud. Had he just damned mankind? He had, he knew—if Gilgaroth should live.

Gilgaroth was guiding Mogra forwards. When she was at his side, the Lord of the Tower returned his attention to his gathered army. "*I will not let Baleron lead you alone. Oh, no. He lacks experience, and clearly respect, and you deserve better. Therefore I appoint Queen Mogra to guide the young prince, the young Heir, to tutor him in the arts of war. I'm sure they will make an ... interesting team. The Seamstress of Shadows, the Keeper of the Womb of Power—SHE shall oversee your General, my Champion, and ultimately it is SHE who will lead you to victory.*"

The Borchstog hordes roared fervently, and Mogra smiled, showing her fangs. The Dark One had an armored arm about her waist, and two of hers rested on his back.

The two Dark Gods—mother and son, husband and wife, father and mother of demons—stood there at the brink of the terrace overlooking their hordes, their children. They were at the apex of their power, the height of their success. They stood, side by side, the wind whipping them, rain lashing them, lightning illuminating them, basking in the worship of their creatures, creatures who at any moment would be given the order to go north, to sweep all opposition aside, to bring ruin to the world.

What was Baleron waiting for? The two gods' backs were turned; he'd get no better chance than this.

But if he acted, there could be no going back.

If he did nothing, he and Rolenya could yet wed and live out their lives, immortals both, as the rulers of some distant land—at least, after he finished playing general; the notion was not unattractive. Indeed, he longed for it, for spending eternity with his beloved.

He placed his hand on Rondthril's hilt.

Coldness exploded in his chest. Icy tendrils shot out from it and drove deep into his soul, into his mind.

You fool! he heard in his head. *Slaying Gilgaroth is impossible. You'll only earn his wrath. If you think the plight of humans will be grim now, just wait!*

It was a strong voice, a voice that brooked no argument, a voice that boomed so loudly within him that there was not room for any other.

And yet one came. It was not so loud, for it was not woven over eons with the power of a god, but it was no less strong, and it said, *No.*

Baleron said *No.*

He thought of the Flower of Itherin and tried to summon its might, if any still remained within him. He felt it stir.

The explosion of ice shrieked and writhed, and that freezing tendril withered. The Flower could not kill the coldness, but it could distract it while he did what he needed to do.

Baleron stepped forward and drew Rondthril with a glorious ring. The battle still raged within him, but he ignored it.

Time seemed to slow.

His guards were so entranced at being this close to their Lord and Lady at such a momentous occasion that they did not immediately notice their prisoner's movements. Only Ustagrot felt something amiss, and he looked over his shoulder, just in time to see the Fanged Blade coming around in a bright, steely arc—

Baleron cut off the necromancer's head with savage glee, and the head and body fell in separate directions. The neck stump spouted a geyser of black blood as the body fell.

Hearing the prince's voice with godly hearing, the Dark One himself began to turn around. Lightning sizzled behind him, and rain beat on his black, spiked armor. His veil of shadow deepened, and from it his eyes burned redly. He was huge, a towering god against a puny mortal.

As soon as Baleron completed the arc that severed Ustagrot's head, he reversed his grip on Rondthril, holding it by the blade in his naked hand, slicing into his tender flesh. He grit his teeth and drew the sword over his head, cocking his arm for the throw that would determine the fate of the world.

The Dark One had half spun around when Baleron released the sword. Rondthril spun, end over end, flashing in the night, spitting tongues of lightning reflected off of its steely surface. Rain lashed it.

Rolenya's blue eyes widened.

The Borchstog guards wheeled on Baleron, but their attention was so fixed on the flying sword that they did not immediately attack him, giving him the chance to wrench a blade loose of its owner's grasp. His hand bled freely.

Mogra still faced the worshipful horde, basking in their love and awe.

Throgmar had seen movement on the terrace and had witnessed Ustagrot's decapitation without stirring. When he saw Rondthril hurled towards his father, he could have sent a lance of flame to incinerate the sword or knock it off course, but he did not. Baleron had not thought he would; after all, he was the Betrayer.

Rondthril flew ...

Rolenya gasped. She'd known this would happen, but it still seemed to come as a surprise to her.

Baleron, who'd been planning his next steps while listening to Mogra's and Gilgaroth's speeches, slashed out with his new weapon, spearing a Borchstog through the throat. With a boot, he kicked another off the terrace. Yet even *his* eyes were fixed on Rondthril!

Gilgaroth was nearly fully turned around when the Fanged Blade struck him, and he had one arm half-raised. If the sword had struck that arm, it might have been deflected, and Baleron's plan would have failed utterly.

Instead, Rondthril, the Fanged Blade, pierced the Dark One's armor at the chest and drove through the Shadow's corporeal body with mindless hunger. It impaled Gilgaroth through the black heart and buried itself all the way to the hilt so that its tip, dripping black blood, stuck out below the Omkaroggen's left shoulder blade.

Gilgaroth, the Dark One, the Wolf, the Shadow, threw back his head and roared. His living shadow began to thin. The tower shook, and the terrace trembled.

Mogra began to turn around, her violet eyes widening.

Light, reddish gold light, poured from Gilgaroth's wounds, as if the very fires of the Second Hell were being let out, and perhaps they were. Indeed, seconds later a plume of flame shot out from around Rondthril's hilt and another from around its tip. The Dark One's inner fires were being loosed. When he opened his mouth to scream, more red-gold light poured out.

The tower trembled violently.

Baleron could not believe it. It had worked! His plan had worked! It crossed his mind that in a way Ungier, even in death, had finally struck at his father. Baleron silently thanked the souls of Logran and Elethris for preparing him, for giving him hope.

Gilgaroth just stood there, roaring, as flame jetted from his wounds. His armored hands gripped Rondthril's handle ... and tried to pull it out.

Baleron blinked. *No*, he thought. *Gods, no ...*

Gilgaroth still lived. Ungier was not mighty enough to craft a weapon that could slay his father.

Baleron had been a fool.

While Gilgaroth tried to remove Rondthril, Mogra turned about to face the prince, and lightning danced in her eyes.

Chapter Fifteen

Baleron did not, could not, stop in his fight with the Borchstogs. He slashed one across the face. Hurled another from the terrace. He dodged one heavy axe, which *thunk*ed into the chest of another, spraying blood. He tackled the one who had struck at him and flung him from the terrace. The Borchstog screamed as he fell.

Baleron turned to fight the next one.

This was a battle he knew to be futile and pointless—there was a whole *army* against him, plus two gods!—yet he could not just surrender. He could not just die.

As he parried the thrust of a Borchstog's sword, sweat flying from his hair, his face contorted in a grimace of concentration, part of his mind reflected that soon he would be with Salthrick, burning in the fires of Illistriv forevermore.

Rolenya, seeing the desperateness of their plight, picked up the sword of a fallen Borchstog. She was far from a trained fighter, but she was motivated.

A gaggle of Borchstogs clamored around Baleron, who was

fending them off breathlessly, weaving his sword in a fury of bright, bloody arcs and thrusts.

One Borchstog sword embedded itself accidentally in another Borchstog's head, and Baleron kicked the body away. Rolling, he knocked another of the hellspawn off its feet. His sword darted up, spearing another through the gut. He fought as if a man possessed, though surely it was quite the opposite.

The soldiers ignored Rolenya. She determined to teach them that this was unwise.

Gritting her teeth, she plunged her blade into the side of one of the Borchstogs battling Baleron. The Borchstog gasped, spasmed on the end of her sword, and slumped to the floor. She yanked at her weapon, trying to pull it free, but it seemed to be stuck; it had lodged between two ribs.

She grunted, trying to pull it loose. Cold rain lashed her, pasting her dress to her skin. Blood from the Borchstog had sprayed her, and she felt sick.

Mogra turned from Baleron to her beloved, Rondthril still sticking from his breast. He needed her attention. She gripped Rondthril's handle and pulled. Reluctantly, as if it had been feasting on his essence and was not quite sated, it moved, and at last she pulled it free. A gout of flame licked from the wound, then subsided.

The goddess stared at the sword's black-blooded, smoking length, while her Son, her Husband, leaned against her for support.

"How could this happen?" she demanded, then frowned. "This is Ungier's blade."

With a moan, Gilgaroth said, *"Treachery."*

Infuriated, she flung the Fanged Blade at Baleron, but he was rolling on the floor locked in combat with a Borchstog, and the sword missed him, bounced off the terrace, and skipped into the interior of the Main Hall.

Mogra screamed in rage. Her eyes fell on Rolenya.

The scream curdled Rolenya's blood, and she shivered at the hate in the Spider Queen's voice.

She turned to see Gilgaroth, one hand over his punctured heart, sink heavily to his knees. The other hand tore his helmet loose from his shadow-veiled head.

Rolenya succeeded at last in jerking her sword free from the Borchstog and turned to face the dying Gilgaroth, if dying he was, the one who had both killed her and raised her from the dead, the one who had presided over her many afterlives—the one who'd eaten her, savaged her, threatened her, and loved her, and listened enraptured as she sang.

Gilgaroth's eyes stabbed into her. He became her entire world. The sounds of battle faded, and she no longer felt the rain on her skin.

"*Rolenya,*" he said, shaping the word as though it were a foreign delicacy. He said it as though he were a lover betrayed, and indeed she felt a pang of guilt.

She pushed his influence away, though it took all her effort. Behind her, she could hear the surviving Borchstogs continue to slice at Baleron, who must still be rolling about on the floor, but she could tell from the sounds of metal on metal that their weapons were striking the terrace, not him.

Rolenya wanted to help him, but she found her eyes irresistibly drawn back to Gilgaroth. His flaming gaze bound her to the spot.

"*My songbird ... Did you know?*"

"I ... I ..." She could not get the words out. For some reason, part of her actually felt *bad* about betraying Gilgaroth. She had to shake herself. "You're evil!" she said. "You're an abomination!

You're the enemy of everything I could ever love. *Now lay down and die!"*

He howled in anguish.

"This cannot be," said Mogra.

"But it is!" the princess said. "Your time is *over*."

A terrible wrath seized Mogra as she fully comprehended the enormity of the events around her, and she stepped forward, fuming in her anger, toward Rolenya, who still held her sword, though limply, in her hands.

Rolenya dropped the weapon in her fright, and it clattered to the slick stone. Stifling a cry, she fell back before the advance of the Omkarog. There was no way she could win. She was dead.

Mogra's shadow fell over her. The goddess opened her mouth as if to release a roar but instead webbing flew out from the back of her throat and shot through the air; the sticky strands knocked Rolenya to the terrace and bound her there. The princess struggled, but the silk was too strong.

The air flickered and Mogra shifted forms, changing into the giant arachnid form of the Spider Goddess. The platform was more than large enough to accommodate her. Now twenty-five or thirty feet tall, an undefeatable monster whose hulking shape blotted out the electric-ribboned clouds above, she stalked towards the princess.

Rolenya struggled against the web, and it tore, but not enough.

One of Mogra's eight legs lifted high and poised over her, ready to spear her to the floor.

Rolenya felt the blood drain from her face. She waited for Gilgaroth to stop his bride before her fury could spell an end to his songbird, but he just stared at Rolenya with his eyes of flame, the eyes of a lover betrayed.

Mogra paused with her leg over the she-elf, waiting for something.

"Yes," Gilgaroth hissed to her, granting her permission.

If a spider could smile, she did so. "At last!" she said. "I've wanted this since the first day I saw you, Rolenya, infecting my spawn with your ... *Grace*." She spat the last word nastily, as though it were an insult, and perhaps to her it was.

Rolenya, who had died many times already, prepared herself for it yet again. It was always painful, and always horrible, and this time she did not expect to be remade. This ... was it.

Mogra's leg started to descend.

"NO," said a voice from above, and the long jointed limb paused.

For suddenly Throgmar was there.

The vast Worm had lifted off his balcony and flown up to the scene of battle, eyes locked on the mother who'd worked against him, who'd seduced him and used him to further her master's ends. He had expected such behavior from Gilgaroth, but not from her, the one who had brought him into this world and invested so much power in him, coddled him and raised him to believe in his own grandeur.

Baleron had been right, it pained Throgmar to admit. He had brooded on the prince's words for days and saw the bitter truth of it. Now, thanks again to Baleron, he had a chance to act, and he would take it.

Mogra had used him and betrayed him, and for that she would pay.

Mogra's great black bulk swiveled to face the approaching dragon.

"Don't you *dare*!" she said.

His claws dug into her back and with a mighty pump of his wings he wrenched her loose from the balcony, lifting her up into the air. Rolenya watched, awed and grateful, as they receded toward the clouds, Mogra thrashing in Throgmar's grip all the way, but Rolenya did not stop in her efforts to tear loose of the white shroud.

"YOU USED ME!" Throgmar cried, high above. "*YOU WERE FELESTRATA!*"

"Fool!" the Spider Goddess snapped. "Of *course* I was! *Now set me down or I will break you!*"

She twisted, wrapping her eight legs about him, and her wicked fangs sank into his chest, injecting him with her venom. He bellowed in pain. The two dwindled with distance.

Gilgaroth, clearly enraged, clenched a fist and a dozen tongues of lightning stabbed into Throgmar, who shuddered and began to lose altitude, his scales smoking. His wings stopped beating, and he spiraled down and down. Then suddenly, his wings beat once, then twice, and Rolenya breathed a sigh of relief.

Gilgaroth made another fist, but this time only one tongue of lightning struck down, and it missed its target. Rolenya did not know if Gilgaroth were truly dying, but he was weakened.

Throgmar, smoking, still bearing his eight-legged burden, began once more to fly away.

"*I WILL FIND YOU!*" Gilgaroth roared at the dragon, or perhaps to Mogra, Rolenya wasn't sure.

Panting, he tore off the last piece of armor on his torso, revealing his wounds, and as Rolenya looked on in wonder he changed shapes as well, assuming the black, sinuous form of the Shadowdragon, perhaps a hundred feet or more long and, in a strange way, beautiful to look upon. He was exotic and wild, and full of power. Fires still poured from his twin injuries in great founts, one from his breast and one from his back.

Angry but weak, he slithered toward Rolenya. Flame licked his lips and between his sharp teeth. His eyes blazed with fury.

"No!" she cried, ripping away the last of the spider-silk.

The tower shook and pieces of it began to crumble off. She started as a gargoyle broke at her feet. What was this? The terrace rocked beneath her. She saw then what must be happening: with the waning of Gilgaroth's power, Krogbur was beginning to fall apart.

Weakened or not, Gilgaroth still looked quite lethal to her as he loomed over her. Desperate, she looked over her shoulder to Baleron. By then, he'd dealt with all the Borchstogs who had not fled at the appearance of the Leviathan and was breathing heavily on the floor, regaining what energy he could. He bled from a score of cuts, and the blood mixed with the rainwater all about. His dark hair was plastered to his skull, and he looked exhausted both mentally and physically, but his dark blue eyes still burned with determination.

She heard the rasp of black scales and, very slowly, turned to face Gilgaroth. She could feel his heat and smell his musk. In fear of her life, she skittered back on her hands and feet, slipping on the wet surface.

"Out of my way!" he bellowed.

She saw that she was directly between him and Baleron, and she knew that this was exactly the wrong place to be if she wanted to survive the next few moments. Gilgaroth wanted to roast Baleron where he lay, but for some reason he was unwilling to slay Rolenya to accomplish it. He may have given Mogra permission to kill her, but it seemed he could not do the deed himself. No matter how much he hated Rolenya, the echoes of her songs still played in his heart.

Her songs had worked! She'd woven her own web, this one of Light and Grace, and she had woven it well. Now Gilgaroth was bound to her, at least a little.

He tried to slip past her. She had to act fast.

Shakily, she rose to her feet. The terrace still shook beneath her, but on bare feet she stood firm. Gathering her courage, she planted herself between her beloved and Gilgaroth.

As commandingly as she could, she looked into the Dark One's eyes and told him, *"No."*

At the roots of the tower, beyond the Inferno, a great panic went up among the Borchstogs and the other races that comprised the army, and the host stirred nervously. They had seen the images of their Lord getting pierced by Rondthril, and fear ran through them unchecked. Huge chunks of Krogbur began to rain down on them, killing many. Their formations began to break up.

The ground shook and split, and the rivers of lava that ran nearby began to rise. Lightning flashed erratically. Thunder rolled.

The Inferno itself started leaping fitfully. It spread outwards, consuming whole battalions of Borchstogs. Worse, it began *climbing the tower*. The fire was burning Krogbur, eating into its ebon face, and the flames rapidly ascended towards the highest terrace.

Baleron, still on his back, had not actually expected to live this long. Perhaps he'd get another chance at Gilgaroth, after all.

All around him, the tower shook and trembled, and pieces of it fell away. The weakened Gilgaroth was not strong enough to focus his energies on keeping it stable, and it was disintegrating. Baleron could hear the roaring of the Inferno that wreathed the lower half of the tower roar louder, growing out of control. The dragons of the aerial moat that protected Krogbur were going mad. Their circles took them closer and closer to the terrace on which the Dark One lay; yet they hesitated to send out their flame for fear of harming their already wounded Master.

On the terrace, Gilgaroth slithered towards Baleron, trying to go around Rolenya, but she determinedly blocked his path, again and again, stamping her bare feet.

"Be gone!" Gilgaroth commanded her.

Stubbornly, she refused. Baleron was impressed by his sister's courage and conviction, but like Gilgaroth he wanted her to get out of the Dark One's way. It was her only chance.

"Move aside!" he shouted to her, but she pretended not to hear him.

Frustrated, Gilgaroth prepared to loose his flame, killing brother and sister together in one deadly blast. He drew in a deep breath and started to let it out, air shimmering around his maw.

Baleron closed his eyes. The end had come.

Rolenya suppressed her panic, despite the fact that Gilgaroth was about to incinerate her where she stood, and Baleron behind her. And afterwards the Dark One would doubtlessly retreat into the depths of Krogbur, to the Black Temple, and there be healed.

She had only one choice.

Summoning all her courage and drowning all her fears, she took a deep breath, closed her eyes, raised her face to the skies and reached deep down inside her, where she found her strength, found that spring of Light, and, tapping it, did the only thing she could do.

She sang.

The sound poured out of her, woven with the innumerable strands of gathered Light, and washed across the terrace, rolling like a wave of white fire over Gilgaroth.

The flames died in his mouth.

He moaned.

Baleron, eyes still closed, heard the opening notes of the song and wrinkled his brow in confusion. He'd expected to be roasted alive where he lay, but instead ... music. Sweet, lovely music.

He opened his eyes.

Before him, facing the long black length of the Lord of the Tower, Rolenya in her torn white dress was singing. A beautiful series of notes cascaded from her, and, to Baleron's shock, Gilgaroth's fiery eyes dimmed ... began to close.

Rolenya's voice rolled on, mesmerizing the Dark One.

Baleron stared. Where had she grown so powerful? Gilgaroth lay there on the terrace, full of a seething wrath, yet too enchanted to move.

Baleron, too, felt roots growing.

Inside the tower, Gilgaroth's creatures went mad. Their Master was an ever-present force in their minds, and now that force was full of fire and pain and chaos. Some Borchstogs fell on each other. Some slew themselves. Some banged themselves against walls. What was more, the interior of Krogbur was trembling and shaking. Collapsing. If not for this, more help would have rushed to Gilgaroth's aid despite the confusion brought about by his pain. Many tunnels were now blocked and help slow to arrive.

Yet there was one being who could navigate such obstructions as a spirit and still take corporeal form when beyond them, one whose reward that was for his service.

He came.

Furious, burning, he came.

Rolenya could feel Light welling up within her like water behind a thin dam and it was all she could do to let it out slowly; she felt that if she released it too quickly she would, like the dam, break apart. The Light would destroy her.

The music felt good. It felt *right*. It made her feel alive just to sing it. All her body tingled and felt aglow, and she gave herself over to it. The notes rose and fell on the brimstone breeze, and Gilgaroth lowered his wolvish head and closed his gaping jaws. Smoke wreathed about his head.

She stepped forward and caressed his face as though she were his mother, his lover—caressed his long jaw, his cheeks, his nose, his forehead. All the while, she sang on.

He fought it, fought *her*, and somehow he found the strength to open his eyes, and she knew she had to open the floodgates a little more. The Light burned her with its power, but she thought she could control it.

His eyes dimmed and shut once more.

Baleron watched on, amazed. Rolenya's song was sometimes white, sometimes silver, sometimes golden, but always it was filled with love and harmony. Rolenya, beautiful Rolenya, had opened the Gates of Paradise with her song, or so it seemed. Dressed in white but stained with blood, she was a shining thorn in a world of darkness. A white light seemed to glow from within her.

Baleron was enraptured. Fortunately the song was not meant for him, and after a few moments he shook himself loose.

He saw what he had to do. The first blow with Rondthril had not been enough. He would have to find the sword and use it again. Ungier was not powerful enough to craft a weapon that could slay his father ... in one stroke. But with two, or many ...

Baleron began to crawl inside, where Mogra had flung Rondthril. He prayed Rolenya could keep the Wolf distracted long enough.

Forcing herself on, Rolenya wove ever greater spells of love and power and binding with her song. Instinct guided her. She only knew about these powers from books and tales—the only experience she'd had using them were during these last few weeks—but she wielded her newfound abilities with all the passion in her heart and all the grace in her being ... and all the desperation of the moment.

Strangely, a large part of her hated to do this to Gilgaroth, he whom she had brought out such gentleness and tenderness in, he who loved her—she knew it. Despite herself, she'd grown to feel almost motherly toward him, and now she abused that trust, twisted it, punished him for it. It sickened her, and she began to cry, tears running down her white cheeks even as she sang, even as she caressed his face, but she sang on. She thought of all the evil he'd committed, all the atrocities done in his name, and that leant strength to her voice.

When she opened her blue eyes, it was as if a blast struck him, and he groaned.

There! Rondthril gleamed in the dark within the Main Hall, near the endless black stairs that led up to the infernal Throne Room. Baleron picked his way towards it, looking back to see if Gilgaroth was still bound by Rolenya's song. He was.

But while the prince watched on, something strange happened. A beam of light broke through the roof of dark clouds above ... *and poured straight into her*. It was as though the Omkarathons, the Light-Bearers, channeled their very power through her. Perhaps they did, Baleron reflected. Perhaps they perceived that this was their moment to act, that Rolenya was their best chance to strike back at the dark powers after all these years. Or perhaps she had simply tuned herself to the goodly energies of the earth and was drawing them up like a plant draws water from the ground—and doing so with such power it stole Baleron's breath to watch it.

All the while, Gilgaroth just lay there lazily, drowsy with imminent death, his lifeblood spilling out onto the terrace and smoking there, his eyes half closed, the ghost of a smile on his whiskered face. Fire still poured from the wounds Rondthril had given him.

Baleron noticed that Rolenya's voice was growing strained. She began swaying a little from side to side, as if about to faint.

Was something wrong? He must hurry.

He wrenched himself loose of the spectacle and crossed into

the shadowed interior of the tower, snatching Rondthril up from the floor. He was amazed at the black blood that coated the blade, and he could feel a hum of joy from the weapon. It had tasted the Shadow's lifeforce and wanted more. Yet it was weary, full and bloated with Gilgaroth's power.

"Just one more strike," he promised it.

He turned back.

Light still channeled into Rolenya, but something was now quite clearly wrong. The power seemed to be too much for her. Perhaps she was too delicate a conduit for such energies, or perhaps she had not had enough experience using them. Either way, it seemed she was using forces she did not fully understand and could not fully control, as the light that suffused her grew so bright and white-hot that a terrible pain filled her; Baleron could see it in her stance and hear it in her voice. The light was eating her up from the inside.

As her voice grew ever more stressed, Gilgaroth's eyes began to open.

Baleron rushed towards her. Before he'd gone five feet, a dark figure emerged from the shadows of the hall where it had been crouched near the archway and blocked his path. Alarmed, Baleron drew back. The hulking beast stood on two legs and had long arms tipped with claws. Long, horn-like ears laid down flat on its wolvish head. The lips of its thrusting snout lifted to reveal terrible fangs, and anger burned in its dark eyes.

"Rauglir!" breathed Baleron.

Dizzy, Rolenya wondered how long she need go on singing. She could not go on much further, she knew. At any moment she could collapse, or worse. It was clear that Baleron's task was incomplete, though, and she had to give him enough time to finish it ... if she could last that long.

Gilgaroth fought her again. His head stirred. His eyes began to open.

Reaching deep inside herself, she opened the floodgates still wider, and her voice rose like the tide. Again it worked, and his eyes half-closed once more. But pain filled her.

Hurry, Baleron! For my sake, hurry!

Murder glittered in the demon's eyes. Venom dripped from his fangs.

"You have gone too far, my love," Rauglir said, his voice an awful growl. "Now you must die."

Baleron glanced over Rauglir's shoulder. When Rolenya turned slightly, he could see that her face was contorted in pain, and her voice was growing more strained by the moment.

Gilgaroth was rousing.

"I don't have time for this," Baleron said.

He rushed Rauglir, Rondthril leading the way. He made as if to skewer the wolf creature through the breast—a feint. Rauglir's long arms swung to knock his thrust aside, but his blade was no longer there. Instead he buried Rondthril in the monster's side. Black blood wept out. Rauglir roared in pain.

A shaggy arm knocked Baleron away. Rondthril stuck in the demon's ribs. Smoke hissed from the wound. With pain-maddened movements, Rauglir ripped the sword free and stared at it even as his own black blood dripped from its length.

"They call it the Fanged Blade," Baleron said, rising.

"It burns," said the beast.

"Good."

"Now it has a new master."

Rolenya's voice washed over Baleron, urging him on. He began to circle around the demon, but Rauglir would not have it. The beast came at him, Fanged Blade flashing, spraying dark blood.

Baleron ducked under Rondthril as it swung at his head.

Rauglir chopped down, meaning to cleave in Baleron's collarbone. The Heir leapt back. Rauglir slashed at his midsection. Baleron dodged, but the Fanged Blade opened a shallow gash on his belly.

Rauglir kept slicing and thrusting, and Baleron evaded desperately.

Gilgaroth's eyes cracked open, and his lips lifted to bare long sharp teeth dripping poison onto the terrace. Flame licked at the back of his throat.

Rolenya was afraid to channel any more power, afraid to open the floodgates wider, but she had no choice. She had to give Baleron more time. She raised her voice and let more Light pour through her. It burned, and she nearly faltered, but Gilgaroth's eyes closed once more.

As the Light welled up within her, scorching her, she continued to sing.

Rondthril struck the floor at Baleron's side, showering sparks. A clawed foot kicked the prince backward. He flew off his feet.

Panting, he stared up at Rauglir from the floor. The demon loomed over him, a towering dark mass of fur and fangs and claws and blazing, furious eyes.

Baleron began to roll aside, but Rauglir was too fast. The same foot that had kicked him now pinned him down. Sharp claws dug into his chest. He struggled, but the demon was too strong. He could not find the air to breathe.

Rauglir raised Rondthril for one final, deadly strike.

"Farewell," he said. Smoke rose from his mouth as he said it.

Baleron swiped his hand across his belly, gathering a handful of blood that leaked from his wound, and flung it up at his enemy. The blood spattered the back of Rauglir's right leg, and Baleron heard the hiss of acid on flesh and smelled the stench of burning fur and skin.

Howling, Rauglir dropped the sword as he stumbled back.

Baleron rolled aside just as Rondthril's blade plunged toward where his face had been just half a second earlier. Then he was picking the weapon up and leaping to his feet.

Rauglir had time to raise one clawed arm, then Baleron was there, thrusting Rondthril up through the demon's chest, right into his heart.

Rauglir's growl died in his throat, and his eyes lost their anger, their fury. Smoke rose up from the wound. Baleron and the demon stood that way for a moment, locked in a mortal embrace, their eyes staring into each other for a long moment.

At last Rauglir slumped and Baleron jerked his blade free. The demon collapsed to the floor in a shaggy, bloody heap, and Baleron spat on Rauglir's corpse.

"That's for my mother," he said.

He saw the smoke rising up from the back of Rauglir's leg and silently thanked Rolenya—and Rauglir himself. If not for the demon's greed, the Flower of Itherin's power would not course through Baleron's blood in the first place.

Rolenya still sang, but her voice was fragile and raw now. He ran towards her just as white smoke began rising from her body.

"Rolenya!" he cried.

Gilgaroth was too enchanted to notice the raggedness of her voice, Rolenya hoped, lulled nearly senseless. Yet if she stopped singing he would rouse.

What was taking Baleron so long? The energies filling her were killing her, she could feel it. She had opened the floodgates too wide, had drawn on powers beyond her skill to handle, and now they were going to consume her. Incredible pain filled her, searing her, and it was all she could do to go on singing.

She had to. For Baleron. For everyone.

The pain rent her voice and made it rough, and then it stole her breath, and she couldn't concentrate on the words. What was happening? Was she really dying? If so, she prayed she would not return to Illistriv.

The pain overwhelmed her. She choked out one final burst, and then the whole world turned to mist. She collapsed in a heap to the wet terrace. White smoke like steam rose from her body.

As soon as the singing stopped, Gilgaroth's eyes snapped open. His horned head lay limply on the floor, but it began to rear up.

Suddenly Baleron was next to it, Rondthril at the ready. He raised the Fanged Blade to strike one last time.

But without Rolenya's voice to keep him spellbound, Gilgaroth was no longer helpless.

Angrily, moaning, he tossed his huge head and knocked Baleron away, then slithered forwards, around Rolenya, towards the archway leading into the Main Hall—and the stairs. The blow nearly flung Baleron over the side of the terrace—doubtlessly that had been Gilgaroth's intention—but as he hit the floor and went sliding on the wet surface, he struck the body of a dead Borchstog, halting his slide just in time.

He glanced down, over the edge of the terrace, and gasped. *The Inferno was consuming Krogbur.* It climbed, even as he watched, the bright red flames licking into the jet black surface, and smoke boiling up in thick sheets. Within minutes the flame would climb to this very terrace.

Baleron glanced back. Gilgaroth was disappearing within the tower. Damn it all! Rolenya had saved their lives and given him enough time to retrieve the sword, but, curse Rauglir, not enough time to use it.

Swearing, Baleron climbed to his feet. A glance at Rolenya showed that she still laid lifeless, white smoke drifting up from her body. His heart twisted violently, and, though it pained him, he knew he did not have time to tend to her.

Reeling from his wounds, he pursued the Dark One as he retreated into his lair, surely going to heal himself in the Black Temple. If he managed to make it there, it would be as if none of this had ever happened. Baleron had to stop him now, stop him and kill him. Now might be the first time Gilgaroth had ever been truly vulnerable, it might be the last, and Baleron knew his window of opportunity would not be open for long—only as long as this stairway was tall, for once Gilgaroth reached his Throne Room with all his servants about, wraiths and Colossi and demons, he would be protected. The only reason others had not rushed to aid their Master yet was the chaos caused by the shaking tower and Gilgaroth's pain.

The Hell-Worm crossed the Main hall and began to slither up the black steps. Dark, smoking blood pooled in his wake, eating into the stairs.

Baleron, cursing, limped after.

Moving with distressing swiftness, Gilgaroth was far ahead of him up the stairs, which seemed endless—in the gloom of the hall, Baleron could not see their top; there must be a thousand steps!—but they would end all too quickly. He staggered upwards.

"I'm coming!" he roared. "You can't run from me!" Breathing hard, blood dripping into his eyes, he said, "But run anyway! Run, Gilgaroth! Run! I want to see you flee!"

He mounted the stairs, one weary step at a time. He tried to avoid stepping on the spilled black blood, hissing on the stone.

Shadows fell on him. Like living pieces of darkness, the wraiths descended in a howling cloud, tearing at Baleron with insubstantial claws. They must have come down from the Throne Room to aid their Master. Ghostly as they were, incredible pain filled Baleron every time they touched him, and he knew they weren't clawing at his flesh, but his *soul*.

He flung his bloody hand at them. The red drops clove

through the half-substantial shadow-bodies, parting them, and the wraiths shrieked in fear and veered away.

Emboldened, Baleron swiped Rondthril against his bloody abdomen, then slicing it at the wraiths, and whenever Rondthril passed through them they wasted away, almost seeming to evaporate. Still they clamored around him, howling and shrieking, tearing at him with their awful claws, but he pressed forward through them, hacking at them as he slogged up one more step. Then another.

Above, the Dark One reached the halfway point, then passed it.

Desperation surged through Baleron. Summoning his last reserve of energy, he sprang up the steps, slicing at wraiths as he went, and at last reached Gilgaroth's tail. With a joyful howl, he stabbed Rondthril through the hard scales and deep inside the Dark One's earthly flesh. He tried to pin Gilgaroth to the stairs, but the stairs were too hard to penetrate, and the Hell-Worm kept going, not even acknowledging the blow with a moan of pain. The blade sliced right through his tail, and fire licked out from the wound.

Gritting his teeth, Baleron followed.

Again he caught up to his enemy, and again he stabbed into Gilgaroth, cursing as he did so.

"Die, you bastard!"

He stabbed, and stabbed again. Black blood sprayed him and he staggered back, nearly toppling. He felt whoozy and sick. *The very blood of the Wolf!* It burned his skin. A weariness came over him, and he almost retched, but something in him fought the poison; he felt the thrumming in his veins. The Flower. He doubted it would be enough to save him, but it would give him time. He had never thought to live beyond this day anyway. *Only let me kill the bastard first.*

He had to hurry. They were nearly to the top now.

Wraiths continued to howl and tear at him, but Baleron had only to fling a few drops of his blood and they scattered.

He rose, though every step seemed like a torture. He had lost too much blood. The world spun and reeled around him.

He saw Sophia and Salthrick; he saw his father and mother; he saw Shelir and Elethris and Celievsti; he saw Felias and Jered; he saw Lunir and Logran and his brothers and all of Glorifel; he saw many others whom Gilgaroth had destroyed. Anger welled up in him, and he marched on.

He caught up to Gilgaroth again and stabbed him, punching through his scales. Gilgaroth hardly noticed. Baleron stabbed again. And again. Rondthril flashed. Thunder shook the tower.

"Die!" Baleron shouted. "Why won't you just die?"

With each strike, fires shot out from the wounds. Baleron knew only vaguely how Gilgaroth and the Second Hell were connected, but they were, one wound about the other, and with every hole Baleron put in the Dark One he seemed to put another in Illistriv.

He struck again and again. Metal flashed. Black blood spurted. Flame shot out. Gilgaroth moaned in pain, but kept mounting the stairs.

As he went, he moved slower ... and slower.

Baleron roared and grunted. Rondthril struck.

"Die!"

As Gilgaroth slowed, Baleron was able to ascend up the Hell-Worm's body, poking holes all through his enemy's length. He slipped on the black blood, got scorched by jetting fires, but he pressed on, all he could hear the thunder of his own heartbeat.

He reached the Dark One's horned and whiskered head.

"Now we come to it," Baleron told him, panting. "Your end is here." He poised the sword so as to drive it through Gilgaroth's eye and into his brain.

Yet Gilgaroth would not be so easily overcome. Suddenly, with one sudden jerk, he reared up and knocked Baleron back. The prince tumbled down a few stairs but caught himself, bracing his weight with Rondthril.

Gilgaroth, eyes flaming as well as body, twisted about and loomed over him.

"Yes," Gilgaroth said. *"Now we come to it. Let me end your Doom, little prince. It is what you have wanted."*

Baleron glared up at him. "It's *king* now. Thanks to you."

The Shadow prepared to strike, to snap up Baleron in his iron jaws and destroy him utterly, but before he could do so the fires that were pouring from his body in great gouts began to consume him, and he bellowed in pain. His whole black length burst into a tortured mass of flame.

He flung himself upon the stairs and writhed. He blackened, his scales blistering, as the fires of his own creation devoured him. Baleron shrank back and watched on, awed. The flames drew sweat from his pores.

From deep within its bowels, the Black Tower rumbled violently.

Baleron shook off his awe. Gilgaroth lived. Baleron stood, spitting blood from where he'd bitten his tongue, and stalked up the length of Gilgaroth one last time. Fires scorched him and smoke stung his eyes, and the writhing coils threatened to crush him, but he endured.

"You made Man," he said, breathlessly, as he went. "You said one from among the Fallen Race would be your Deliverer, and so it is. I, Baleron Grothgar, King of Havensrike, deliver you into darkness. Farewell!"

Reaching Gilgaroth's head, he swiped Rondthril across his belly, gathering a coat of blood, and plunged the unholy sword into the Dark One's skull. A shock ran up his arm, but he felt Gilgaroth's flesh and bone give beneath him. Gilgaroth roared. His whipping head knocked Baleron back down the stairs.

The Hell-Worm thrashed and moaned, writhing in his death

throes, Rondthril embedded in his brain. Flames shot from his fanged mouth and washed across the glistening black stairs.

Baleron retreated down the steps, stumbling, his eyes on Gilgaroth, as Krogbur shuddered and broke apart.

The shadow-wraiths swarmed about their Master, trying and failing to help him. His fury drove them away, so they circled him at a distance, wailing in terror and sadness.

The Dark One's thrashing finally ceased, and his body slumped to the stairs and was still. Thunder boomed and the walls shook and broke. Fissures spread. Cracks split the stairs. Wind screamed and howled.

Gilgaroth did not move.

Awe fell on Baleron. *The Wolf ... is dead.*

As he watched, insubstantial shapes, like shadows of shadows, suddenly poured from the holes Rondthril had dealt the Dark One. They boiled out of the Second Hell, some screaming, some wailing, all in haste to be gone as Illistriv collapsed. More and more poured from Gilgaroth's wounds—thousands, perhaps millions of them—and Baleron watched in wonder, completely transfixed.

Illistriv was breaking. It must be. And all its prisoners were being set loose. Even now Baleron might be watching Salthrick's soul escape its torment, along with millions of others. Baleron felt a smile spread across his face. The wraiths, seeing the imprisoned souls go free and fearing retribution, scattered.

Baleron turned about, meaning to go down, and his smile faded instantly.

Rolenya, white and smoking and still, lay in a heap down on the terrace.

Calling her name, Baleron leapt down the stairs as fast as he could, slipping and cursing, but at last he reached her and, sinking to his knees, cradled her in his arms.

"Rolenya!" he said. "Can you hear me?"

She didn't move. The wind blew her hair, fluttered her dress, but she didn't move. She was still warm, but Baleron had no idea if that would last. She was already cooling under the frigid rain.

Bitter tears welled in him. *After all this, for her to die ...*

A large slab of Krogbur smashed into the floor near him, pelting him and the princess with shrapnel, and he knew it was only a matter of time for them both. The tower would fall, and he and Rolenya would be obliterated in its collapse.

A great winged shadow fell upon the terrace.

Baleron looked up to see a familiar form descend from the skies. Wounded and bloodied in a hundred places, weakened by his mother's poison, Throgmar landed on the platform and inspected his father's smoking remains, which could still be seen high up on the black stairs, smoldering.

In the air about the tower, the moat of dragons was breaking up and scattering. They felt their Master's passing and knew that Krogbur was the wrong place to be at the moment. At any second it would collapse, killing anyone near it. Even the Borchstog army at its base was beginning to flee, though it was too late for them. The leaping fires of the Inferno spread, consuming all in its path, burning itself out. All was chaos and pandemonium.

Baleron could smell thick smoke on the suddenly-hot breeze. The Inferno must be close to the terrace. At any moment the terrace would be consumed in fire. The very air shimmered with heat, and the floor burned him. Its wet surface began to hiss.

Slowly, Throgmar lowered his horned head from inspecting the ruin of his father to regard the shape of Baleron cradling Rolenya at his feet.

Wind whipped Baleron and rain tore at his flesh, but the heir to the throne of Havensrike did not attempt to flee.

Throgmar met his eyes.

Thunder shook the tower, and another slab crashed right near the prince, spraying him and the princess with shards.

"YOU," said Throgmar slowly. He did not seem to be in a rush. Indeed, far from it.

Rolenya's flesh was growing colder. If she was still alive, Baleron had to get her to shelter quickly. As for himself, he felt sick from his contact with Gilgaroth's blood. It felt as though a fire were spreading throughout his body. The Wolf might kill him yet.

He blinked, looking deep into Throgmar's amber eyes.

"Help us," he said.

The Betrayer just stared at him. The dragon said nothing. Wind shrieked through his horns.

"Or," Baleron pleaded, "if you don't want to help me, save *her* at least. *She* deserves better than to die like this."

"FELESTRATA DESERVED BETTER THAN WHAT YOU GAVE HER, TOO."

"But she did not exist!"

Heatedly, the Worm shouted, *"SHE EXISTED TO ME!"*

The rawness of his voice was painful to hear. Desperately, Baleron proffered Rolenya to him. "Take her. Fly her far away from this. Release her somewhere safe."

"PERHAPS I WILL TAKE YOU AND LEAVE HER. THAT IS WHAT YOU DID TO ME."

Baleron gnashed his teeth. *Damn him!*

A crack developed in the terrace to his right, and part of it fell away. Smoke from the Inferno drifted up, wreathing the platform. The soles of Baleron's feet began to blister, as if he wore no boots at all.

"I will not go without her!" he said.

Ul Mrungona appraised the body of his father. "IT SHOULD HAVE BEEN ME," he said, almost quietly. "*I* SHOULD HAVE HAD THE PLEASURE OF SLAYING HIM. FOR DENYING ME THAT ALONE, I SHALL HAVE TO PUNISH YOU." Another chunk of Krogbur fell away, smashing into the terrace and taking some of the platform with it. "YET I DON'T HAVE TIME TO THINK ON IT HERE. I'LL HAVE TO TAKE YOU WITH ME,

WHERE I WILL PONDER YOUR PUNISHMENT AT MY LEISURE."

Warily, Baleron let the dragon scoop Rolenya up in one huge claw and himself in another. She still lay limp and smoking, like a doll that had been steamed, her eyes closed and her clothes plastered to her skin.

Throgmar chuckled darkly as, with a mighty pump of his wings, he lifted off from the terrace and flew away from a disintegrating Krogbur. Baleron watched the Black Tower recede through a gap in the dragon's claws. Within seconds of Throgmar departing it, the terrace broke and fell away, flaming.

Its stump grew small with distance until it was lost in the chaos of the night. Baleron watched Krogbur collapse, one chunk at a time. The fires of the Inferno had consumed nearly its whole length. The tower was a rod of flame stretching from the ground into the lightning-rent heavens.

On the endless black stairs, Gilgaroth moved. He moved only slightly. Not even the tail twitched.

But the eyes, the two burning portals to a vanishing Illistriv, opened, then narrowed in hate.

Summoning his last strength, Gilgaroth sent out his will to the brooding storm clouds that thronged the tower, and lightning struck down.

"*Revenge,*" said he.

A thousand bolts of lightning, the very last effort of Gilgaroth, split the skies. Their electric snake-tongues chased Throgmar as he fled the devastation. Air whistled through his claws as he picked up speed, trying to outrun his death.

In his one hand Baleron gripped a claw, steadying himself. This was the Wolf's work, he knew. He could taste the stench of Gilgaroth's hate on the heavily charged air.

Across the gap of Throgmar's chest he could see the limp

form of Rolenya encased in a mighty dragon-hand. She did not stir.

White whips struck all about the Worm, hounding him. Throgmar flew faster, frantic to be away.

Other dragons flew at him, breathing flame. Their fires scoured his armor, torching some patches of hair, but did no real damage. One blast came close to roasting Baleron but managed only to bring a flush to his skin. When the smaller Worms came close, the Leviathan's own fires chased them, and his fires were more deadly. Some of the dragons fell smoking from the sky.

Throgmar flew ever faster—faster—but the storm was too swift, even for him. A bolt of lightning struck one of his wings, and he roared. Dove. Baleron's stomach leapt to his throat. They were all going to die!

Another bolt of lightning speared the Betrayer's back, and Baleron yelped as ribbons of electricity webbed Throgmar's talon, then faded.

Another bright blue tongue struck the Worm, and another. It was a wonder he was still alive at all.

The other dragons put distance between them and Throgmar. His immediate vicinity was not a safe place to be.

He maintained the presence of mind, at least, to put himself into a large spiral, all he could do with the full use of only one wing, and it slowed them enough so that they would not necessarily die on impact. Baleron wondered if this is how Ungier had felt, falling from the terrace.

They fell forever. Down, down, down, Baleron had long moments to contemplate the coming darkness—or would it be darkness? What happened to loosed souls in Oslog now that Illistriv was no more?

The land pitched up at them.

Baleron gritted his teeth and braced himself.

Throgmar struck the ground with his chest, nearly horizontal to the land, and went sliding forwards across the blackened wastes, tearing a scrabbled swath. Baleron was bumped up and down, jostled terribly in the dragon's fist, but Throgmar held him tight, fingers closed, sealing Baleron in.

At last the speed of Throgmar's slide diminished, and he ground to a halt.

The roar in Baleron's ears faded enough so that he could pick out individual sounds, but in the scaly enclosure of Throgmar's fist, all he could hear was his own ragged breathing.

Throgmar's fist half opened and Baleron could see the bleak surroundings, a flat wasteland of charred earth.

An avalanche of pebbles as Throgmar shifted his weight. Dust rose up. The dragon moaned.

Reeling, Baleron climbed out of the claw, coughing and wheezing; their landing had churned up a great deal of dust and ash. He saw that they were on an open plain cut through with many fissures, many miles from Krogbur, which still stood in the distance, a fiery line disappearing into a black sky. Piece by flaming piece the tower crumbled away, and the pieces were like fireflies filling the air around Krogbur.

Baleron looked down at himself in surprise. He was alive ... at least for now. Gilgaroth's poison still coursed through him.

What of Rolenya?

Heart in his throat, Baleron made his way over to the other scaly fist and pried her loose of the Leviathan's claw. Hefting her limp weight in his arms, he carried her some distance away and set her down as gently as he could on the plain of ash.

Her eyes were closed. She did not move. He stared down at her for a long time, praying.

The rain didn't reach this far, and he shivered in the cool air, his skin still wet. For the first time he noticed that Rolenya was covered in gooseflesh.

His eyes widened.

Could it be ... ?

He waited, staring, hardly daring to breathe.

Suddenly, her chest rose and fell. Relief washing through him, he raised his head and whooped in joy. Laughing, he kissed her forehead and cheeks.

"Rolenya!"

He looked around. The Great Army was far away, and the soldiers would be busy fleeing the earthquakes and leaping flames. The dragons had already broken off. Rolenya, he realized, was safe. He would die, yes, but she would not, and that was just fine.

She stirred.

"Sleep," he told her, stroking her hair.

All of a sudden, he grimaced in pain, clutching a hand to his chest. His concentration wavered in and out. It was only a matter of time, he knew. He had to make the next few minutes count.

He returned his attention to the Leviathan. Throgmar lay on the charred ground, his body blackened in places and smoking, and he looked too weak to move. His amber eyes were partly open, and he and Baleron regarded each other for several moments silently, sullenly.

Unable to put it more diplomatically, Baleron asked, "Can you go on?"

Throgmar grunted. "I DO NOT KNOW WHY I TRIED." He seemed to sag, and rested his weary head on the earth. Deflated and hollow, having perhaps killed his mother and helped the murderers of his father escape their rightful deaths, he seemed both angry and racked with guilt. At the same time, he also seemed strangely uplifted, as if a weight had been removed.

Blood from dozens of wounds along his massive bulk leaked into the blackened earth, and his scales glistened redly. Perhaps Mogra's venoms were even then running through his system, finishing him off.

"Was vengeance sweet?" Baleron asked him, thinking of the Spider Goddess.

"VERY," answered the Worm.

"So she is dead, then."

Throgmar did not answer for a long span. His eyes clouded, and Baleron thought the dragon was likely imagining the moment he slew her. He must have been right, as the Worm soon said, "I DROPPED HER FROM A GREAT HEIGHT AND SET HER AFLAME. I DESCENDED AFTER HER, MEANING TO WATCH HER STRIKE THE GROUND, MEANING TO WATCH HER DIE ... BUT A PLUME OF SMOKE ROSE UP AND I LOST HER ... AND THEN A SCORE OF MY OWN SPAWN FELL ON ME, SHRIEKING THAT I WAS A TRAITOR ... I SLEW MY OWN CHILDREN, BALERON. *AND THAT IS AFTER I SLEW MY MOTHER!* WHAT DOES THAT MAKE ME?"

"I don't know," Baleron admitted. "But I thank you."

"DO NOT. I WOULD HAVE SLAIN YOU, AS WELL—*IN TIME.*" He added this last part sinisterly.

Baleron spread his arms wide. "Then, if these are your last moments, and you were going to kill me anyway ... "

Throgmar studied him for a long time, and Baleron waited.

At last the dragon lowered his eyes. "I LIED. VENGEANCE WAS ONLY SWEET AT THE MOMENT. TELL ME, WAS IT SWEET FOR YOU? YOU TASTED IT TWICE, IF NOT THREE TIMES."

"Sweet the first time," Baleron told him truthfully. "But afterwards bitter. And now I find out I didn't kill anyone, not then, but ... it hurt the intended target—"

"ME."

"You," he agreed. "So—the job was done. The second time? It feels great. I *ached* to kill Gilgaroth. I know he was your father, but ..."

"OH, I HAVE HATED HIM FAR LONGER THAN YOU. MY HATRED IS OLDER THAN YOUR COUNTRY!"

Aloud, Baleron mused, "It's hard to believe he's gone. To live without the constant threat of war and oblivion will be strange ... I suppose. Others will know that peace, not I."

It was odd to talk with Throgmar like this, Baleron reflected, as though they were two old friends, but in a way that's exactly how it felt, that they were two comrades sharing a last talk before their deaths overtook them. It was only a question of who would fade first.

"AND ME?" Throgmar said. "HOW DID IT FEEL WHEN YOU HAD YOUR REVENGE ON ME?"

"You? Oh, that was the best, the sweetest of all."

Chuckling, Throgmar took a large deep breath and let it out in one great, melancholy sigh. His golden eyes dimmed.

Baleron waited for the dragon to take another breath, but he did not, and after a few minutes the prince realized the truth of it. He hung his head.

Silently, oddly morose, he closed the dragon's eyes.

"Sleep well," he said. "And may your spirit have no need of further vengeance."

On the black stairs, Illistriv had burnt itself out, leaving only a smoldering husk where once had been a mighty being. Gilgaroth's eyes were still half open, and they were still flaming, but the flames were dying. Within seconds, they would be out.

The Dark One opened his maw one last time and groaned, a long, sad groan of lament, and then his fire faded.

Krogbur broke around him. The fires of the Second Hell engulfed the whole of the Black Tower and consumed the last of Gilgaroth. In the end, his own Inferno claimed him. And then it too went out.

The cold shadow in Baleron's chest throbbed once, swelled, and he heard a horrible cry inside him. Then something left him. It was as though there had been a cloud on him for years, so long he'd grown used to it, had not even been aware of it, when suddenly it was no more.

It shocked him, and he staggered, almost drunken.

Gasping, he looked toward the Black Tower. Gilgaroth must be dead. Really, truly dead.

The Doom was no more. Baleron ... was free.

For a little while.

Returning to Rolenya, he found her still breathing. As he bent over her, he brushed dark hair from her face, and she stirred. He continued to sit beside her, and it was not long before her blue eyes opened.

"Thank the gods," he breathed.

She gazed up at him tearfully. She must have been having a nightmare, as she looked panicked, frightened. He stroked her head to calm her.

"Did we ... die?" she asked.

He shook his head. Tears leaked out. "Not yet. There is none to claim us. Gilgaroth is dead."

Wonder filled her eyes. "Truly?" When he nodded, she embraced him tightly. "Oh, *Baleron*! You did it!"

"No," he told her solemnly. "It was—"

The Black Tower exploded.

With Gilgaroth's death, the energies he had stolen to raise and bind the tower were loosed, and that coupled with the destructive element of the out-of-control Inferno ...

Baleron and Rolenya watched with astonishment as the immensity of Krogbur, flaming like a torch, flamed suddenly brighter, then erupted in a shower of fire and molten stone in a line from the ground to the sky, an immense eruption that showered millions of tons of death out over the wasteland ... and the army camped at the tower's base. Baleron and Rolenya, even many miles away, could hear their screams. The army that would have spelled the end of the Crescent was no more. A few dragons still wheeled about the spire, but as it exploded it took them with it.

As the countless pieces of the tower smote the wasteland, the earth split and broke, laying ruin to mountains and fields of ash and filth, burning them all away in a bath of fire and red hot magma. Baleron never could have imagined the *BOOM* or the shock of the rushing air that followed. He could feel it in the very land, feel the vibration as the shockwave swept outwards. The wind of it ruffled his hair, burned his skin.

He and Rolenya huddled tighter as the devastation drew nearer. More wind howled around them, carrying with it the spirits of demons and innocents loosed by Illistriv's obliteration, as well as the heat from the Inferno's fires.

Such a huge cloud of dust and ash billowed up from the ruin that Baleron could hardly see what happened next, but he did. All the volcanoes in Oslog seemed to erupt at once, jetting lava into the sky and sending glowing rivers of the earth's blood down their black slopes. Great earthquakes were triggered, and the land was broken again and again. Lava spewed up from the ground. Old mountains fell and new ones thrust up. The world was sundered and remade.

Baleron and Rolenya, frightened, looked all about at the breaking land. The destruction that radiated out from the site of Krogbur's fall edged closer and closer. Baleron tensed. It looked as though the ruin would swallow them.

"I love you," Rolenya whispered, and held him tight.

The destruction rolled toward them, closer and closer. He could feel the earth vibrate. His teeth rattled together.

Then, suddenly, miraculously, the destruction ceased rolling in their direction. The earth continued to split and quake, but the devastation came no closer to the two lovers. They seemed to be too far away to be in immediate danger, even though the ground still shook beneath them, and he could still smell the smoke of the fires.

At last the earth calmed as much as it could, and the former brother and sister breathed sighs of relief.

"It's over," Baleron said. Wind howled in the silence that followed. "They're gone. Gilgaroth and Mogra. Dead. The Black Tower fallen."

"We ... won." She said it in a small voice, sounding surprised.

He almost didn't believe it. For a moment he was absolutely convinced that this was yet another trick of the Dark One's, and that any second all this would go away and he would be back in Krogbur's pits, hallucinating, Ghrozm standing over him with a scalpel.

"We did," she said. "We truly did."

He winced as a sudden jolt of pain nearly knocked him over, and he had to hold on to her tightly to steady himself.

"What is it, Bal?" she asked. "What's wrong?"

He grimaced again. "I'm dying, Rolenya. The blood of Gilgaroth ..."

A look of terror crossed her face.

"I'm sorry, Rol," he told her. "So sorry. After all this ... and I desert you now..." He was short of breath. His insides were baking.

An odd calmness descended on her. Her eyes flashed with confidence and surety and her usual prideful stubbornness. With conviction, she said, "Gilgaroth said once that he had enough darkness to counter my Light, but he was wrong, and he paid for it. Now let me prove it once more."

"Don't try. You're still too weak."

"I'm strong enough for this. Now be quiet."

So saying, she pressed her lips to his and held his face against hers. Her lips were soft and warm and moist, and he felt he could drown in her touch.

Slowly at first, but then more quickly, he could feel a strange power coursing through him, countering the poison of the Shadow. It washed him of the taint and corruption of Gilgaroth, and he was like a withered plant suddenly given light and water. It seemed to awaken, if accidentally, the remains of the Flower of

Itherin, and he felt a glow inside him. Renewed energy and vitality rose in him, burning the poison out.

Their lips parted, and he gasped, staring at her in wonder.

"How do you feel?" she asked.

"I feel ... good." He laughed. "Very good."

She smiled, her blue eyes wet, and for the first time he contemplated a future in which the two of them lived, in which *they walked away from this.*

She half sat up, and he helped her. For a while he just held her in his arms, and together they surveyed the bleakness of the wastelands. A great blaze shot up to the south where Krogbur had fallen and the Inferno loosed. Illistriv's fires were dying, but new ones sprang up. The rest was grim and dark. Occasionally, the earth trembled, and all the volcanoes in the area were erupting like great fountains, sending the burning blood of Oslog high into the charcoal sky. The Dark Country was wounded—perhaps mortally. Rivers of fire cut through it, but the prince and princess were safe for the moment. Just the same, Baleron recognized the need to move while they could. A hot breeze blew down from the mountains, carrying the stench of sulfur.

"I hope our homes don't look like this when we return," she said.

"Me, too."

"Will the armies still be there? Will the war still go on without him?"

"I doubt it. They'll turn back and hide here for another thousand years, and we'll rebuild."

"Rebuild? But you have no home. You have no country."

"There will still be survivors, hiding somewhere in the north. I'll unite them and found a new capital."

She looked at him strangely. "That's right. You're ... you're King now."

He sighed. "Of Ungoroth?"

"Of whatever we make of the ruins."

"We?"

She took his face in her hands and kissed him again. "Of course."

He reminded himself to be vigilant. The great army of Gilgaroth might be destroyed, but there were still countless creatures out there, prowling the waste. And dragons. Many, many dragons. Baleron realized that he and Rolenya were without weapons, food or water, and had only each other to keep them warm. It would have to be enough.

They climbed to their feet.

"We have a long road back," she said, her blue eyes scanning the bleak, jagged horizon to the north. To the south, all was ruin: fire and clouds of smoke.

Taking a deep breath, he held out his hand and she took it.

The sun, he saw, was rising to the east, a white disc behind jagged black mountains. The storm clouds were breaking up, revealing the last visible stars. It had been a long night, and he doubted the day to come would hold much light, but it was more than he had expected. Many horrors of the night were likely seeking shelter from the sun; it was probably the first time Brunril's Torch had been seen in this land in many years. A hot breeze blew.

"Come," he said. "Let's go."

Wearily, bleeding and barely able to stand, Baleron and Rolenya left the body of Throgmar where it lay smoking on the ground and marched out into the wastelands, bound for home.

THE END

Made in the USA
Monee, IL
06 May 2022

96000475R00138